Praise for *Tanglewreck*

'A fantastical, imaginative and impressive parable'
Financial Times

'A volume to treasure. Outstanding ... ambitious, a cracking satirical tale, full of memorable characterisations and mischievous humour' *Daily Telegraph*

'After reading *Tanglewreck* I felt I'd read something that had fulfilled all of my imagination. It was the most original, exciting and best adventure story I've read in a long time' Jennifer, aged 14, *First News*

'An exceptional book: big, ambitious and awash with Winterson's usual inventiveness ... a book that is very funny and which holds you, enchanted, right through to the bitter-sweet ending' *Observer*

'Quantum physics, Ancient Egyptian mythology, secret societies and a procession of Popes happily mingle ... No one could fail to enjoy the book's exuberance of ideas and wacky charm' *Evening Standard*

'[Jeanette Winterson] has produced her first full-length novel for children, and her humour, soaring imagination and passion makes it irresistible' *Daily Mail*

Blackbirds

JEANETTE WINTERSON

TANGLEWRECK

A & C Black • London

Acknowledgements

Thanks to everyone at Bloomsbury, especially Sarah
Odedina and Georgia Murray. To Caroline Michel, Suzanne
Gluck, and the William Morris team. To Leah Schmidt, at
The Agency. To Philippa Brewster and Henri Llewelyn
Davies for their detailed reading, and to Lysander Ashton,
quantum physicist and film-maker, who checked the science,
and to my godchildren, Eleanor and Cara Shearer, who
checked the science fiction. To Fiona Shaw who was always
Mrs Rokabye as I was writing. And to Deborah Warner for
the generous loan of her parents, Roger and Ruth, a house
full of antiques, and a sense of possibility.

First published in Great Britain in 2006 by Bloomsbury Publishing Plc

This educational edition published 2008 by
A & C Black Publishers Ltd
38 Soho Square, London W1D 3HB

www.acblack.com
www.acblackbirds.com

Copyright © Jeanette Winterson 2006

ISBN 978-0-7136-8689-0

A CIP catalogue for this book is available from the British Library

Printed on natural, recyclable paper made from wood grown in
well-managed forests. The manufacturing processes conform to
the environmental regulations of the country of origin

Typeset by Dorchester Typesetting Group Ltd
Printed in Great Britain by MPG Books

To Eleanor and Cara Shearer with love

CONTENTS

THE TIME TORNADO

At six forty-five one summer morning, a red London bus was crossing Waterloo Bridge.

A group of school children, sitting at the back, were copying each other's homework and fighting, when one of them looked out of the window, across the river to Cleopatra's Needle, and saw something very strange.

The boy elbowed his friend. The dark finger of ancient Egypt was pointing towards the sky as it always did, but today the tip of the obelisk was glowing bright red, as it had when it was new and painted and glorious, four thousand years ago, in the Temple of the Sun.

'Look,' said the boy, 'look!'

Riding the river as though it were a road was a phalanx of chariots and horsemen.

The white horses were pulled up on their haunches; the nodding ostrich plumes on their head-collars rose and fell; the fan bearers came forward, the troops stood at ease, and above the kneeling priests was the Pharaoh himself, inspecting his new monument from a burnished car.

Other people turned to stare at the mirage, and the bus

driver slowed down, though he did not quite stop; he seemed to be hovering over Time.

In the slowed-down silence no one spoke and nothing moved – except for the river, which to all observation was running backwards.

Then, from downstream, there was a sudden terrible crack, like the sky breaking. A cone of wind hit the bus, knocking it sideways over the bridge and shattering glass across the seats where the children were sitting.

The bus should have crashed down into the river, but instead the wind whirled through the punched-in windows and lifted the bus high above the bridge and out towards the obelisk.

A great wave of water swelled up against the stone piers of the bridge, battering the concrete underside with such force that part of the supporting wall was torn away.

As the tidal wave slammed back down on to the water, the river resumed its normal flow. At the same second the bus spun crazily into the line of chariots. On impact, bus, chariots and horsemen vanished, leaving nothing behind but traces of red-gold sun on the surface of the water.

Big Ben struck seven.

A few days later police found an exercise book floating on the Thames; the name printed in the front of the book identified it as belonging to one of the boys on the bus. The pages had thickened to parchment, and the writing inside was not English, but signs of long-legged birds and half-turned figures under the eye of the great god Ra.

The bus and its passengers were never found.

It was the first of the Time Tornadoes.

THE VISITOR

A t 4:30 p.m. precisely, Abel Darkwater drove his Rolls-Royce Silver Cloud through the gates of the great house called Tanglewreck.

Abel Darkwater was never late – unless he intended to be; and his watch was never wrong – unless he wanted it to be.

Some people are always short of time, but Abel Darkwater had all the time in the world – well, nearly all of it – and it was the *nearly* that was the problem, and the reason why he had come to Tanglewreck.

He steered the big car up the long ragged driveway. He glanced at the round green dials on the dashboard. The speedometer told him he was travelling at precisely 10mph. The rev counter registered 30 revs per minute. The luminous clock assured him that he was punctual, and the Age-Gauge steadied its hands at 1588, the year Tanglewreck had been built.

Abel Darkwater had invented and fitted the Age-Gauge himself. In town it computed the age of the houses. In open countryside it could calculate the date of the limestone or the shale or the clay, and he knew what dinosaurs would have roamed there once, or what desperate hunters had leaned over rain-driven ledges to drop a boulder on a boar.

The Age-Gauge worked on radioactive emissions – faint but traceable echoes of time. Abel Darkwater knew that all time is always present, but buried layer by layer under what people call Now. Today lies on top of yesterday, and yesterday lies on top of the day before, and so on down the layers of history, until the layers are so thick that the voices underneath are muffled to whispers. Abel Darkwater listened to those whispers and he understood what they said.

Now he was at Tanglewreck, and the house was telling him the beginning of its own past – the day when it was a young house new-made. When Now was Then and Then was Now. He was curious to hear more, but he had come here today on business, and he must not keep that business waiting.

He pulled up outside the black and white timbered house, and switched off the engine. The dials fell back to zero. He heaved himself slowly out of his car, and consulted his heavy gold pocket watch: the hour hand marked four. The minute hand thirty-five past the hour. The second hand moved swiftly from forty to fifty. The fourth hand, in red, like a warning, pointed towards eleven o'clock. Abel Darkwater looked up, following the direction of his watch. Sure enough, there was a face at the window. It drew back. He smiled, though you would not call such a smile pleasure or kindness, and then he raised the door-knocker in the shape of an angel.

Silver drew back from the window. She knew why he had come.

20

From below she could hear Mrs Rokabye bawling from the hall.

'Silver! Get down here at once, this split second of the minute.'

'Yes, Mrs Rokabye.'

Silver ran down the stairs to the closed arms of Mrs Rokabye, her mouth open like a crater, the words steaming out.

'Look at the state of you!'

Silver looked at the state of her in the big mirror in the hall. Her hair was orange and curly and it stood on end unless she plaited it. Her eyes were green. Her nose was straight. Her face was freckled and she was small. Small and untidy; it is hard to be tidy when you are doing jobs all day.

'Get down into the cellar and stoke the furnace with coal. Do you expect me to do it myself?'

'No, Mrs Rokabye.'

'No indeed! I am slaving for our future. Without ME, there will be no future!! Without me, YOU would have to go into a children's home. Would you like that?'

'No, Mrs Rokabye.'

'No indeed! When I think what I gave up to come here and look after you. Why, I gave up a whole life. It was all goodness on my part, and it has been all ingratitude on your part. Do you think I like being here?'

'No, Mrs Rokabye.'

'Great, draughty, crumbling monstrosity. I had a lovely home in Manchester with carpets and central heating and

Darts Nights with all my friends, and now I live on a windswept hill in this ruin, with YOU.'

'Yes, Mrs Rokabye.'

'Mr Darkwater – you remember him? He proved a very good friend to us after the . . . er, tragedy, accident, misfortune. We sold him the clock and some watches to pay off your father's debts.'

'Yes – he took my secret night-clock.'

'Oh, don't be such a baby – we lived on that money for a year.'

'*You* did . . .'

'What was that?'

Mrs Rokabye was looking at Silver with eyes as narrow as arrowheads. There was going to be trouble – but then there was a knocking at the door, and Mrs Rokabye smoothed her pinned-back hair and whipped out her compact to powder her nose. It was like dust settling on a rock.

'Here he is! Quick, quick, now get downstairs into the cellar and don't come out until I tell you. Bigamist will be watching.'

'Yes, Mrs Rokabye.'

My name is Silver and I have lived at Tanglewreck all of my life, which is to say, eleven years.

I live here with Mrs Rokabye: my father's sister and my legal guardian.

My parents and my older sister Buddleia disappeared in a railway accident, one Friday, four years ago, when I was seven. Then, after it had all been written about in the newspaper, and there was talk of what to do with me, Mrs Rokabye appeared, all in black, which is normal, I suppose, after a tragedy, but then she never took off the black tragedy clothes. She always wears black, and I think her soul is black too.

My father had never talked about his sister, my aunt, but she signed all the papers and everything is legal. I'd rather live by myself, but it's not allowed.

Mrs Rokabye has a pet rabbit called Bigamist, on account of his habits. The house is full of small-scale Bigamists, so that wherever you go, there's a pair of yellow eyes watching you, and a black nose twitching, and an ear cocked at your business, and a scut just hiding under a chair as you come into a room. They're all her spies, but Bigamist is the worst. He tells her everything I do.

Today, I've been trying to sneak into the kitchen and find the cake intended for Abel Darkwater. But Bigamist is following me and I haven't got a carrot to throw him off the scent.

The cellar is black and filthy and lit by a dusty electric 25-watt bulb. We're on an economy drive here at Tanglewreck – at least the house is, and I am. Mrs Rokabye eats fish and chips and puddings and chocolate bars, and then she keeps her 100-watt bulb on all night watching television. She sleeps until eleven o'clock, and then she takes a taxi to go shopping. She comes back laden with ready-chopped carrots and fresh washed lettuce for Bigamist, and Fast Fish 'n' Chips Ahoy! for herself. And slabs of chocolate the size of rafts. Family size *it says, but as we're not a family, I don't get any of this.*

I eat soup most days, and I make it from what I grow in our vegetable garden. Tonight I'm having dandelion, nettle and cabbage. I shut my eyes when I eat it, but that doesn't make it taste any better.

Still, I tell myself, tasty or nasty, it's better than what Mrs Rokabye would give me – which is next to nothing.

'Girls should know how to cook,' she always tells me, putting her own extra-large portions of cod 'n' chips in the microwave. 'I am preparing you for life.' Then she doles out a few scraps of meat and bread, and takes her own laden tray into the library.

I started shovelling the coal and thinking about my mother and father. My father was a scientist who worked at Jodrell Bank on Alderley Edge in Cheshire. He did something with stars. My mother was a painter but she had to spend a lot of time looking after my sister Buddleia, who had a twisted leg from when she was born. My parents and Buddleia had gone to London for something important on the day that they didn't come back. I don't know what it was, but it was something to do with the Timekeeper . . .

'So you understand, Mrs Rokabye, I must have it, and I will pay you a large sum – oh yes, a very large sum to get it.'

Abel Darkwater clinked his teacup. Silver heard the cake knife hitting the plate as Mrs Rokabye sliced through the Victoria sponge.

'I will make you rich, oh yes.'

'Mr Darkwater, I have searched the house from chimney to cellar for the last four years. There is not a cobweb of this horrible house that I have not mapped. I simply do not know where the clock or watch or whatever it is could be hidden.'

'You do not, but the child Silver must know.'

'What on earth does she know? On Mondays she is simple, on Tuesdays she is stupid, on Wednesdays she is stubborn. On Thursdays she is silly, on Fridays she is silent, on Saturdays she is SO cross, and on Sundays she is sullen. Don't you think I've quizzed her day and night since the moment I arrived?'

'Perhaps you ask the wrong questions, Mrs Rokabye.'

Silver leaned back on her shovel. The funnel of the furnace was acting like a speaking tube – or rather, a listening tube, because she could hear everything they were saying in the library. Quickly, she shovelled some more coal to keep them warm, and then she pressed herself close to the funnel. Bigamist was looking at her suspiciously but he didn't dare to come closer because of the roaring fire.

Abel Darkwater was speaking again.

'When the child's parents so strangely disappeared, her father was carrying the Timekeeper – or so everyone thought. I happen to know beyond a second of doubt that he was supposed to bring the clock to me. But the clock, like the parents, has never been found.'

Mrs Rokabye was silent for a moment. Then she said, 'It is my belief that the watch was stolen from his body and sold. It is probably in Timbuktoo.'

'Believe me, madam,' said Abel Darkwater, his voice dry with irritation, 'if that watch had belonged to anyone else, anywhere in the world, these last four years, I would have known about it.'

'I realise you are very well connected in the trade,' said Mrs Rokabye, by way of appeasement, but this only fuelled Darkwater the more.

'In the TRADE? You call Tempus Fugit a trade? It is a lifetime! It is many lifetimes. What began in the pyramids of Egypt is not done yet. Isaac Newton was a member of our "trade", as you call it. I have a clock of his in my possession.' Abel Darkwater looked up, startled. 'What's that rabbit doing in here?'

'He looks after the child,' said Mrs Rokabye, getting up. 'Like Nana in *Peter Pan*, you know.'

'Yes, I do know,' said Abel Darkwater. 'There was a croco-dile in *Peter Pan*, and a clock. Very important part of the story – now get rid of that rabbit, and listen to me.'

And so Bigamist was not able to impart to Mrs Rokabye his suspicion that Silver was up to no good. He found himself dropped briskly out of the window, then Mrs Rokabye returned meekly to her chair.

In the cellar, Silver crept closer to the funnel. What on earth was Tempus Fugit? She had to try and remember the words. But now Abel Darkwater was speaking again.

'I buy and sell watches and clocks – the rare, the valuable, the curious. There is only one watch of any interest that has never passed through my hands, and that watch is the

Timekeeper. Now answer me this question, Mrs Rokabye, and answer it well; have you ever noticed any – shall we say – disturbances in Time, here at Tanglewreck?'

'You mean, like the things I have been seeing on the television? What are they called?'

'Time Tornadoes.'

'No, nothing like that – I get up in the morning and I go to bed at night.'

(*You do not*, thought Silver, from the cellar, *you stay up all night watching old films and then you leave me to get up on my own and do the washing up.*)

'So Time here has not halted at all – even for a few moments, or seemed to be running out? Are some days shorter than others?'

'No, every day is the same length.'

(*Oh no, they're not*, thought Silver.)

'And have you been disturbed at all by anything, or anyone from the past?'

'Ooh, I heard about that Woolly Mammoth appearing on the River Thames – is it troo-oo-oo?'

'Yes, it is true.'

'No!'

'Yes.'

'And that people have disappeared? In London?'

'Yes, it is true, though nobody knows why.'

'I blame mobile phones.'

'Why is that, Mrs Rokabye?'

'They emit, don't they?'

'Emit what?'

'Rays – waves, whatever you call it, can't be good for you, and people are talking on them all the time – all those signals bouncing off satellites. I mean, what's going on in space? That's what I'd like to know.'

'It is true, Mrs Rokabye, that at present we are experiencing strange disruptions in the fabric of Time – once so constant and so certain. People vanish, as you say, Time stands still – temporarily – then it jerks forward far too fast. The best minds are considering it.'

'Well, thankfully it isn't happening here.'

'I am glad to hear it. It is what I expected you would say. Now listen carefully. I believe that the Timekeeper is still here in this house, although you have failed to find it for me.' Abel Darkwater held up his hand as Mrs Rokabye opened her mouth in protest. She closed her mouth. He continued. 'So now I have another plan. I would like you to bring the child to London – tell her it is a special treat. I shall provide train tickets and expenses, and you shall both stay at my house. That will give me an opportunity to question the child about the Timekeeper, and, perhaps, if you don't mind – and please take this money for your troubles – I would like also –'

At that moment there was a terrific crash as Bigamist flung himself down the cellar stairs. Silver missed whatever it was 'also' that Abel Darkwater wanted – and she wondered why he didn't just ask her his questions here and now in the house. She didn't have anything to tell him anyway. Nobody seemed to believe her, but Silver had absolutely no idea where the Timekeeper could be. She had never even seen it.

As she swept up the last of the coal to throw on the furnace, she noticed something sparkling in the coal dust. She picked it up carefully, so that Bigamist couldn't see what she was doing. It was long and thin, like a man's tiepin, with a sharp pointed end, and it seemed to be made of diamonds. Hurriedly, she dropped it in the pocket of her overalls.

Overhead, she heard the library door open and the floorboards creak as Mrs Rokabye and Abel Darkwater went towards the front door. She sneaked up the cellar steps, past Bigamist, and darted into the library. Quick as a whistle, she stuffed the leftover ham sandwiches and Victoria sponge down her overalls, and filled her pockets with chocolate biscuits. From the window, she could see Abel Darkwater slowly lowering himself into his car. Mrs Rokabye was turning back towards the house, counting the wad of money in her hands.

Silver grabbed the jug of milk from the table, and slipped out past the enraged rabbit and upstairs to her little bedroom that she loved. It was where she felt safe.

The room was high up in the attics of the house. It had a big wooden bed carved in the shape of a swan, and a fireplace, where she always kept a fire burning, fetching sticks from the orchard, so that the room smelled of apples and pears even in the worst of winter.

Silver began to heat the milk on the little fire, and lay out the sandwiches and cake. She would save the biscuits for later.

She looked at the photograph of her mother and father

and sister on the mantelpiece, but she didn't cry. Instead she said, half to herself, and half to the photo – *Help me to find the Timekeeper.*

The room breathed in. The fire paused in its burning. The milk that had boiled to the rim of the pan bubbled and stopped. It was only the smallest hesitation in time, but Silver knew what she had to do. Something in her and something outside her leapt together and waited in the leaping. She said, *Yes, yes.*

Then the moment landed, and the milk boiled over, and everything was as it usually was, but Silver knew that she had made a promise – to something inside herself and to something outside herself. She would have to find the Timekeeper now, because the Timekeeper had to be found.

TOAD IN THE HOLE

Three days later, Silver was in her vegetable garden weeding the cabbages, when she heard Mrs Rokabye calling to her from the house.

It sounded as though Mrs Rokabye was shouting something like 'Toad in the Hole', but Silver knew it couldn't be that, because Toad in the Hole is something to eat and Silver never got anything to eat from Mrs Rokabye.

She's probably found a frog stuck down the sink, thought Silver. *I'd better go and rescue it.*

Silver shut the gate on to her little garden so that the hens couldn't get out, and walked towards the kitchen. She could smell food – hot food, which was very strange.

Mrs Rokabye was standing at the low kitchen door, smiling. It was a horrible sight; the corners of her mouth were drawn up towards her eyebrows, and her eyebrows were pulled up towards the hairnet she always wore in the house. She had been practising smiling all morning, but it was not nearly for long enough.

'Welcome, dear child!' she said. 'Come and eat your lunch while I tell you something very exciting.'

Silver came slowly into the kitchen. It was not a modern kitchen at all. It was enormous, like a bus depot, and it had a stone floor, and a huge iron oven, and a long wooden table with long wooden benches placed on either side. There were hooks from the ceiling for hanging hams and herbs. There were two stone sinks side by side with plate racks nailed on the wall above them. There was no fridge, no washing machine, no dishwasher, no lino, no TV, no nothing at all, except what had been put there four hundred years ago. Oh, and there was Mrs Rokabye's microwave, sitting on its own at one end of the twenty-foot long oak table, where twenty servants had eaten every day, when the house had been a great house.

The microwave looked very out of place in the old kitchen, as though a Martian had left it there and gone back to Mars.

Today, though, Mrs Rokabye was not heating up Ready-Meals for One in the blue microwave. She was bending over the great oven and lifting out a huge tin dish of sausages cooked in egg batter.

'Toad in the Hole!' she said, placing it on the table in front of the hungry and amazed Silver.

Quickly, she washed her hands and sat down, as Mrs Rokabye cut two portions with a gleaming knife.

'You never said you could cook,' said Silver.

'I have been very busy,' said Mrs Rokabye.

'You've been here for four years.'

'Is it really four years? All that dusting I've had to do – the place was a shambles, as you know. Well, well, four years, how time flies – tempus fugit, as Abel Darkwater would say.'

'What?' said Silver, her mouth full of delicious sausage.

'Tempus fugit,' said Mrs Rokabye. 'It means "Time flies".'

'What language is that?' asked Silver.

'Latin, I think,' said Mrs Rokabye. 'You must ask Mr Darkwater yourself. Ask him tomorrow – for that is my wonderful news!'

While Silver ate seconds and thirds of Toad in the Hole, Mrs Rokabye told her of their trip to London the very next day.

'We will have a picnic on the train. We will stay in Mr Darkwater's magnificent house – nothing like this – all modern inside, and we will be taken to a musical in the evening. Mr Darkwater loves children and all he asks in return for his kindness is that you talk to him as though he were your own father. If he asks you a question – any question, do you hear me – if he asks you a question you must answer it.'

'What if I don't know the answer?' said Silver.

'I am sure you do know the answer,' said Mrs Rokabye. 'All questions have an answer.'

Silver wondered if that was true, but there was no point asking Mrs Rokabye. Privately, Silver thought that the answer to some questions was another question.

'Be ready to answer,' said Mrs Rokabye, 'it will be better for everyone that way. Then we shall all have a lovely time.'

She said it still smiling, though by now the strain was beginning to show, like somebody desperately trying to hold on to the edge of a cliff by her fingertips.

She turned away to get Silver some chocolate, but really to give her face a chance to relax into its customary scowl.

As she stood with her back to Silver, relaxing and scowling, she didn't realise that she was reflected in the polished metal door of the Chocolate Cabinet. Silver could see the real look on her face, and she knew that nothing had changed.

The Chocolate Cabinet was where Mrs Rokabye kept her supplies of caramels and cake bars. The cupboard was made of steel and fastened with a metal padlock of the ferocious kind. Silver was never allowed in there.

Carefully, and with something like pain, Mrs Rokabye took out two tubes of Smarties, then put one back, then took it out again. She reminded herself that she was a nice kind lady, at least for the next twenty-four hours, and she guessed that a nice kind lady would not be mean with her sweets.

'London!' she said brightly, forcing pleasure and happiness into her voice, like the ugly sisters forcing their feet into Cinderella's slipper. 'London! We are going by train at eight o'clock in the morning and we will have a lovely time.'

'When are we coming back?' asked Silver. She loved the house and she hated the thought of leaving it. The house was her friend. The house felt alive. Since her parents had disappeared, it was the house that had looked after her, not Mrs Rokabye.

'Such an ungrateful girl!' said Mrs Rokabye, keeping her voice light, her fists clenched with fury under the table. 'Here I am, doing my best to win influence with important people like Mr Darkwater, just so that you can have a holiday like other children, and do you say thank you? Not you! You ask when you are coming home.'

'Well, I need to know so that I can pack my suitcase,' said Silver evenly. She knew better than to fight Mrs Rokabye.

'Ah, well, indeed,' said Mrs Rokabye, mollified. 'Then take whatever you like, but only a small bag.'

'How many pairs of knickers?'

'Two,' said Mrs Rokabye.

By now, Mrs Rokabye had been pleasant for a whole hour, and she had smiled through most of that hour, and she had spent the morning cooking instead of lying in bed reading Murder Mysteries, and she had given away some of her chocolate, and the whole business had exhausted her. She decided to go and lie down and take a pill. She told Silver to wash the dishes, and then she disappeared up the stairs.

As soon as she had left the room, Silver ran over to the Chocolate Cabinet because Mrs Rokabye had left the padlock off.

'1603,' said Silver, reading the lined-up numbers. 'Now I can get in here whenever I like.'

She grabbed a couple of extra chocolate bars, and hid them in her jeans. Then, hearing Mrs Rokabye returning, she turned away and ran to the sink.

Mrs Rokabye swept into the kitchen like a hailstorm and went straight to the Chocolate Cabinet and locked it.

'Do your packing in good time tonight,' she said. 'I will

leave you ham sandwiches and milk for supper, and I want you in the hall, washed and dressed by seven o'clock tomorrow morning. A taxi will take us to the station. Do you understand?'

'Yes, Mrs Rokabye,' said Silver, without turning round.

That afternoon Silver went to talk to the house.

The house was very quiet but she knew it was listening to her. She often talked to the house, but she preferred to do it in her special place. It was a room where nobody had ever been but her.

It was triangular room with triangular windows on three sides, and a strange old window in the sloping roof. Silver called it the Sky Window, because all you could see through it were the clouds floating by.

When Silver sat in the special room, she felt like a bee in a hive.

She sat in it today, cross-legged, making a triangle of her body, and closing her eyes so that she could listen to the house. It was here that she knew the house was alive, and it was here that the house spoke to her – not with words, but she understood what it was saying.

'What will happen to me in London?' she said.

For a minute the house was silent, then she saw a red light flooding the window in front of her, and colouring the thick wide floorboards red, and her legs and hands red, and the front of her sweatshirt, right up to her neck, but not her face.

'Danger,' the house was saying. 'Danger.'

'Then I won't go,' said Silver. 'I'll hide in you and she'll never find us again.'

The house said nothing.

'Do I have to go?' said Silver, who knew the answer in the pit of her stomach.

'Yes,' said the house.

And for the first time in her life Silver realised that sometimes you have to do something difficult and dangerous, something you don't want to do at all, and that you have to do it because something more important depends on you.

'Will I find the Timekeeper?' she said, but the house didn't answer.

'Will I come back here one day?'

'Yes,' said the house, 'one day.'

Silver sat on the floor as the long shadows of the afternoon filled the room.

What did she know? She knew that something had happened to her parents. She knew that Mrs Rokabye and Abel Darkwater were in league against her, and against Tanglewreck too, and there was the thing called the Timekeeper, but she didn't know exactly what it was, or why a watch could be so important.

She knew that in the world beyond the house very strange things were happening to Time. She took all her knows and her don't knows and asked the house what she should do.

And then, without waiting for an answer, she suddenly stood up, because the house had already given her its answer.

And that is how Silver and Mrs Rokabye caught the 8:05 from Manchester Piccadilly to London Euston, leaving the great house watching behind its hedges of beech and yew.

THE JOURNEY

M rs Rokabye was in high spirits on the train, even though she had left Bigamist behind.

At the station she ignored all the newspapers with their headlines about Time Traps and Time Tornadoes and the future of the world. Instead, she bought all the glossy magazines about the lives of film stars and celebrities. Like most people she longed to be a film star herself, though it was difficult to imagine what parts she could play, except for nasty aunts with odious pets.

She sat with a bucket of sweets on her bony knees, and she gave Silver four caramels, then she remembered she was a nice kind lady that day, and fished out another eight of the hard centres she didn't like.

'What a blessing to be away from that awful house!' said Mrs Rokabye. 'I sometimes think it is listening to me, ha ha ha.'

'It is listening to you,' said Silver. 'Tanglewreck is alive.'

'Children are the most ridiculous things ever invented,' said Mrs Rokabye. 'Houses do not have ears.'

'My father said that Tanglewreck has listened to everything for four hundred years, and that the house never forgets. Even if you talk to yourself the house can hear you,' said Silver.

Mrs Rokabye did not like the sound of this at all. Suppose the house had overheard her conversation with Abel Darkwater? Suppose the house knew that she was intending to cheat Silver out of her inheritance and sell Tanglewreck to a developer who wanted to build Executive Homes on the site?

No! No! No! A house is a house is a house. The sooner a bulldozer came and flattened it the better. Mrs Rokabye's eyes darted about as she thought these thoughts and her big teeth crunched her chocolate peanuts. *Calm down*, she said to herself, *first things first*. First the Timekeeper and all the money she would get from Abel Darkwater, and after that the horrible house. She had a Plan; all clever people had a Plan. She would follow her Plan step by step and not let this unsettling child distract her. Tanglewreck was an old ugly house, and anything else was a silly superstition.

'I don't know why you like that house as much as you do,' said Mrs Rokabye, sighing, 'but however much you like it, it is not alive.'

The ticket collector came and clipped their tickets. 'Delays at Macclesfield,' he said, and went on down the train.

Mrs Rokabye buried herself in her star-studded magazine. She had decided to ignore Silver until they reached King's Cross.

'I'll tell you about Tanglewreck,' said Silver, ignoring Mrs Rokabye ignoring her. 'Then you'll know why it's special.'

Silver had told this story to herself many times before,

when she was on her own, which, since her parents had died, was always.

'There was a field,' said Silver, 'and the field was empty, but some said they saw a house there long before it was built; a shimmering house, made of fog, and standing in birch trees.'

'What nonsense you talk!' said Mrs Rokabye, glancing up from her magazine, but Silver was repeating word for word just what her father had told her.

'In 1588 the first stones of the house were laid, but although it was a fine house, it was a wild place and no one wanted to live there, and so the house waited.

'In those days, in the days of Queen Elizabeth the First, our family, the Rivers, were called Rovers, and because they were wanted for crimes in England, they stole a ship and put out to sea –'

'That's right!' said Mrs Rokabye. 'What a disgrace to be descended from pirates!'

But Silver wasn't listening to Mrs Rokabye; it was her father's voice she could hear now, reassuring and low, in the days when she had sat on his knee in his study, with the fire blazing, listening to stories about Tanglewreck . . .

'It is true, Silver, that the Rovers were pirates, but they were successful pirates, and in those days, England and Spain were enemies, and so when the Rovers finally limped back into Deptford with a broken ship and a hull groaning with stolen Spanish treasure, they begged the Queen for an Official Pardon and a Quiet Life.

'*Queen Elizabeth liked treasure, and she didn't like Spaniards, and so she graciously agreed to take three-quarters of the pearls, each the size of a baby's head, and half the bars of silver, each one the length of a man's leg.*

'*Roger Rover was knighted Sir Roger, for his services to the Treasury, and, for the sake of his new status and his new wife, he changed the family name to River, and River it has been ever since.*'

'And now there is no heir to Tanglewreck, is there?' said Mrs Rokabye, her eyes gleaming. When her eyes gleamed she looked just like Bigamist, and Silver half expected her to chew on a carrot.

'My father made me the heir,' said Silver, looking straight at Mrs Rokabye. 'He said it was time that the old house had a girl to look after it. That's why he called me Silver, as a reminder of the treasure that began it all. Oh, and because he said I was like his favourite pirate.'

'What pirate?' said Mrs Rokabye suspiciously.

'The one in *Treasure Island*. Long John Silver.'

'Never read it,' said Mrs Rokabye, who never read anything except celebrity magazines and Murder Mysteries.

'I brought it with me,' said Silver. 'Here it is, and there's a picture of Long John Silver on the cover. It's really good. You can read it to me if you like.'

'No thank you,' said Mrs Rokabye, who would rather have lain face down under the floorboards than done anything to please Silver.

'I'll read it by myself, then,' said Silver, who was used to doing most things by herself.

She wrapped herself deep into her old duffle coat and opened the book, but before she could begin, a strange thing happened. The ticket collector came back and said, 'Delays at Macclesfield.'

'You told us that already,' said Silver, 'and we have gone past Macclesfield.'

But they hadn't, because the train had got jammed in Time.

'What do you mean, we are jammed in Time?' demanded Mrs Rokabye. 'I have paid for my ticket, two tickets, as it happens.'

The guard shrugged. 'Nothing I can do about it. Happens here a lot lately. The train can't go forward until Time goes forward. Simple as that.'

'But have we gone backwards?' asked Mrs Rokabye.

'No,' said the guard, 'and praise the Heavens for that or I'd have to get out of bed all over again. We haven't gone backwards, but we haven't gone forwards either, which for a train is a misfortune.'

'I should say it is!' said Mrs Rokabye. 'So how long do we wait?'

'Until your watch starts again,' said the guard. 'You will notice that your watch stopped ten minutes ago.'

'Ridiculous!' said Mrs Rokabye. 'Something should be done.'

Silver looked out of the window. Everything seemed

normal, except that the train was at a standstill and so was the little wristwatch her father had given her. He would know what to do, if only he were here, and then she wondered if he too had got jammed in Time somewhere. After all, he had been on a train, and none of them had ever been found, even though there had been a funeral. Perhaps if she could find the Timekeeper . . .

'Are we getting older while we're sitting here?' Silver asked the guard.

'I don't think so,' said the guard. 'You will be older when you get to your next birthday, but if Time stands still, you won't get there and so you won't be any older.'

'Well, what if we stayed on the train for the rest of our lives?' asked Silver.

'Impossible,' said the guard. 'Time or no time, the buffet closes at six o'clock, and that's that.'

'I want to get off the train!' shouted Mrs Rokabye suddenly. 'I shall get off the train and on to a bus.'

'Sorry, ma'am, it's against company policy to let anyone off the train while it's in a Time Trap. We do not know what is happening out there, and we can't be responsible for your safety. If you leave the train you might be stuck on this section of track for ever.'

'FOR EVER??' said Mrs Rokabye. 'Outside Macclesfield for ever?'

'Regrettably, yes,' said the guard.

Silver was fidgeting with her hands in her pockets and

wishing she had a hard-boiled egg to eat, when she felt something sharp at the bottom of the torn lining in her old duffle coat. She felt round the edges of it with her fingers, and she realised it was the pin or whatever it was that she had found on the floor of the cellar the day she had been shovelling coal for Abel Darkwater.

Maybe if I point it towards London, we'll get there quicker, she thought, and she turned the pointed arrow tip South, and closed her eyes and concentrated as hard as she could.

Nothing happened. Nothing happened at all, in fact that was just the point; the nothingness of what was happening was so intense that it was like waiting for a thunderstorm to break. And then it did.

Silver opened her eyes just as Mrs Rokabye's sweets and magazines came flying past her ear.

'Hold on!' shouted the guard, as the train roared forward.

It was like being in a rocket. Silver felt herself forced back against her seat, and she heard a noise like something whirling round her head. She held on tightly, as the other people in the carriage screamed with panic. Mrs Rokabye was lying across the table in a dead faint.

Silver was scared but she tried to notice what was really happening, and what was happening was that the hands on her watch were going round and round faster and faster, and everything outside the train had gone dark. Then there was a terrific thud, and she heard announcements coming over the tannoy system.

'Ladies and gentlemen, we have now arrived at London Euston. Please take all your belongings with you when you leave the train.'

'What time is it?' said Silver, as the guard got up from under the table.

'An hour earlier than it should be,' he said, consulting his pocket watch, 'if that means anything to you.'

'I want my money back,' said Mrs Rokabye. 'This journey has taken years off my life.'

Silver hoped this was true. She picked up her little bag and followed Mrs Rokabye off the train.

London was a bewildering place, full of roars and noises and dust, and bright red buses and black taxis with yellow lights on top like lit-up wasps.

They got into a black taxi and Mrs Rokabye gave the driver the address on a piece of paper.

'Just visiting, are you?' said the cabbie. 'You come to the wrong place here, Missus. This place has gone barmy. Don't know if it's the Little Green Men or the hole in the Ozone Layer, but Time ain't wot it used to be.'

'I blame mobile phones,' said Mrs Rokabye, who had said this before and was not one to change her mind.

'I think it's our own fault,' said the cabbie. 'We're all going so fast that we're taking Time with us. Nobody's got any time nowadays, rush, rush, rush. Well, here we are, and there's no time left. I reckon Time's running out like everything else on the planet – like oil and water and all that.'

'Very interesting,' said Mrs Rokabye, who was bored rigid,

but Silver thought it *was* very interesting, and she decided that if she had to spend two days with Abel Darkwater she would find out all she could about Time. After all, if she knew a bit more about Time, she might get to know something about the Timekeeper.

Suddenly they drove into a huge crowd of people waving banners.

'What's all this?' demanded Mrs Rokabye.

'Demonstrations against the Time Tornadoes an' all that. People want the Government to do something – but it says there's nothing it *can* do. Time is like the weather, you can't control it, can you?'

'There was an item on last night's news,' said Mrs Rokabye. 'Very worrying for all of you, I'm sure. Look out!'

The taxi had slid to a stop in front of a woman on a bicycle waving a banner that said, 'Time is not Money.'

'Ridiculous!' snorted Mrs Rokabye, who would have sold all the time in the world if only she owned it.

'Civil unrest,' said the cabbie. 'We're heading for big trouble, I tell you.'

Silver watched out of the window as the taxi moved through the modern streets and into an older part of the city where the houses were tall, with square-paned windows.

'Spitalfields,' said the cabbie. 'Old part of town, this, used to be outside the City walls in the days when London had walls all the way round it. Leper colony used to be here, and mad houses and slums and rats the size of Scottie dogs and just as black.'

Mrs Rokabye was not looking impressed. Nobody in her *Beautiful Homes* magazine lived anywhere like this.

'Here we are, then,' said the cabbie, as they pulled up outside an old brown shop, its windows full of clocks and watches.

'Tempus Fugit,' read Silver, looking at the peeling sign over the door. 'And in the window there's a golden chariot with wings, and there is –'

Her heart sank because she didn't like him.

There was Abel Darkwater standing in the doorway waiting to greet them.

TEMPUS FUGIT

Abel Darkwater was a round man.

He had a round face, and a round body, and round rings on his round fingers. The gold loops of his pocket-watch chain were round, and when he drew out his watch, which he did as the taxi pulled up at his door, his watch was round and fat and gold.

'Early,' he observed.

'It was the train,' said Mrs Rokabye. 'First it hardly moved at all, then it shot down here at the speed of light.'

'Are you speaking loosely or accurately?' asked Darkwater. 'Did you actually travel at 300,000 kilometres per second?'

'No,' said Silver, 'but we didn't get any older – the guard said so.'

'He was a ridiculous man,' said Mrs Rokabye. 'I am quite exhausted.'

'And then there was a demonstration in the street,' said Silver.

'Yes, indeed,' said Abel Darkwater, 'and this is only the beginning.'

The beginning of what? thought Silver, but Mrs Rokabye was dragging the bags out of the taxi and complaining about her trials.

'Come in, come in,' said Abel Darkwater. 'This is a treat, an outing, an expedition, no one shall be exhausted, we shall all be happy, oh yes.'

The house was a tall wide house with a broad doorway into the hall, and a flight of stairs at the far end of the hall. The way into the shop was off this hallway, and Abel Darkwater's private apartments were upstairs. The shop was lit by electric light, and looked bright and welcoming, but as the three of them went slowly up the stairs into the house, the only light was from an oil lamp burning on the window ledge. The other rooms were lit with candles.

Mrs Rokabye did not look at all pleased; she had hoped for central heating and plasma-screen TV and thick carpets and leather sofas and one of those fridges that beeped when you were out of milk. Abel Darkwater was very rich, so why did he live in a house that didn't even have electricity?

'I haven't done much to the house since it was built,' he said, reading her thoughts. 'Time passes so quickly, as you discovered on the train.'

Mrs Rokabye sniffed. 'I thought you lived in luxury!'

'Oh, I do, Mrs Rokabye. I live in the luxury of time, and how many of us can say that?'

'When was this house built?' asked Silver, looking at the wooden panelling that lined the rooms, and the heavy shutters folded back on either side of the windows.

'1720,' said Abel Darkwater. 'I – that is, my forebears – moved here in 1738. It has hardly been altered since.'

'Like Tanglewreck,' said Silver, 'but not so old.'

Abel Darkwater smiled, Mrs Rokabye glowered. Why did everyone she knew live in horrible old houses? She longed for a white settee and a glass coffee table and one of those plastic palm trees you didn't have to water.

'Where is the bathroom, please?' she said.

'It hasn't been put in yet,' replied Darkwater. 'There was some talk of it in 1952, but the plumber never came back. I must telephone him soon. For now, dear lady, please use the commode in your bedroom. Sniveller will show you the way.'

'Sniveller?'

'My manservant.'

Abel Darkwater took a bell from his pocket and rang it loudly. There was a sniffing sound from somewhere downstairs in the shop, and then the man Sniveller appeared. He was a short wiry man with no hair at all on his head, and black bunches of it protruding from his bright red nose. He bowed to Mrs Rokabye and begged her to follow him up the stairs. Very dubiously she did so.

'Ah, my dear child. Now we are alone, oh yes, and I have tea ready for us in my study.'

'It's not tea-time,' said Silver.

'Time is what we make it,' said Abel Darkwater, leading the way, 'and in my opinion, there is always time for a piece of chocolate cake, oh yes.'

What a place it was, Abel Darkwater's study!

The floorboards were painted with a circular sundial that

told the hour as the light fell through the window.

There was a grandfather clock on one wall, its pendulum tick-ticking from side to side.

Around the window that overlooked the street were more clocks than Silver could count, and each one told a different time, with its place in the world written underneath it – New York, Tokyo, Los Angeles, Sydney, the North Pole.

There were other names too, ones she had never heard of, with little pictures of stars beneath them.

'Where's Alpha Centauri?' she asked.

'It is the star nearest to ours. It is four light years away. If you were invited to tea on Alpha Centauri in four years' time, you would have to set off now and travel at the speed of light if you wanted to get there before all the cake had been eaten. Fortunately, you are here today, and there is plenty of cake left.'

Abel Darkwater smiled. He was better at smiling than Mrs Rokabye, but Silver had the feeling he had just been practising for longer.

The bookshelves were stuffed with old leather-bound books about clocks and watches. The table was covered in diagrams of cross-sections of old mechanisms. A chronometer lay in pieces in a box on the floor.

Silver looked up at the ceiling; a clock like a children's mobile was gentle swinging round and round.

Everything in the study was ticking, even the two of them, their hearts beating like human clocks.

Silver had a feeling that they were sitting inside Time, and then she wondered, though she knew it was silly, if she could ever climb outside Time?

The second that she had the thought, Abel Darkwater glanced at her.

He's reading my mind, she said to herself, and immediately forced herself to think about cabbage.

Abel Darkwater gave Silver homemade lemonade, with the lemons still floating about in it, and chocolate cake thick as a mattress.

'After tea I will show you my shop,' he said. 'People come from all over the world to buy and sell clocks and watches here. That's how I became acquainted with your dear departed father; he was coming to visit me about the, er, Timekeeper.' He said this last word very quickly, watching Silver's face with his shiny round eyes.

Cabbage, thought Silver, *cabbage, cabbage, cabbage.*

Darkwater frowned and continued, 'Yes, sadly, he was trying to put that remarkable object into my care. It would be safe here, you see, oh yes, safe, and such a thing should be in safe hands, not left alone or neglected or used as a plaything, perhaps?'

'I don't know where it is,' said Silver. 'Don't ask me because I don't know. Mrs Rokabye asks me every day.'

Abel Darkwater smiled again, and continued.

'You don't like Mrs Rokabye, do you? I can't say that I am surprised. I do not like her myself. If I had the Timekeeper, we – that is you – could be rid of Mrs Rokabye for ever.'

'She's my aunt,' said Silver. 'She's signed all the papers. It's legal.'

'Anything is possible,' said Abel Darkwater. 'You could be cared for at Tanglewreck until you are old enough to do as you please. If you were to sell me the Timekeeper, I would arrange everything on your behalf.'

'I don't know where it is! I've never even seen it,' said Silver. 'I'll just have to wait to grow up, that's all.'

'It might be too late by then,' said Abel Darkwater. 'The world is changing. Time is running out.'

He stood up and went over to a cabinet and took out what looked like a golden egg-timer, except that it was about a foot tall. He turned it upside down and the sand began to run through it.

He paused, watching the sand and rocking back and forward on his heels, like a clock pendulum himself.

'I will tell you a story,' he said, 'because children like stories.' He paused for effect, and began.

'Long ago, in the pyramids of Egypt, the great god Ra, the Sun God, told his people that one day the Earth would roll up like a scroll, taking Time with it. The Pharaohs consulted their best magicians, and the magicians told them that before the End of Time there would be one chance left for the world to save itself.

'What chance? To imagine and design and set in motion a device that could regulate Time. Look at all the clocks on the wall telling me the time in every part of the world – and look at those other clocks, that tell me the time in different parts of the universe!

'On Earth, a second in Tokyo is the same length as a second in London, but a second on Jupiter is not the same length as a second on Earth. A clock in a rocket ship runs slower than a clock on Earth. Time is the most mysterious force in the Universe, and the most powerful, oh yes, and whoever controls Time will control the Universe.'

As he said this, his round eyes grew wide as two orbs, and he seemed to float a few inches above the floor. The sound of the clocks ticking was deafening and Silver put her hands over her ears. Abel Darkwater continued to talk.

'In our world, Time is becoming unruly. Some seconds, some minutes, some hours, last longer than others. Some are shorter. We do not know how this is happening, but it is happening.

'The fabric of Time is beginning to tear, and when it tears, the past pokes through, and sometimes the future too. You have heard of the Time Tornadoes that have struck this city, and today you were caught in a Time Trap. So far these things are small enough, but they are signs, signs that, as the great god Ra predicted, Time as we know it may be coming to an end.'

Abel Darkwater went and tapped his hourglass.

'When Time comes to an end, you too will come to an end. I am sure you don't want that to happen.'

There was a knock on the door and Sniveller stood outside with Mrs Rokabye, who was wearing a pair of bright pink earmuffs and complaining about the cold.

'Let me take you down to the shop,' said Abel Darkwater cheerfully, his eyes returning to their normal marble-size. 'The shop has underfloor heating of the most up-to-date kind – for the watches, you know. In the meantime Sniveller will light the fires in all of your rooms, and you will soon be quite warm.'

'Quite warm,' said Mrs Rokabye, 'is not warm enough.'

They went downstairs to the shop. There was a polished glass counter filled with beautiful wristwatches lying on deep red velvet. Clocks lined the walls, and in the corner was a twelve-feet-tall stuffed black bear, his whole body pinned with military and naval operational watches – watches that were also compasses and depth-meters.

In the front window was a golden chariot with wings.

'The emblem of Tempus Fugit,' said Abel Darkwater, 'which I am sure you know means "Time Flies".'

'I told her that,' said Mrs Rokabye, wondering if she could steal a very particular lady's jewelled wristwatch she liked the look of.

'But why is it a chariot with wings?' asked Silver.

'Ah,' said Abel Darkwater, 'it is from a poem written in the sixteenth century by a member of our Society, for we are a Society, you know. Tempus Fugit has a very distinguished history. We are Collectors, and everything here is a Collector's Item. You might say that we collect Time . . .'

'The chariot . . .' said Silver, who knew that grown-ups

can never remember what it was you asked them only five seconds ago.

Abel Darkwater closed his round eyes and rested both hands over his round waistcoat, and began to recite:

'Yet at my back always I hear
Time's winged chariot hurrying near:
And yonder all before us lie
Deserts of vast eternity.

'It is a poem written by a man named Andrew Marvell about Time. We thought – that is, the people in the Society in 1666 thought – that the winged chariot should become our emblem. Here, have one of these.' And he gave Silver a little enamelled badge in the shape of the chariot.

While Abel Darkwater was reciting poetry, Mrs Rokabye had stolen the watch she wanted. Sniveller had seen her, but his Master had instructed him to let Mrs Rokabye alone, whatever she did. So, feeling much warmer, now that she had committed a crime, Mrs Rokabye's temper improved and she agreed to take a small glass of sherry with Abel Darkwater in his study.

And she wanted to know what was happening to the men he had sent to search Tanglewreck.

THUGGER AND FISTY

Thugger and Fisty were crouching in the bushes at Tanglewreck waiting for the taxi to take Mrs Rokabye and Silver to the railway station. Mrs Rokabye had promised to give them the All Clear sign, and she did this by throwing a carrot out of the window as the taxi drove through the gates. She always had carrots in her handbag, in case Bigamist got hungry, so Silver was not surprised to see a carrot appear, though she was surprised to see her throw it out of the window.

'Can't take my country habits to the big city,' she said by way of explanation. 'Suppose when I opened my handbag, the carrot fell out? What would everybody think of me?'

They'd know what a mad old bat you are, thought Silver, saying nothing, and privately concluding that even if Mrs Rokabye were to drag a whole sack of carrots through the London streets, it wouldn't make her seem any worse than she already was.

The taxi drove on, and as soon as it was out of sight, Thugger and Fisty scrambled out of the bushes.

Thugger was a thick-set nasty-looking man who always wore a dark suit and a fitted overcoat. Fisty had to call him Mister Thugger, because in their organisation, Thugger was the boss.

Fisty was thin and sinewy with a face like a ferret. He was a featherweight boxing champion, known in the ring as Flying Fisty, because of his punches. He was very fit and very mean. Not even animals liked Fisty, and animals forgive most people their crimes, but Fisty was the kind of man who kicked dogs and drowned kittens. His only friend in life was a robot-dog called Elvis, who didn't need food or love or taking for walks or stroking or brushing. Elvis had been computer-programmed to love Fisty and bite anything that wasn't Fisty, except for Mister Thugger.

Thugger and Fisty walked up to the house.

'Shall I smash the door in?' said Fisty eagerly.

'How many times have I told you?' said Thugger crossly. 'Darkwater said this is a delicate operation, all right? The Ugly Mug 'oo lives 'ere 'as left the door open. Just turn the 'andle, all right?'

'All right, Mister Thugger.'

Reluctantly, Fisty turned the handle, the door swung open, and the two gents walked into the hall.

Neither of them had ever seen anywhere like Tanglewreck. The hall was wide as a barn, and it had two fireplaces built into the walls. The floor was laid with big slabs of polished stone, and the ceiling was supported by wooden vaulted beams. A rusty dusty suit of armour stood next to a stuffed peacock. Benches and oak chests were lined up along the walls. Somebody's hat had been left where it was, but that was four hundred years ago.

Fisty was smacking his leather-gloved fist into his leather-gloved palm. This job was too quiet for his liking.

'All right, then,' said Thugger, 'one floor at a time, search the place. We're looking for a clock or a watch with an angel on it. No mess, no damage. We got forty-eight hours before the Ugly Mug and her ugly little Muggins come 'ome. Have you programmed Elvis for the scent?'

'I programmed 'im with downloads of watches and clocks from the *Antiques Roadshow* website. Trouble is, what if he eats it when he finds it?'

'He's a robot, he doesn't eat.'

'He swallows things, though, and then I 'ave to git me 'and up the back end an' git 'em out again.'

'Oh, shut up, Fisty, and get on with it. This place is spooky, all suits of armour and big fire grates and them pictures of their ancestors following you with their eyes, I don't like this 'ouse at all. It's a good thing I'm brave. Now go on!'

Thugger and Fisty split up to search Tanglewreck.

Now that Thugger was on his own, he was not feeling at all brave. He always claimed that he didn't believe in ghosts but that was because he had never met one. Today, he had the distinct feeling that someone, or something, was walking behind him.

Never mind. He took out the infrared Searcher that Abel Darkwater had given him, and began scanning the walls and floors of the library. The Searcher was another of Darkwater's own inventions, and it was used to reveal the whereabouts of secret panels and disguised doors, and cupboards hidden behind pictures. Whenever it found something, it began to beep, and then a picture showed up on its screen. It was beeping now, straight at a portrait of Sir Roger Rover wearing his Elizabethan ruff.

Thugger staggered under the weight of lifting the picture from the wall. 'Why couldn't they use a camera in those days like everybody else? This thing weighs a ton, and 'e's an ugly mug too.'

Thugger finally got Sir Roger off the wall, and sure enough, where the picture had been, there was a little door set in the plaster and covered in cobwebs. Thugger got out his multi-tool knife and prised open the door. He put his hand inside and pulled out an old dusty piece of paper.

Must be a clue, he thought. *Spooky houses like this always have clues behind the wall.*

He unrolled the paper, and with difficulty made out the letters written in faded ink.

WHOEVER SEEKS THE TIMEKEEPER WILL NOT FIND IT HERE BUT THE HOUSE WILL FIND HIM.

Thugger didn't know what this meant, but he didn't think it was friendly. He slammed the little door and shoved Sir Roger Rover back on his hook, a bit skew-whiff, but serve him right.

The Searcher found nothing else in the library, so Thugger moved across the wide stone-paved hall into a small room with diamond-leaded windows and a lectern with a big old book lying open there. Thugger didn't read books, he preferred DVDs, but the Searcher was beeping fast as an emu, so he had to stand in front of the lectern and look at the book.

It was a book of poetry written by some demented old dead person who thought he was marvellous. *A Marvell*, it said, and Thugger thought it a bit rich, calling yourself a marvel, especially when you couldn't even spell it properly, but then there were a lot of things they couldn't do in the past, like fly aeroplanes and send text messages. Thugger was glad he didn't live in the past.

Then, as he was wondering why the Searcher was beeping so much at the book, and why he couldn't get an image on his screen, two things happened at once; he got a text message from Fisty that said, 'HELP WHERE R U?' and before he could reply, the lectern was creaking round and round like something in a horror movie and a flight of stone steps had opened up beneath it. The Searcher stopped beeping.

Gingerly, Thugger put his phone back in his pocket, took out his torch, and started off down the stairs.

Things were not going well for Fisty.

He had gone through all the cupboards and drawers in all the bedrooms and tried to make it look like nobody had been there, but whatever he did, he left a trail of socks and knickers and hair brushes and towels, and then there was Elvis the robodog lifting his leg against the beds and savaging the pillow cases.

Spooky dump, this, thought Fisty, who had never seen a four-poster bed and couldn't understand how you could watch TV with all those curtains drawn round you. But then, there were no TVs in the bedrooms – very weird.

'Come on, Elvis, find the watch, there's a good robodog, find the watch and bring it to me and we'll get a big fat reward, that's right, and I'll buy you a new Attack programme for your lovely little microchip brain.'

Elvis barked happily, and the two of them trotted off down the corridor towards the west wing of the house. That would have been all right, but then Bigamist appeared.

Elvis had never seen a rabbit. There were no rabbits in London and his circuit board had never had to memorise one. Fisty had seen rabbits, but never one like this, coal black, the size of a tabby cat, and wearing a diamond collar.

Bigamist had seen dogs, but not dogs with metal legs and 360-degree swivelling ears, and not dogs that HAD NO SMELL. The rabbit twitched his nose, then twitched it again. The man smelt of chicken nuggets and tomato sauce, but the dog had no smell at all.

For a few seconds, the three of them looked at each other, then Fisty decided he'd have a bit of fun. He bent down and pressed Elvis's KILL button.

The dog's Mohican run of purple fake fur down his orange metal back stood on end, and his yellow tongue slavered out of his steel jaws. His black eyes flashed light-up red, and with one bound he leapt on Bigamist, took him in his mouth and threw him across the room.

'Ha ha ha,' laughed Fisty. 'Rabbit pie tonight.'

But Bigamist had other ideas, and he was just as nasty and mean a creature as either Fisty or Elvis, so instead of acting like any normal rabbit and dying of fright, he shot down the corridor with his enemies in pursuit.

Bigamist knew a thing or two about Tanglewreck that Fisty and Elvis didn't know, and he led his pursuers to the one place they least wanted to go – the dungeon.

At the last second the wily rabbit leapt over the false floor-boards, while Fisty and Elvis crashed down on them, and straight through into the dark damp dungeon below.

As they lay in a heap on the floor they saw the rabbit's eyes gleaming down in triumph.

Elvis had lost one of his metal ears in the fall, and was whimpering sadly, but Fisty didn't care about Elvis's ear. It was his phone he was worried about – what if it had broken when it had fallen out of his pocket?

He scrabbled round in the dark, until at last he found it, in a puddle on the floor, and keyed in his desperate text message to Thugger: HELP WHERE R U?

But Thugger

by now

was very lost and very frightened in a room that opened on to a room that opened on to a room that opened on to a room that opened on to a room that opened on to a room that . . . room, opened, a, on to, room, room, room, room, room, room, ooooooooooooooo!

MIDNIGHT EVERYWHERE?

I t was late at night.

Abel Darkwater and Mrs Rokabye were sitting over the fire in the study. Silver was fast asleep in her bed. The great house Tanglewreck was keeping watch over its new prisoners.

At eight o'clock that evening, Sniveller the manservant had delivered fish, chips and peas and jam roly-poly pudding to Silver in the little wooden-panelled rooms that sat by side on the third floor of the house. He put down the plate, and knocked out a huge dollop of tomato sauce on the side.

'The more you eat the bigger your feet,' Sniveller had said, putting down the plates. 'Eat today, gone tomorrow.'

'Are you talking to me or someone else?' said Silver.

'I don't know who and neither do you. Ignorance is a closer friend than knowledge.'

'Why is this house full of clocks?' asked Silver.

'Why is the sea full of fish?' replied Sniveller.

'Why do your trousers only come down as far as your knees?'

'But my legs come down as far as my feet.'

'But you aren't wearing any socks or shoes,' said Silver.

'It's after eight o'clock. No shoes or socks after eight o'clock. Wouldn't want me to run away, would you?'

'Would you run away if you were wearing socks and shoes?'

'Oh, I would, if it was past eight o'clock. Yes, I would, everybody knows that. Now eat your supper and go to sleep. Tails and heads in the bed. Which is which?'

Sniveller spun a coin in the air.

'HEADS,' shouted Silver.

'Heads to the window, tails to the door,' announced Sniveller, pocketing the coin, and re-arranging the pillows on the little iron bed. 'That's your head lying North and your feet lying South, all compass-like and content. Goodnight.'

Sniveller had made a little bow and backed out of the door, sniffing his way down the stairs.

Silver was sleepy after the journey, and the strangeness of the place, and although she wanted to keep awake, her eyes kept dropping shut. The room was warm and soft, with its low fire burning in the grate, and its two candles flickering on the table. The food was plentiful and hot, but as soon as Silver had finished eating, she forced herself to get into her pyjamas before she went to clean her teeth at the little wash-stand in the room. She was so tired that she couldn't even pull faces at herself in the mirror, which was what she usually did while she cleaned her teeth.

She was busy scrubbing away with the toothbrush when she suddenly looked up. In the mirror she saw Abel Darkwater's face – yes, it was his face! She spun round, but the room was empty.

Silver was feeling uneasy. She went through into the connecting room, with its little iron bedstead. The bed looked soft and inviting. She swung up her legs, then suddenly, for no reason, decided to turn round the pillows and sleep the other way. Yes, that felt better. She leaned on her elbow to blow out the candle, then changed her mind.

'I won't blow out the candle. I'll play a game with the shadows until I fall asleep. I'll pretend I'm on a ship sailing out to sea with Sir Roger Rover.'

Then she thought of her daddy, and how he would have kissed her and told her not to worry about anything at all.

'I wish Daddy was here,' she whispered to herself. 'He'd tell me what to do.'

And Silver's eyes were full of tears but she was brave too. She burrowed herself deep under the blankets and let herself go to sleep.

Down in the study, Sniveller was serving wine to his Master and Mrs Rokabye.

'I am going to hypnotise Silver,' said Abel Darkwater.

'I was once hypnotised,' observed Mrs Rokabye. 'I was told I was a chicken and I laid an egg.'

'This is not seaside entertainment,' snapped Darkwater. 'I shall draw Silver back through Time until I reach the moment where her father tells her what he intends to do with the Timekeeper.'

'If he ever did tell her,' said Mrs Rokabye. 'I believe that child is as ignorant as a cockle.'

'Even cockles have their uses,' replied Darkwater. 'Silver has already fallen into a deep sleep. All that remains is for Sniveller to bring me to the child and I shall do my work.'

Mrs Rokabye had no worries about what might happen to Silver, but she was brooding about Bigamist.

'I hope your horrible henchmen haven't upset my rabbit,' she said. 'When I said you could search Tanglewreck, I told you to be especially careful of Bigamist.'

Abel Darkwater's eyes swelled with irritation. 'My henchmen, as you call them, seem unable to answer their mobile phones. We must assume they have failed in their mission and that possibly they are dead.'

'Dead!' cried Mrs Rokabye. 'What are you saying, Mr Darkwater? Is it not enough that I have to pass my days in a horrible house without carpets or central heating or even a fridge, and now you tell me that there are two dead bodies there as well?'

'I cannot say, but I can say that Sniveller will go back with you if you prefer, and remove any offending objects.'

Mrs Rokabye was about to say that she found Sniveller himself an offending object, but he had returned to the room to tell Darkwater that the child was ready for hypnosis.

'Are you sure she is quite asleep?' said Darkwater urgently.

'Quite asleep, Master. I put opium in the tomato sauce.'

'What a marvellous idea!' said Mrs Rokabye, looking at Sniveller with new eyes. 'I hope you will tell me where I can buy some. London has everything!'

'I get mine from a Chinaman in Whitechapel,' said

Sniveller. 'Three stops on the Underground and a hundred years back in Time.'

Mrs Rokabye was looking confused and Darkwater was glaring. He took out his enormous gold pocket watch, and examined it closely, like a face in the mirror.

'Excuse us, Mrs Rokabye. Help yourself to wine and chocolates, won't you?'

'Don't mind if I do,' said Mrs Rokabye, settling down as best she could in the hard high-backed wooden chair. Still, the wine and chocolates were very nice and she was suddenly feeling sleepy herself.

'Don't mind if I do . . .' she said, as the glass slipped from her hand.

Abel Darkwater and Sniveller made their way slowly up the stairs.

'What did you put in her wine?' asked Darkwater.

'Chloroform drops,' said Sniveller. 'Undetectable in claret.'

'Excellent,' said Darkwater. 'Help me with the child, then carry Mrs Rokabye here up to bed. Are we heads or tails tonight?'

'Heads is North-facing. Wind quite bracing,' said Sniveller.

'Heads,' repeated Darkwater, opening the door into the shadowy room. 'Heads.'

Silver heard the door open, as the boards creaked under

the weight of the two men. She pretended to be asleep.

Sniveller stepped forward quickly and clipped a thick cloth, stretched like canvas, to the four upright rails of the little bed. It was like lying under a flat tent.

Abel Darkwater drew what looked like two interlocking triangles, making a pointed star on the canvas, and in the middle of the star, he placed a ticking clock. Then he said something in a language Silver couldn't understand, and a bright green flame lit up the room. She could see the outline of the men clearly now, at the foot of the bed.

Abel Darkwater began to pass his hands across the top of the canvas and directly over her feet.

'You are going back in Time,' he said, 'back in Time, not far, not far at all, but a few years, oh yes, just a few, and your father and mother are still alive.'

Silver lay absolutely still and rigid with terror. Then a very strange thing started to happen.

As Abel Darkwater spoke on and on in the language she couldn't understand, she felt herself slipping and shifting, like she was disappearing from her own body and going somewhere else. She felt very light. She was moving very fast. She was crossing time like it was a street. She was moving from Time Now into Time Then.

Then she saw it. She saw it exactly as though someone was projecting it on to a wall. Behind Abel Darkwater was the face of her father. Her beloved father!

Darkwater turned, and because Silver was lying the wrong way round, she risked raising her head on the pillow, hoping he wouldn't see her under the canvas. They were back at Tanglewreck...

It was a cold day and the bear in the garden was covered in snow. It was a hedge bear, made out of box plants and shaped and trimmed by their father. There were foxes too, and a deer standing with its face towards the forest.

'Once,' said her father, 'these creatures lived here when the forest came as close as the edge of the garden. There were still bears in England when this house was new.'

Her father was wearing a knitted tie and a thick wool shirt, and a big loose heavy jacket. He took something out of his pocket and the children looked at it in wonder.

'This is the most beautiful object in the world,' he said, 'but I think it is alive too.'

'Is it a watch or a clock?' said Silver.

'It's called the Timekeeper,' said her father. 'Its mysteries are hard to understand. I don't really understand it myself. I'm taking it to London tomorrow to show it to a man who will tell me everything about it. He wants me to sell it to him, but I won't do that.'

'Can I come with you?'

'Not this time. Next time. This time we'll take Buddleia because she needs to see a doctor about her leg.'

Their father was gazing at the clock. 'Our ancestors were given it to keep safe by someone who was very unsafe himself. It was a long time ago, and they looked after him, and he asked them to keep this for him. It's been in the family for hundreds of years – nearly as long as the house – and now it's my turn to look after it, and one day, it will be your turn.'

'You never showed it to me before.'

'No. I keep it hidden.'

'Why do you hide it?'

'Oh, just because I have a feeling that someone else might want it.'

'Where do you hide it?'

As she said that, the image of her father holding the clock became bigger and bigger, then it began to waver and fade. Abel Darkwater started shouting at the top of his voice, and the light in the room was so bright that Silver fell back and closed her eyes.

Abel Darkwater was leaning over her feet. 'He hid it somewhere, didn't he? Where did he hide it? He hid it in the house or the garden, didn't he? Take me there, follow the day that I have given you – follow your father. Where is it? Where is it?'

Suddenly the room went dark. Abel Darkwater was breathing heavily. Silver felt in her body that whatever had happened to her was over.

Sniveller and Abel Darkwater left the bedroom and went into the adjoining room where Silver had eaten her supper. She could hear them talking in low voices, but they had shut the door and she couldn't hear what they were saying.

Without really planning it, Silver slid quickly out of bed and pulled on her jeans, fleece and socks over her pyjamas.

She slipped out on to the landing and padded silently

down the stairs. How dark it was! The stairs wound down and down like the spring of a clock, and as her fingers felt the walls to steady herself, her body made giant shadows thrown by the candlelight.

She reached the wide hall. There was the telephone on the table. It was a funny-looking thing; upright, like a black candlestick, with a microphone at the top to speak into, and a listening tube hanging at the side, and a dial at the base that you had to spin round to get the numbers. She had seen Abel Darkwater using it that afternoon, so she knew what to do.

Looking round nervously, she lifted the tube and dialled 999.

A voice answered. 'What number are you, caller?'

'I don't know,' said Silver. 'I want the police, please.'

'Yes, tell me your number, caller.'

'It's not my phone. I want someone to help me.'

'Details, please. Name. Address.'

Before Silver could say anything else, there was a great roar from upstairs, and she heard Abel Darkwater shouting at the top of his voice, 'You snivelling idiot. Where is the child?'

Silver dropped the phone and ran to the front door. It was locked and bolted. She slid back the big bolt at the bottom of the door, and turned the hoop-topped iron key in the boxy brass lock, but she couldn't reach the top bolt, and Abel Darkwater was coming down the stairs. She turned away and frantically shook the door handle into the shop. It opened. She rushed inside and closed the door behind her. Was she trapped or was there another way out?

In the shop there was no sound at all except for one ticking clock – just one. The time was five minutes to midnight.

The display cabinets of watches and clocks were lit by dim red lights that made the gold and silver casings glow like the bodies of luminous insects, and the shiny glass faces of the watches were like great round eyes. Like Abel Darkwater's eyes, she thought.

Silver was too frightened to be frightened. Her whole body was numb but her mind was racing. She had seen that the door at the back of the shop led into a small courtyard. Perhaps there was a way out there.

As she made her way towards the door, the one and only ticking clock suddenly paused, and then began to strike midnight. As it did so, every single clock and watch in the shop, all the ones that hadn't been ticking at all, chimed and belled and rang the hour, MIDNIGHT, MIDNIGHT, MIDNIGHT.

Silver put her hands over her ears. There were cuckoos flying out of wooden clocks on the wall, and brown-faced men wearing fezzes walking out of a clock shaped like a pyramid, and a dog that flew from its kennel barking the hour, and a woman banging a kettle with a stick, and a bell tolling from side to side in the steeple of a church, and over the top of all of them was Abel Darkwater's voice coming from nowhere.

'The universe was not born in Time but born with Time. Time and the Universe are twin souls birthed together. Whoever controls Time controls the Universe. Whoever has the Timekeeper controls Time.'

Abel Darkwater was standing in the open shop doorway in a triangle of light. As he came towards Silver, she dashed between his legs, but he reached down and caught her, and picked her up and slung her over his shoulder.

'Let me go! Let me go!'

Laughing, Darkwater stepped slowly into the hall, and stood with his back towards the front door of the house, looking up the stairs as Sniveller came down with a steaming purple glass.

'Drinking stops you thinking,' he said. 'Give her this and she'll be asleep in no time, Master.'

'You said that earlier and the child is wide awake, as you can see.'

'I dosed the tomato sauce, yes I did,' said Sniveller, cowering.

'I hate tomato sauce!' yelled Silver, her legs kicking, her head staring at the door. Then suddenly she saw what to do, yes, now that Abel Darkwater had lifted her up, she could pull back the top bolt, then if only she could just . . .

She wriggled forward with such a thrust that Darkwater lost his balance, and Silver had the bolt in her hands before he stumbled and dropped her. Sniveller lunged forward to catch her but tripped over Darkwater, who was too heavy and slow to move quickly. Silver knew that the door was fully unlocked now and if only she could just turn the knob . . .

She was free! She was outside in the street! She had no

shoes on her feet, but she could run, and run she did, she didn't know where, until the lights of the city seemed far away and, breathless and sweating, she stood on one sore foot, on a bank by the River Thames.

RABBITS!

Midnight was chiming as Fisty and Elvis lay in the damp cellar, hands and feet tied.

Bigamist was not the only rabbit in the house, and once he had his enemies safely dropped down the hole, he signalled to a few of his friends and relations, and they all came along with twine from their carrot sacks and ran round and round the unhappy pair until they were as tightly bound as wasps in a spider's web.

Fisty had tried kicking them at first, but they were all black, all identical, and if he sent one of them flying through the air, another one bit him. Elvis was no use at all. His KILL button had been disabled in the fall, and the rabbits had taken away his remote control. He was a dog without means or purpose.

'What am I supposed to eat?' demanded Fisty, wondering why he was talking to a rabbit, but Bigamist seemed to understand, and before long half a sack of soft mouldy carrots was pushed down into the cellar. With his hands and feet tied, the only way that Fisty could eat them was to lie on the floor and dig in the sack with his head.

'Fur 'ats, every one of 'em,' he said to himself between mouldy miserable bites. 'I'll make 'em all into 'ats and sell 'em on eBay.'

But no one was listening, because Elvis had lost his ears, the rabbits had gone, and Thugger was in another part of the dungeon having some very unpleasant problems of his own.

MIDNIGHT
EVERYWHERE

The River Thames at Limehouse bows away from the City. The river glitters darkly. The river reflects the starless London sky. The river flows on to the sea. The river flows in one direction, but Time does not. Time's river carries our spent days out to sea and sometimes those days come back to us, changed, strange, but still ours. Time's flow is not even, and there are snags underwater, hesitations in Time where the clock sticks. A minute on Earth is not the same length as a minute on Jupiter. A minute on Earth is sometimes a different length all by itself.

Big Ben was chiming midnight.

When Silver heard the chime, she thought it was one o'clock in the morning and that she had been running for an hour. But then the clock went on chiming its grave and solemn toll, and she knew it was still midnight, or that midnight had come again.

The city was still. Faint car noises came from the road behind the old warehouses and wharf buildings, but in front of her was the river, no ships, no barges, only the stretch of water from one side of the bank to the other.

What should she do now?

She sat down, her back against a stone wall, her knees drawn up to her chin, her arms round her knees. She wanted to cry, but she knew she mustn't. She pictured Tanglewreck in her mind, solid and secure and waiting for her, and she had a feeling that the house was doing its best to help. Then she remembered why she had come to London in the first place; because there was something important to do. If it was important, it was bound to be difficult. She wouldn't cry and she wouldn't give up.

Then, as these thoughts began to make her feel better, she sensed that the ground underneath her was shaking faintly, as though a big train was passing below.

She had the feeling of something enormous, invisible, and very near. Her heart tightened.

Gingerly, like a cat, she edged forward on all fours. How dark and quiet it was, the city breathing like a sleeping animal.

Then, she saw it, head down, just underneath her on the bank, drinking from the river, the water pouring off its tusks as its head came out of the water. It looked like a cross between a bull and an elephant. It had dark curly hair all over its body, and huge thighs and shoulders, and legs that sunk into the mud as it walked.

It took a lumbering step forward and the wall she sat on shook.

It was a Woolly Mammoth.

Silver didn't know what Woolly Mammoths liked to eat but she wanted to make sure it wasn't her, so she kept very still as its great head swung round to stare up the bank.

Then she heard a voice, a boy's voice, but high and piercing.

'Get thee back into, Goliath! Get thee back into, afore thee be seen by Devils.'

The Mammoth turned and shuffled off towards an open culvert in the bank. Silver couldn't contain her curiosity. She stood up and looked down on to the muddy stretch where the river lapped, and the second she looked down, the boy looked up. He was the oddest-looking boy you ever saw.

'Do you laugh at me?' he said.

'No,' said Silver, 'course not.'

But before either of them could say anything else, they heard a shrill whistle, like at the start of a football match, and then the sound of running feet.

'Dive!' shouted the boy, disappearing. 'Devils!'

Silver looked round, and saw that Abel Darkwater was behind her, with Sniveller dressed in a policeman's uniform, but a very old-fashioned policeman's uniform. His feet were still bare and he was carrying a cage with a blanket in it.

'Put the child in the cage,' commanded Darkwater, and before Silver could run or fight, she found herself upended by Sniveller's wiry arms and thrust inside the metal bars.

'Got her this time, Master, snug as a bug in a rug.'

'Let me go!'

Abel Darkwater laughed and put his face near the bars. His eyes were like two deep wells with faint lights at the bottom. Silver felt herself going dizzy.

'I knew you would come here, to this very river, to this very spot. You can't help yourself finding the way.'

'I don't know where I am,' said Silver, weakly now.

'Oh yes, Silver, yes you do, though you do not. The Thames is an old river, a dirty river, centuries have been pumped into it. The ancient Britons lived by its waters, and fought the Roman armies as they drew slowly up the river from Gravesend. Elizabeth the First sailed down this river to greet your ancestor Roger Rover at Deptford.

'Now it is your turn, Silver. We are going on a boat journey together, and whether or not you ever return will depend on what you tell me about the Timekeeper.'

'I haven't got it!' Silver jumped back to life, shaking the bars. 'I keep telling you I haven't got it. I don't know where I am and I don't know where it is.'

'But you will lead me to it. I am certain, oh yes, very certain. Sniveller, pick up the cage and carry it down to the water, and signal for the boat.'

'Help!' shouted Silver. 'Help!'

'There is no one to hear you,' said Abel Darkwater.

But there was someone to hear her. Out of the darkness flew a figure of fury followed by half a dozen yapping dogs who set on Darkwater and Sniveller, biting and snapping, while the feet-flying, furious odd boy wrenched open the cage door and pulled Silver out.

He grabbed her hand and together they ran over the rough ground until they came to a manhole with its cover half off.

'Down!' said the boy. 'Fast as a flea.'

Silver did as she was told and the boy followed her, pulling the lid over them.

'My dogs will come down the Swan Hole,' he said.

'I can't see anything,' said Silver. 'What swan hole? 'Where are you? Where are we?'

There was a groping noise, then a flaring sound, and suddenly Silver could see everything by the light of a makeshift torch that seemed to be rags wrapped round a pole and soaked in paraffin. They had plenty of paraffin heaters at Tanglewreck, so she knew the smell.

There was the boy; about four and a half feet tall, heavily built, wearing a dirty blue coat fastened here and there by brass buttons, over a collarless shirt. His legs were in knee breeches, like the ones Sniveller wore, and he had no socks under his big heavy laced-up boots. His hands were like the front feet of a mole; spade-square with thick fingers. He had black hair, a very pale face, big moony eyes, and, *this was it, this was the thing*, he had the biggest ears on either side of his head that Silver had ever seen on a human being.

If he was a human being . . .

The boy watched her looking him up and down, and then he said again, 'Do you laugh at me?'

'No,' said Silver. 'You saved me. Thank you very much. My name is Silver. Who are you?'

'I am called Gabriel,' answered the boy. 'A Throwback.'

'A what?' asked Silver.

'A Throwback. That be my Clan and my Kind. We dwell

under the earth, and we do not live as Updwellers do.'

'What's an Updweller?'

'You be an Updweller.'

Silver looked at the strange boy, with his strange speech and ragged clothes, and she felt two things simultaneously; two feelings so twinned together that she couldn't separate them. She felt that she had known this boy all her life, which was silly because she had just met him, and she felt that she could trust him. Since her father had died, and Mrs Rokabye had come, and everything had gone wrong, this was the first time that Silver felt she had a friend. She didn't think about what she felt, she just spoke straight away, without explaining.

'I am in trouble. Will you help me?'

The boy nodded. 'Let us go together to the Chamber.'

'The Chamber?'

'Come,' said Gabriel.

GHOSTS!

Thugger was having an underground experience too.

He had gone down the hidden flight of stairs into the cellars, and as soon as his feet had touched the bottom step, the opening to the reading room above had closed with a dreadful grinding noise. However he was going to get out would not be the way he had come in.

He swallowed hard and decided to be brave. It was very dark so he got out his torch and flashed it around.

Cobwebs everywhere, YUK! which meant spiders everywhere, big YUK! And the biggest YUK! of all was the slime. His fingers turned green from feeling their way along the walls. Suppose he was walking into a sewer?

Sewers meant rats, and Thugger didn't like rats.

At last he found a door and opened it thankfully. Doors meant rooms or passageways, and rooms and passageways led out of sewers.

He went into the room – nothing there, but there was another door. He opened it into a room with two doors, tried one, and found it led into a room with three doors. He went back and tried the second door of the second room. It led into another room with three doors, which led into

103

another room with four doors, and now the doors were like mirrors, every one identical, every one showing him the same thing, but multiplying themselves, so that he no longer knew which doors he had tried and which doors were untried.

He panicked, and ran through the rooms, pulling open the doors. There were echoes too – footsteps, his own, they must be his own. The rooms were an echo chamber and the noises were delayed, because even when he stood still he could hear footsteps in the other rooms.

'Who's there?' he called, and the voice answered, 'THERE THERE THERE.'

He spun round. Where where where?

'Who are you?'

'YOU YOU YOU,' the voice said.

'I'm not scared!'

'SCARED SCARED SCARED.'

'I've got to get out of 'ere,' Thugger whispered to himself so that the Echo wouldn't hear him, but it did hear him, and chased him step by step and room by room, as he went on through the endless house.

'HERE HERE HERE.'

'It's just my voice,' he said. 'I'm lost and I don't like it, that's all, but there's nothing to worry about.'

Then he fell over. No, he didn't fall over, he was tripped up; someone or something had put out their hand and pulled him flat on his nose. Punching wildly, his closed fist hit a solid object that straight away hit him back right over the head. As he lost consciousness he had the feeling that he knew what, or who, it was.

THE THROWBACKS

S ilver had never seen anything like the underground world of the Throwbacks.

She followed Gabriel down a narrow passage about six
inches deep in water. She had no shoes on, and running
through the city had torn her socks. Now she was footsore
and soaked, but she didn't say anything, just hoisted up her
jeans and pyjamas to keep them dry, and walked as quickly as
she could. Bits of rubbish were floating about in the water;
old crisp packets and burger boxes, and she was glad when
they began to move slightly uphill, and the water shallowed
out to indented puddles in the clay floor.

Gabriel didn't speak to Silver until they were able to walk
side by side.

'This be the way to the Chamber, but we must go by the
Devils.'

'Who are the Devils?'

'You shall see them.'

The roof of the passage was getting higher, when suddenly
Gabriel doused his torch in a puddle and pulled Silver into an
opening in the wall. As they stood still and silent as statues,
she could hear voices approaching, and then she saw four men
wearing red waterproof suits and full-face helmets with some

kind of air filter on the front. They carried high-pressure water guns. She guessed they were for the maintenance of the drains or something like that. Whatever they were, they weren't devils, but Gabriel was trembling.

As soon as the men had gone by, towards the culvert where the Mammoth had come in, Gabriel took Silver's hand and they started on their journey again. He was fearful, and kept looking round.

'It's all right, Gabriel,' said Silver. 'They are human beings like us. Um, well, like me, but men, and grown up. They aren't devils.'

'Did you not see their red bodies and their heads of monsters and their weapons?'

'Those were just waterproof clothes and water guns and some sort of safety helmet, that's all. When they take it off they look like humans, like Updwellers.'

'They cannot take off their heads and bodies,' said Gabriel, 'and I have seen them use their water-weapons. Water is soft but the Devils magic it hard as iron.'

'It's pressurised,' said Silver.

'You do not know them,' said Gabriel. 'It is Goliath they seek.'

'The Mammoth.'

'Yea. The Devils will kill him with their weapons.'

'Gabriel,' said Silver, 'do you ever go above ground?'

'We cannot live Upground. We can go there but we cannot live there. We would be killed.'

'Who would kill you?'

'Devils or Wardens or the soldiers, or the White Lead Man.'

Silver couldn't understand this at all, so she fell silent and looked around her to see what these tunnels and passages were.

They were built of brick, and here and there steel ladders were anchored to the walls, leading upwards, she supposed, to the pavement and all those metal plates and grilles that you can see when you walk around the city. She had never thought about what was underneath all those plates and grilles. She had never guessed that there might be a whole world.

A rumbling through the wall made her think that they must be near a Tube train station. She glanced at Gabriel; he didn't seem bothered by the noise.

'What's that?' she said, to see if he knew what it was.

'That be the Long Wagon,' said Gabriel. 'Updwellers use him when they come down here. They fear to walk here by themselves. They come all together in the Long Wagon.'

'Why do they come down here – the Updwellers?'

Silver knew that everybody used the Tube to travel round the city, but she wanted to know what Gabriel thought about it.

'It be their loneliness,' he said. 'Updwellers be lonely for the ground they come from. They come here to remember.'

Silver was beginning to realise that Gabriel's world was not like her own world one bit. But then her world had a lot wrong with it, so she wasn't going to say anything rude about his.

'Updwellers lived here once. Look and see.'

Gabriel opened a little door in the wall and led her on to a deserted platform.

At first it looked like any other Tube station platform, but then Silver realised that the posters on the walls were from the Second World War, because all the people in them were wearing gas masks.

'Updwellers,' repeated Gabriel, and sure enough, they came to a row of rotting stripy mattresses, with blankets still thrown on them, and here and there old newspapers and magazines.

'Air-raid shelters,' said Silver, who had read about the war.

'This be the time when all people dwelt underground,' said Gabriel.

Silver didn't believe this was true, but she didn't want to argue, and she was fascinated by this caught moment of Time. It was as though Time had got trapped here and couldn't move on. She didn't feel like she did when she went to a museum and saw lots of old things; she felt as though Time existed differently here. Even though the people had gone away and gone forward, Time itself was left here, or a piece of Time, anyway, as real and solid as the mattresses and tin mugs.

The dirty faded signs on the wall said ALDGATE WEST.

'My work be to find supper,' said Gabriel. 'I may not return without our supper.'

'Where are you going to find that?' asked Silver, wondering why anyone ate supper in the early hours of the morning.

'Here,' said Gabriel, and he disappeared.

Now Silver was alone in the dark, listening to the rats and mice scurrying about their business. She shut her eyes and visualised her little room at Tanglewreck, with the fire lit, and whatever food she had been able to steal from under Mrs Rokabye's selfish and sharp eyes. She supposed that Mrs Rokabye had arranged everything with Abel Darkwater, but did that mean she was really bad, or just greedy and stupid? Grown-ups were always worrying about money, she knew that, but what did you need if you could eat and sit in front of the fire and read books? That was what Silver would do with her money.

She wondered if the Throwbacks had any money . . .

Just then Gabriel reappeared, dragging a large sack.

'Pizza,' he said, 'from the Pizza Hut.'

'You've been to Pizza Hut?' asked Silver disbelievingly.

'My mother Eden be from the Kingdom of Italy. There be a Hut up a stretch from this place and at this hour a Short Wagon comes and two Updwellers bring these boxes to the Hut. It be a depot for food. Come.'

Dragging his sack, he hurried along the deserted platform and disappeared into the tunnel where the trains came through. Not wanting to be left behind, Silver ran after him.

It was now pitch black, and there were heavy dripping noises coming from above. Every five seconds, Silver felt another cold drop slither down her neck or her nose. She was damp all over and beginning to shiver. All she wanted to do was sleep.

Something is following me, she thought, and looked fearfully behind her into the solid darkness. There was nothing to be seen, nothing to be heard, except for scurrying and dripping, but she was sure that that there were more than two of them in the tunnel.

Suddenly, coming towards them, she saw a flare, then another and another, and Gabriel ran ahead, while she hesitated, and then a man appeared like an apparition out of the half-light. He was heavily built, like Gabriel, taller, though not much, and he wore a black fur coat. Gabriel said something to him, and he nodded, before striding up to Silver.

'We greet you as a Stranger. Micah will hear your story, he will.'

'You've got to help me,' said Silver. 'There's a terrible man who . . .'

But she said no more because she fainted clean away.

When she came round she could hear low voices, and she sensed the low light on her eyelids. For a moment she didn't open her eyes, because she wanted to be awake without anybody knowing.

She was warm. The air smelled of petrol and dogs. Someone was playing what sounded like a recorder.

She opened one eye just a little. A group of men, women and children were sitting round a fire dug into a shallow pit and piled with old crates and pallets. Most were drinking something out of what looked like giant tin mugs. Some had mending, or knitting or carving on their knees.

The men were short and square with their hair tied back in brief ponytails. Silver knew better than to stare at their ears, but they all had ears the size of hands. The women were taller than the men, and slender, like shoots growing up towards the light. The children looked strong, and some of them were playing with the dogs, or riding round the edges of the chamber on the smallest ponies Silver had ever seen.

'Bog ponies,' said a voice by her ear. 'The dogs be Jack Russells, the ponies be bog ponies, and my name be Micah, and I be the Leader of the Clan.'

Silver opened both her eyes and looked at the man who had come out of the shadows. The others were all dark haired, but Micah was blond. He wore a shirt with the sleeves rolled up, a torn waistcoat embroidered with flowers, and a pair of blue seaman's trousers. He had a long clay pipe in his hand, and on his fingers he wore gold rings three deep.

Silver sat up. She was feeling stronger but she was starving.

'Hello,' she said. 'Gabriel rescued me. Can I have some food, please?'

'Eden! Bring you food for the child?'

A woman came forward with a wooden dish. There was a piece of pizza in it, and some thick yellow soup. *'Eccola bambina bella!'* said Eden. Silver didn't care what it was, she ate and ate, and all the time Micah watched her.

Then Silver started to tell the whole story of her parents, and Mrs Rokabye, and Abel Darkwater, and the opium in the tomato sauce.

'And what be the reason of all this doing?' asked Micah.

'It's a clock called the Timekeeper, and a house called Tanglewreck.'

Micah's face changed, but he did not say what it was that had caused his pale face to redden, and then turn paler than before. He knocked out his pipe and stared into the low fire.

Then he said, 'We will help you, we will. We know the man Abel Darkwater.'

'You know him?'

'We did know him, we did, once upon a time, yea, and we know of his business.'

Micah clapped his hands and everyone stopped their work or their drinking, and the dogs stopped jumping over each other, and the ponies stood quietly at the back.

'We have no traffic with Updwellers,' said Micah, 'but you be a child and a Stranger, and it be in our beliefs to help Strangers. All of us that you see here before you were Strangers once, so we were.'

And Micah, in his high singsong voice, began to tell of how it began that the Throwbacks had come to be.

'There be a hospital called Bedlam – though not what you would call a hospital now in your own time, but a terrible tall torture of a place where a man or a woman might be tied to a chair for days at a time and fed no food but dead mice.

'It was a Mad House. It was a place for the Insane, though many of us who went there had no insanity, no, none at all, but we were an offence to our masters. Many ways there be to get into Bedlam but only one way to get out. And that was the narrow way that all must take. Yea, Death.

'I be in Bedlam myself in the year 1768 and that year the Warden minted the name of the Throwbacks for us, and hung the names round our necks in these medallions – yea, these medallions, look you here.'

Micah reached round his neck and took out a circular metal disc on a chain. On one side was his name, MICAH, and on the other side the word BEDLAM.

'Throwbacks we be, and by his cruelty he called us after angels too, for our Christian names, to make the visitors laugh, for in those times visitors come to Bedlam and other Houses of the Mad, to laugh at us like wild beasts.

'Strong I be, and clever too in my way, yea, and I see one day that there be a rusty door in a rusty cell, and I contrived to get time in there and I found it led out and away, if only we digged enough, and for three years long we digged enough, and we found a way to be free, and many of us escaped underground, and hid here.

'When we were free we discovered a strange thing, yea, that underground we be not living and dying as Updwellers do, but that for us, Time moves more slow, creeps like darkness. We live long lives, not like to Updwellers, and we know not Time as you know Time.'

'But how do you know Abel Darkwater?' asked Silver.

'He be that man,' answered Micah. 'He be that man who named us.'

'What, in the Bedlam place?'

'Yea, he be the Warder of Bedlam.'

'But that was like two hundred and forty years ago, or something. He isn't that old – I mean, he's old, but he's not, like two hundred and forty or whatever.'

'I be as old as he.'

'Nobody lives to two hundred and forty! Even Mrs Rokabye isn't a hundred!'

'In thy world I would be dead. In my world, I am alive.'

Silver fell silent. She didn't know whether to believe him or not – she wanted to believe him, but how could he be so old? And Abel Darkwater too?

Micah put his hand on her shoulder and smiled. 'You be young. Our story be strange to you. Rest now. Sleep.'

'I left my shoes behind,' said Silver, looking sadly at her torn socks and blistered feet.

Micah gestured to one of the women, who brought Silver what looked like a pair of clogs with shiny buckles. She gave them to her, and a pair of hand-knitted woollen socks. When she saw the state of poor Silver's feet, all bleeding and sore, she went away and came back with a tin of something thick and yellow and nasty-smelling, and rubbed it all over Silver's feet. It felt wonderful.

'What's that?' said Silver.

'Dog grease and cloves.'

'Dog grease!'

'When a dog of ours be dead, amen, we renders him in a cauldron, and we forms him into this good grease.'

'You do that to your dogs?'

'Yea, but not afore they be dead, amen. What do Updwellers make with their dogs that are dead?'

'Um, we bury them or the vet takes them away.'

'Wasteful,' said the woman. 'Wicked wasteful.'

Silver felt quite sick to be covered in boiled-down dog, but she didn't dare say anything. She just pulled on her socks quickly and tried to forget about what was on her feet as she drank the delicious hot apple cider she had been given.

Soon she fell deeply asleep.

STRANGE MEETING

M rs Rokabye was eating breakfast.
It was rather a good breakfast of kippers and toast and hot chocolate, and she was glad that no Silver had appeared to come and spoil everything. She had promised herself the last kipper, and she was eyeing it so greedily that Sniveller got up with a sigh and slapped it down on her plate.

'If the child wants to sleep, she can't expect breakfast,' announced Mrs Rokabye.

'Sleep she may, but not today,' said Sniveller.

'What are you talking about?' asked Mrs Rokabye, who longed to be alone with her kipper.

'She's run away.'

Mrs Rokabye put down her knife and fork. 'Run away? From here? From me?' She bit the head off her kipper. 'How sharper than a serpent's tooth.'

'Found a bone, have you?' said Sniveller.

'How sharper than a serpent's tooth is a thankless child,' finished Mrs Rokabye, who only ever quoted the nastier bits of the Bible.

'Last night, what a sight!' said Sniveller. 'Master blames me. You never said she didn't eat tomato sauce.'

'I have never given her any tomato sauce! Children should

not be indulged.'

'Master hypnotised her, and –' Before Sniveller could continue, the door to the dining room opened and in came Abel Darkwater in his outdoor clothes.

He sat down heavily, and motioned to Sniveller to fetch him coffee.

'Have you found the child?' asked Mrs Rokabye, who had no interest in Silver's welfare, but every interest in her own get-rich-quick opportunity. Mrs Rokabye had slept soundly, not knowing she had been drugged, and she had awoken to find herself happy, in her own mean-minded way. Yes, happy at last, and now the wretched child had upset everything.

'I have not found her but I know where she is,' said Abel Darkwater. 'I know a number of things that I did not know until last night, oh yes.'

'Was the hypnosis successful?' asked Mrs Rokabye eagerly.

'It was, and it was not,' replied Darkwater opaquely.

'Well, what are we to do now?'

'Wait,' said Abel Darkwater, 'and see.'

He got up and left the room. Mrs Rokabye had the distinct feeling that she was being left out of something important. She poured herself more hot chocolate and brooded.

As she brooded and sipped, and sipped and brooded, there was a horrible howling from the landing, and Sniveller came tumbling through the door, with blood pouring from his nose.

'What on earth?'

'He's beating me again, oh, oh, oh, no, no, no.' Sniveller

fell into a chair. 'It's the prophecy.'

'What prophecy?'

'You don't think he wants the bloody clock, tick-tock to tell the time, do you?'

'I have no idea why he wants it,' said Mrs Rokabye. 'All I know is that he will pay me a magnificent sum of money when he finds it.'

'If he finds it. He's been looking for it all his life and never had a wife.'

'What nonsense you talk. Tell me in plain English why he wants this clock.'

Sniveller spat out a blood-stained sentence. It was all he could manage, and anyway, he didn't rightly understand it all himself.

'Whoever controls the Timekeeper controls Time.'

Mrs Rokabye pricked up her ears. If she could get it she would never have to wait for the bus again.

'But only the Child with the Golden Face can bring the Clock to its Rightful Place.'

'You can't mean Silver?'

Sniveller nodded and mopped his face with his neckerchief. 'And now we've lost her like a penny down the floorboards.'

'But she has no idea where the Timekeeper is, I am quite sure of that.'

'Yes, Master knows that now, but Master says . . .' Sniveller lowered his voice. Mrs Rokabye's eyes grew wide, but before Sniveller could finish his snivelling sentence, Abel

Darkwater had burst into the room, his round face excited.

'It is of great importance that you stay in the house today, Mrs Rokabye. I can feel faint changes in the surface of the Earth. There is a Time Tornado approaching us.'

'A Time Tornado!'

'Yes indeed, oh yes indeed!'

'I think I had better go back to Tanglewreck,' said Mrs Rokabye, who never thought she would hear herself say such words. 'This London living is very bad for my nerves.'

'You cannot go anywhere,' said Abel Darkwater, 'unless you want to run the risk of being swept up in Time and deposited who knows where?'

'Why does no one here speak plain English?'

'Madam, it is very simple. Since the Industrial Revolution, which you will recall began with the invention of the steam engine, our world has been moving faster and faster. For most of his evolutionary life, a man could go no quicker than his legs or his horse could carry him. Now he may travel in a jet plane across the world in a matter of hours. His factories churn out more goods per hour than an artisan could make in his entire lifetime. We have no more interest in the slow round of the seasons; we grow our food by artificial light, and our hens lay eggs all year because they do not know when it is winter. Children are given Easter eggs, but they do not know it is because Easter is the Spring point of the Equinox, when hens would begin to lay again as the light from the sun increased.

'It is strange, but the machine age and the computer age

both promised to give mere mortals more time in their lives, but less time is what it seems we have. We are using up Time too fast, just as we are using up all the other resources of the Earth.

'Human beings do not understand Time, but they have tampered with it. In consequence, Time is not what it used to be. Time is becoming unreliable.'

'But what is going to happen?'

'That remains to be seen,' said Abel Darkwater. 'Hark!'

Mrs Rokabye heard a terrible noise, like an air-raid siren.

'That is the warning! You are quite safe in this house, but under no circumstances should you do more than look out of the window, and do not try and interfere, whatever it is that you may see. Now I recommend you wait here. I shall stand at the front door out of curiosity.'

'But –'

'Oh, I shall be quite safe, oh yes.'

Mrs Rokabye sat by the window just in time to see a ginger cat fly past, followed by a satellite dish. That was enough for her; she hated upset, though she liked to cause it. She decided to go and lie down.

As she climbed the stairs, it occurred to her to search Silver's bedroom. What had the child taken with her? Had she packed her clothes?

Mrs Rokabye went quietly up the stairs, and loudly shut the door to her own room, so that Sniveller would not suspect anything. Then she hurried on to the little rooms at the top of the house.

The bed was unmade. Silver's clothes were lying about. She had gone without her shoes! *She must have wanted to get away very badly*, thought Mrs Rokabye, and wondered what it was that had taken place here. There was her duffle coat . . . Mrs Rokabye fished through the pockets; a conker, a pencil, a few sweets from the train, a little plastic wallet with a picture of her mother and father and Buddleia inside. Nothing else. Nothing . . . or, what was this? She rummaged inside the lining and pulled out the diamond pin. She gasped. Where had Silver found this? It must be worth a fortune if it was real. Perhaps it was part of the treasure she had heard was buried at Tanglewreck? Never mind the clock! If there was treasure . . . Her face hardened from surprise to anger. Horrible wicked child to keep the treasure to herself. Well, now these diamonds belonged to Mrs Rokabye!

She hid the pin in her knickers, slipped back down the stairs and lay on the bed. Her heart was beating fast. Abel Darkwater had taken her for a fool, but he would see who was the clever one! Perhaps she would have to persuade Sniveller to help her. Yes, she would have to use her charm. It would need practice, like smiling, but she was up to the task.

Her brain was whirring. She put on her pink earmuffs and lay on the bed with the pillow over her eyes, and both hands on the diamond pin.

Abel Darkwater went downstairs and opened the door.

Men and women were running down the street into shops

and cafes and offices. Drivers pulled over anywhere they could, and lay down on the seats of their cars.

The sky was dark. Rain began to fall. The rain turned to snow.

The snow melted. The sun shone so brilliantly that the windows blazed like fire. Then there was a moment of absolute stillness in the deserted street, before a huge wind pulled through that part of the city like a beast dragging its prey behind it.

Abel Darkwater braced himself in the doorway and consulted his pocket watch. The hands were spinning wildly, and he could see from his Annometer that Time was lurching backwards and forwards in short bursts, like a learner driver crashing the gears.

The Annometer was another of his own inventions. This one told him whether or not Time was slipping. Even before the time troubles had begun, Darkwater had noticed that in certain places Time could slip. People who experienced that strange feeling of going backwards or forwards in Time were sometimes right. Time slipped its gears occasionally and went into reverse, then it could lurch forward. Now this was happening so fiercely that everyone could feel it. But it had always happened here and there.

The Time Tornado hit, and a whole building across the street was torn from its foundations and carried up into the air, like a child throwing a doll's house. Darkwater watched with interest as the occupants of the building waved wildly out into the air, shouting for help. There was no one who could help them. The house disappeared into a black cloud.

Abel Darkwater studied the gap opposite him in the street. It was not a gap like a bomb or an explosion would make, but more like the house had been cleanly sliced away from the ground by a knife.

Darkwater checked the Annometer. It was registering 2060. The wavering images of two buildings appeared in outline in the now vacant plot. Since the future was not fixed it was not possible to see what would definitely happen in 2060, but possibilities of happening could be seen. The first possibility was a stainless steel tower. The second possibility was a museum called the Time Museum. Underneath them both he thought he could see the outlines of a children's playground with swings and slides. He smiled. That was a very faint possibility indeed.

There was another rending crack in the sky, and to Abel Darkwater's surprise, books began to rain down on the street. He ducked under his lintel to avoid being hit on the head, then he stepped out to pick up the nearest volume. It was old and leather bound. He read the spine:

THE ORIGIN OF SPECIES by Charles Darwin.

Hmmm . . .

March 17th 1859. John Samuel Martin, a bookseller of Charing Cross, London, was walking to dinner with a book under his arm when a great wind of the day snatched it from his fingers and flew it into the air. To his surprise it did not seem to fall back to Earth, which is against the laws of gravity.

Consulting his Annometer, Darkwater realised that Time was behaving differently today. It was like a child throwing a tantrum. It had taken a book from the past, and hurled it into the future. It had taken a house, and hurled it – who knew where?

As he stood in the street, indifferent to the chaos around him, he said out loud, to himself, 'This hasn't happened before.'

'Is Before a Time or a Place?' said a voice, silky and soft and edged with some harder material.

Darkwater turned round. He was taken aback, and he was displeased.

'It's been a long time, hasn't it?'

'I rather hoped it would be for ever,' said Abel Darkwater.

'If there is such a thing,' said Regalia Mason.

And there she was – in her white suit and white shoes, her long blonde hair simply tied back. Only her eyes were as dark as he remembered them.

Abel Darkwater switched off his Annometer.

'Still using your Home Inventions?' said Regalia Mason, in a voice full of sympathy. 'Here, try this. It's only a proto-type, of course.'

Regalia Mason took out a sleek black box, about the size of an Ipod, and pressed the buttons. 'Who was it you were trying to find?'

'I'm not trying to find anyone!' snapped Abel Darkwater.

'Oh, pardon me,' said Regalia Mason. 'I had the distinct impression that you were.'

'I am following the Time Tornado. That is all.'

'That's why I'm here,' said Regalia Mason. 'I flew in from New York this morning. I have a meeting with the Committee.'

'At Greenwich?'

'At Greenwich. They are very concerned about these distortions in Time. The public don't like them at all. It seems you may need my help.'

'I certainly don't,' said Darkwater.

'The Government does. They need to get Time back under control. To do that they need money and they need expertise. That means America.'

'When I think that you were once a colony,' said Abel Darkwater.

'I was never anyone's colony,' said Regalia Mason.

Abel Darkwater looked at her with dislike. 'Are you still running your little business?'

'Well, I'm not selling clocks and watches, if that's what you mean.' She glanced briefly into the windows of the shop. 'Time to move on, don't you think? See you later, alligator.'

Tall, elegant, unperturbed at the sight of overturned cars and smashed windows, Regalia Mason walked briskly away.

Abel Darkwater watched her. There was no reason at all for Regalia Mason to be walking past his shop that morning. In any case, she was not the kind of woman who walked anywhere.

All through the night he had been thinking about the hypnosis, and how Silver could not take him further, and how she claimed to have had no knowledge of the Timekeeper at all. He did not like the child but he was sure that she usually told the truth. There had been a memory – he had found it – but something or someone had blocked that memory, and done it so powerfully that even Abel Darkwater had not been able to recover it from its hiding place.

Something

or

someone.

A black Bentley Continental drove silently past him and pulled up a little way down the street. Regalia Mason got in. She did not look back.

Darkwater felt something pressing against his chest. It was his Warning Signal. He took it out. DANGER, it flashed in red number nines. DANGER.

REGALIA MASON

I n New York City the tops of the buildings tear the sky. When the snow falls the tops of the buildings look like mountain peaks. The most important people in the city live and work as high as they can on their man-made mountains. When they want to travel, a helicopter lands on the roof and carries them away, just as enchanters on glass mountains whistled for eagles.

Regalia Mason had an office in a part of New York City called Tribeca. She was so high up that the clouds sometimes snowed outside her window while lower buildings were still in sunshine.

In her vast white office she gave orders to people who had never seen her. People knew her name and they were afraid of her, but only a very few knew what she looked like.

She was beautiful.

And cold.

Regalia Mason was the Chief Executive and President of a company called Quanta. Quanta made its money by only selling things that people had to buy – like air and water and oil. Whatever was in short supply, Quanta sold. Sold it very expensively. Sold it to people who could not afford it. Sold the Earth and the stars and the sun. Yes, they had even sold stars to rich men worrying that Earth was too full, and they had sold solar energy to people who had run out of all fossil fuels. They had sold everything out of the Earth – its gold, its titanium, its plutonium, its iridium, its rivers, sea, forests and coral.

Quanta controlled National Parks, where the last few animals lived, and Quanta controlled all the oil reserves of the Middle East.

Quanta controlled most of life, and Regalia Mason controlled Quanta.

There were only a few things that Quanta didn't control; one of them was Time.

Regalia Mason was sitting in her white office, wearing her white fox-fur coat and gazing out of the window at the flat plain of sunlit clouds.

She was above the skyline, the way you are in an aeroplane, and when she looked out, the clouds seemed solid, like after snow has settled on land. White infinity stretched before her.

On her desk she had an egg-timer made out of white gold, and she idly turned it over and over, and tiny fragments of diamonds fell from one sphere to the other.

Regalia Mason was a scientist. Underneath her white fox-fur, she wore a white coat. She analysed, quantified, measured, and experimented. Her latest experiment was to take Time from people who had too much of it – useless people, lazy people, unemployed people, children, perhaps, yes, children, perhaps, and sell the Time she had taken from them to people who didn't have enough of it – important people, rich people, successful people, old people, dying people, if they could afford it.

She had a file on her desk marked Top Secret. Inside were the rough outlines of her new idea.

Time Transfusions.

She was going to sell Time Transfusions.

Faintly, overhead, she heard the whirr of the helicopter blades coming to take her to the airport. She was going to London.

PETROL PONIES

Micah and Silver were sitting cross-legged in the Chamber.

'The question be this,' said Micah, puffing on his long clay pipe. 'Be you the Child with the Golden Face?'

'Who's she?' asked Silver, who had told Micah everything she knew about everything.

'There be a prophecy to do with the clock, the Timekeeper, but there also be a story about the clock that you know not.'

'Tell it to me . . . please,' said Silver. Gabriel came quietly out of the shadows and sat down by Silver, listening to what Micah had to say.

'There dwelled a man in Yorkshire, by the name of John Harrison, who made clocks. His life's work lay to solve the matter of longitude at sea, so as sailors could always know their position without having to consult the stars.'

'What's longitude?' asked Silver.

'Longitude be the angular distance, East and West, from the prime meridian, which is a central line – imaginary, mind – belting the Earth, like a great hoop, from North to South.'

'Where's the prime meridian?'

'Why, Greenwich, child! Greenwich here in London, on the banks of the Thames! Ain't you never been at sea?'

Silver shook her head sadly and Micah laughed and explained that in the days when he went to sea, Greenwich wasn't the prime meridian either.

'Took 'em till 1884 to make up their minds on that one, but in my day what you did was choose your own central line and calculate from that to find out where you be. Trouble is, a man can't find out where he be, unless he got his longitude, and that meant the devil of a calculation with the stars. My master John Harrison wanted to invent a clock –'

'The Timekeeper!' shouted Silver.

'Nay, child, not that, but much to do with the story . . .'

Silver could hardly sit still for excitement.

'We dwelled in his house, his son and myself, for I was his apprentice. I remember it, the day that he had made his Chronometer Number Four, and he had one of the clocks he made by a blazing fire in his study, and one outside in the snow, and he ran back and forth such as a fiend in hell will run back and forth, watching the measure of heat and cold on his mechanisms, to see if the hot or the cold made either run too fast or too slow – for no clock yet made had run right in too much of heat or cold.

'He says to me, "Micah, take you one of these Chronometer Number Four on a voyage to Jamaica, and you fetch it home again, and keep you a record of all that happens inside and outside of my clock."

'Now, in Jamaica, I was drunk like a sot one night, and a man wagered me all my pay on a last throw of the dice. Nay, I should have said nay, but yea, I did agree, and thanks that I be fortunate, for I won the dice, and I turns to him and asks him what he will give me for my winnings. He laughs like an open grate in the ground, and throws a rough bag at me.

'I opens the bag, and in it there be a clock, yea, broken and beautiful, lost of many jewels, and with a double face, and strange pictures marking it. I took it back with me on the voyage, and I tried to mend it as I went, and mend it I did, but no matter what I did, it ticked awhile and stopped, ticked awhile and stopped, and there was nothing I could do.

'One night, the waves like toppling towers, the wind like the wind at the ends of the earth, a cabin boy from Jamaica creeps up to me, his eyes wide as the road to damnation, and, says he, the clock be voodoo, only bring bad luck, says he. He says to throw it overboard, and he gives me a piece of paper, no, not paper it wasn't, it was human skin dried like parchment, and on the paper was the writing, "The Child with the Golden Face shall bring the Clock to its Rightful Place". Inside that piece of paper, that skin of paper, and wrapped up like swaddling babes, were two pictures belonging with the clock, and one was a road, and one was a child.

'Well, I paid no attention to his fearful voodoo, but when our ship comes to port, a man be waiting for me on the dockside. Round-faced he be, and in a woollen cloak, and he offers me on the spot two hundred pound for the clock. *Nay,* says I, I be taking the clock to my right master, John Harrison.

'As I made journey up country, back to Yorkshire, I sees one following me, and following me, and following me as close as my own shadow but without speaking. I manages to give him the slip, one wild and lost night, and I finds myself at a great house in Cheshire, and it was there, to save myself and the clock, that I begged the master of that house to hold the clock for safekeeping, promising I would return with my own master as quick as one moon's passing.

'I never did return. The man following me was Abel Darkwater, and he caught me, and, with his men, had me slapped in Bedlam, for theft of a clock, he said, and many a night he had me read drawings for him, and explain how such a clock as he desired could be made.

'I could have told him where the clock was hidden but something prevented me. I cannot even say what prevented me, for many a time I would have told him and been set free, and yet when I opened my mouth to speak, I swear honestly that I could not remember where I had taken it, and I swear honestly to this day that when you said the word, my tongue was loosed for the first time in all these hundred hundred years and more.'

'What word?' said Silver.

'Tanglewreck,' said Micah. 'Thine own house be the place.'

Silver was very silent for a moment, then she burst out,

'But the Timekeeper isn't there any more. Nobody knows where it is!'

'It must be found,' said Micah. 'The time has come. It must be found.'

'But I don't know where to look!' Silver was beginning to cry with frustration.

'Have you no clue, child? No clue whatever it be? Think with all thy might!'

Silver thought. But whenever she thought about the Timekeeper she could not imagine it at all. It was as though someone threw a cover over it, just as she was about to speak. But there was something . . .

'I found a pin – I forgot that bit – it was in the coal dust. It was shiny and pointy and . . .' And as she described the pin, Micah closed his eyes and began to describe it too.

'. . . gold, three inches long, diamond-covered, with an emerald at the top and the bottom. Child, that is no pin nor jewel, it be the first hand of the Timekeeper!'

'Are you sure?'

'Have I not seen it with mine own eyes and told it to you truly just now?'

He had. Silver's face fell. 'But I left it in Abel Darkwater's house. It's in my duffle-coat pocket in the house!'

'We must haste there!' said Micah. 'He shall not have it!'

'But I can't go there again. He'll capture me and put me in a cage!'

'We will journey with thee, and enter with thee.'

'But –'

'Not as Updwellers do. There be a way. Come! Hurry! Make ready! Balthazar! Gabriel! The Petrol Ponies!'

The four of them set off through the Chamber, where most of the Throwbacks were now asleep on pallets covered in animal skins and blankets.

Silver was expecting another long walk through mud and water and disused tunnels, so imagine her surprise when Micah opened a door into a dry, warm, concrete vault, to reveal three neat lines of motorbikes.

'Petrol Ponies,' said Micah proudly. 'Built in your world in your years 1930s.'

'Where did you get them from?' asked Silver, touching the soft polished leather seats and bright chrome lights.

'Your world keeps not its possessions. When I be an Updweller, more than two hundred and fifty years ago, a man kept to him the same spoon and dish and coat and chair all his life. His boots wore out, his horse wore out, but whatever did not wear out, he kept to him. For a long time now, Updwellers have thrown away what they have so that they can have new things. I do not understand the wicked waste, but I have profited from it. These Petrol Ponies were saved by us and restored by us. They be called Enfields.'

'I thought I could smell petrol,' said Silver.

'That be here,' pointed Micah. 'Above us now is a place where Updwellers take their wagons and carriages. There be plenty of petrol. Now come, ride behind me.'

Micah pulled out the biggest of the Enfields, and Silver

climbed on to the seat behind him. She had never seen a motorbike like this; instead of one long seat, it had two saddles, like old-fashioned bicycle saddles, resting on heavy coiled springs.

Micah steadied the bike upright with one short sturdy leg, and brought his other foot down hard on the kick-start. The bike roared to life, the headbeam lit up the tunnel ahead, and suddenly they were off, at what felt like breakneck speed, tearing through passages sometimes so narrow that Silver had to squeeze in her elbows to stop them scraping the walls.

The low roar of the bikes was amplified by the stone and brick. Silver wanted to cover her ears, but she was frightened to let go of Micah, in case she fell off.

'Why do you call them Petrol Ponies?' yelled Silver to Micah. 'We call them motorbikes.'

'Yea,' said Micah, 'but the Throwbacks have no use for your bicycles, with motors or without motors. We have always used ponies. When we first came here, one of our number brought bog ponies from Ireland, for they are small and light and can work underground. Then we found these Enfields, and we called them Petrol Ponies. You have one name for them, we have another. You have one world, we have another.'

He braked so hard that Silver nearly tumbled off. The bikes behind had to swerve and screech to avoid a collision. Micah switched off his engine. Now everything was dark and silent again.

'Listen,' said Micah. Silver strained her ears but she could hear nothing. Micah turned to Balthazar. 'Do you hear it, brother?'

'Yea.'

'What?' whispered Silver, twisting round to talk to Gabriel.

'Ticking,' said Gabriel.

'We be beneath the house of Abel Darkwater,' said Micah.

Micah signalled to Balthazar to stoop so that he could stand on his shoulders. He balanced cleanly as a monkey, and worked with his square spade hands to free a rusty metal plate in the roof of the vaulted tunnel.

He pushed it to one side, and swung himself up, motioning for Silver to be passed up through the opening.

She found herself in the little courtyard behind the shop.

As Balthazar was pulling himself through in turn, Micah warned Silver not to speak until he gave her permission. 'Throwbacks neither read nor write, they were not learned in Bedlam, though I be one who can read. In that place we learned each other to speak without words, so that our cruel Warders did not hear us. I will read Balthazar's mind, and he mine.'

'What about me?' asked Silver, who had never been good at guessing games.

'You must be quiet. We risk much to come here. Gabriel will wait for us, and bring us help, should we be catched like rabbits by him that is a living snare.'

Micah moved silently over to the door that led into the

shop and tried the handle. It opened. He frowned. He feared a trap. As he felt this fear, Silver saw a picture of a metal mantrap in her mind – the kind they used to hide in the woods to catch poachers, even though it tore off their legs. For the first time, she noticed that Micah had a limp. She shivered.

Now they were all in the shop and creeping past the watchful clocks out into the hall where Silver had made her escape. She suddenly wondered how much time had passed since then, and realised she had no idea whether it was hours or days.

The house was eerily silent. Micah led the way up the broad stairs and when they arrived at the first landing, Silver tugged at his sleeve. She wanted to warn him that this was Abel Darkwater's study, so she thought it in her mind as fiercely as she could, and Micah nodded.

They crept past, and now they were on the second landing, where Mrs Rokabye slept. Silver paused at the closed door. Mrs Rokabye always snored, but there was no sound from her room.

They passed on, up to the set of rooms on the top floor where Silver had eaten and slept. Both of the doors from the landing were open.

Micah went inside, first one room and then the other. There was no one there.

The bed was neatly made up. Silver's case was open on a chair where she had left it, her old duffle coat hung over the back.

She ran forward and grabbed the coat and turned the pockets inside out. Nothing! She scrabbled down on her hands and knees under the chair; nothing! She wriggled on her tummy under the bed; nothing!

Micah and Balthazar exchanged glances, then went to work searching the room. Silver knew the pin had been in her pocket. She knew that someone had taken it. Sniveller? Abel Darkwater? Not Mrs Rokabye, she was too stupid to know anything . . .

She put on her duffle coat, stuffing her trainers into her pockets. She left the case of clean clothes. Somehow they didn't seem to matter any more.

Softly, the three of them retraced their steps downstairs towards Mrs Rokabye's room. Impulsively, and before Micah could grab her arm as he read her thoughts, Silver opened the door.

The room was empty. Mrs Rokabye's latest Murder Mystery and her pink earmuffs were on the bed, but she was not.

Micah and Balthazar glanced at each other uneasily. They would have to search the whole house, and that included Abel Darkwater's study. If he had found the pin, he would certainly have taken it there to examine it.

The first floor of the house had three interconnecting rooms that Darkwater used as a bedroom, sitting room and study. Silver motioned to the Throwbacks to open the door into the bedroom and begin that way. No one wanted to go straight into the study.

Abel Darkwater's four-poster bed was tidy and not slept in. Quietly, they opened the cupboards filled with clothes, and Silver noticed that his clothes were not from one century or one time, but a jumble of breeches, frock-coats, top hats and tweed suits, like a dressing-up box or costumes for a play.

In the sitting room were the remains of a meal on the table, and a candle that had recently burned out, spilling wax on the cloth.

Now they were outside the study door. It was a panelled door covered over with green baize, like the kind on a snooker table, and the green baize was held on the door with shiny brass tacks that caught the firelight and the candlelight and reflected your face like tiny distorting mirrors. Silver looked at herself and her new-found friends, and they all listened to the absolute silence.

There was nothing else to do; they had to open the study door.

Silver heard Micah breathe in as he stepped forward and walked firmly into the room.

Then she heard a low cry like a whipped animal.

Abel Darkwater was waiting for them.

'You have not found what you were looking for, I think,' he said to Micah, without smiling. 'I sympathise. I am in the same sorry situation myself.'

Silver rushed into the room, forgetting what she had been told about keeping quiet.

'You don't know what we were looking for!'

'Ah well, that tells me you were looking for something!'

Silver fell silent, caught in her own trap. Abel Darkwater smiled at her. 'I wonder what it was?'

'I'll never tell you anything! Not ever never!'

She stepped forward, brave and defiant. Abel Darkwater raised his hand to slap her. Micah stepped in between the two of them. Darkwater looked surprised, and then angry.

'So, John Harrison's man, as you used to be known, would you stand against your Master?'

'Thee be neither my Master nor my Better,' said Micah.

'Wretch, have you forgotten who ruled over you? Have you forgotten this?'

Abel Darkwater turned to one of his cabinets and took out what looked like a short leather truncheon. Silver saw Micah wince. Darkwater laughed.

'Have you forgotten this already?' With a sudden swing, Darkwater hit Micah on the side of his head. Blood spurted out on the carpet as Micah fell on to his knees. Silver dived at Abel Darkwater, who grabbed her wrist. She bit him. He pushed her away, nursing his hand.

'Foolish child! None of you can stand against me. I will bide my time, oh yes, for I have more of it than you, Silver. You will lead me to the Timekeeper, whether you know it or not, whether you like it or not.'

Micah stood up unsteadily, mopping his face. He said to Abel Darkwater, 'Be she the Child with the Golden Face?'

'Ha ha ha, ha ha ha,' laughed Abel Darkwater, 'so you

remember a thing or two after all, do you? Well, I will tell you as much as you will tell me: nothing! Now, go back to your filthy underground bog, and take the child with you. You will spare me the expense of feeding her.'

Micah and Balthazar did not speak. They shuffled out of the door and down the stairs as though they had been broken by something heavy and evil. Silver followed them, not knowing what she should do. Abel Darkwater stood at the top of the stairs watching them go.

She turned round. 'Where is Mrs Rokabye?

'Mrs Rokabye is at the theatre. She has gone to see *The Lion King*. Sniveller has taken her. She quite grew to like Sniveller when she discovered he is a poisoner by profession. You remember Sniveller, don't you, Micah – although you knew him as the White Lead Man in those days?'

Micah did not reply.

'Doesn't she care about me at all?' asked Silver, who knew Mrs Rokabye was bad, but had held out a faint hope that she was not all bad.

'Of course she does,' said Abel Darkwater cheerfully. 'We all do, very much, but it would have been a pity to waste the tickets.'

He turned and went back into his study and closed the door.

As soon as the three of them were back down in the tunnel, Gabriel, waiting for them patiently, could see that things had gone very badly, but he did not break the oath of silence.

They rode back on the Petrol Ponies, and parked them without speaking.

Only when he was back in the warm circle of the Chamber, with a bottle of something strong-smelling to drink, did Micah speak.

'Certain it is that he has not discovered that pin, that hand of the clock.'

'Then where is it?' demanded Silver.

'That I know not,' said Micah.

'But what can we do now? Shall we go back to Tanglewreck?'

'I know not,' said Micah. 'I must dwell on this awhile, but there is something I know.' He paused to light his pipe. 'Someone else has knowledge of the Timekeeper. Someone who thy mother and father and sister met with on the day you tell us of, the day they were journeying to Abel Darkwater.'

'How do you know?' asked Silver.

'They vanished, yea. The Timekeeper vanished, yea. The one man who has sought it for centuries has lost it once more. Someone else must be nearby.'

'But who?' wondered Silver.

THE COMMITTEE

Regalia Mason liked to be early to meetings; it was an interesting way of making others feel uncomfortable. If the most important person in the room is early, even those who are on time feel as though they are late.

It amused Regalia Mason to manipulate someone's idea of Time in these small ways. Soon she intended to be manipulating Time in much bigger ways too.

She was reading through the notes supplied by the Committee. Since the first Time Tornado had hit Waterloo Bridge and the school bus had disappeared, there had been a number of other incidents, and in all of them the pattern seemed to be the same; Time stood still, then jerked forward at terrific speed. There had been seven sightings of a Woolly Mammoth on the banks of the Thames, and yesterday, as well as the disappearance of several buildings and cars and people, certain artefacts from the past had been found in the street.

She made a note on her pad. 'Time is coming forward, coming towards us. We are not going back in Time.'

The advisors were coming into the room. She knew some of them; the Astronomer Royal, Sir Martin Rees. The Cambridge Professor of Cosmology, Stephen Hawking; the quantum physicist, Roger Penrose; the neuroscientist, Susan Greenfield, always elegant in her short skirts and long boots – Regalia Mason made a note of the boots. Then there were two members of the Government, and a senior civil servant everyone knew as Sir Bertie. A last-minute addition was a man from MI5, whose name was a secret, and who suspected that the whole thing had something to do with the Chinese.

There was the usual rustling of papers and clattering of coffee cups and eyeing up of the biscuits that went on at important meetings, and even though the world might be coming to an end, the men still chatted about their golf and their children.

Regalia Mason smiled to herself. She never chatted and she never ate biscuits.

She waited to be introduced. She waited to hear the facts she already knew about the Time Tornadoes and yesterday's perplexing events. Some of the physicists thought that Time had ripped – that a hole had appeared in the fabric of Time, rather like the hole in the ozone layer.

The geophysicists, who studied the impact of volcanoes and earthquakes on the spin of the Earth, were asked if the tsunami in Thailand had anything to do with the strange behaviour of Time. Everyone agreed that after that disaster the Earth had shifted about one millimetre on its axis, but no one could agree that such a thing could make a difference to Time.

The sinister man from MI5 wanted to know if human

activity could affect Time, just as human activity had affected climate change.

Regalia Mason could see the impatience on the faces of the scientists. They wanted equations, calculations, not James Bond-style plots.

Regalia Mason spoke. 'I think it highly likely that human beings *have* affected Time.'

There was a pause in the room.

'Is it not strange that the faster we have learned to go, the less time we seem to have? The whole of the Western world is in a hurry, and the developing world is racing to catch up.'

'I said all this was something to do with China,' said the sinister man from MI5.

'I do not believe it is anything to do with China,' said Regalia Mason.

'Well, Pakistan, then.'

She ignored him. 'Which of you here has not said, this week, that you are running out of time, that you have no time, that time is short, or how time flies?'

'Those are merely figures of speech,' said Sir Bertie, adjusting his red silk white-spotted tie with irritated fingers.

'I disagree,' said Regalia Mason. 'I believe they are clues.'

Stephen Hawking tapped a single sentence into his voice computer.

'Einstein and the clock in the city square?'

'Of course, of course,' Regalia Mason nodded.

'What's that story? I don't follow,' said the sinister man

from MI5. Regalia Mason smiled at him. He had the vague idea that this was frightening, but he didn't know why. She was such a beautiful woman. She began to explain, as though talking to a rather nice child she might eat afterwards.

'Einstein's Theories of Relativity always began with simple pictures in his mind. As a boy, he wondered what it would be like to race alongside a light-beam. Later, he imagined himself zooming away at the speed of light from the big clock in his city square. As he looked back, he realised that the hands on the clock were standing still. This is because when we travel at the speed of light, Time seems to stand still. Travelling faster than the speed of light, Time would appear to go backwards.'

'Could you just remind me what is the speed of light?' said Sir Bertie.

'300,000 kilometres per second,' the whole room answered at once.

'That's quick,' said the man from MI5.

'Indeed it is quick,' agreed Regalia Mason, 'and it is a paradox that at the speed of light Time slows almost to a stop, but at lower speeds, our speeds here on Earth, we seem to be forcing Time to move faster.'

'You're saying that our planes, our computers, are speeding up Time?' said Sir Bertie.

'I am saying that Time is distorting. We have evidence of that. I am saying that people commonly perceive Time differently than they once did. We feel that our days are not long enough. Well, perhaps they are not.'

'What Dr Mason says about perception is absolutely right,' said Susan Greenfield. 'The human brain is highly subjective.'

'But Time is not subjective!' said one of the men. 'There is such a thing as Time, and it passes! However we perceive it, it exists outside of ourselves.'

'I am not sure of that,' said Regalia Mason simply.

'The human race has only a fifty-fifty chance of survival,' said Sir Martin Rees. 'Perhaps we will never reach the future, however much time we have, or however we perceive it.'

'That would be a pity,' said Regalia Mason. 'A future where we could control Time would be a future worth having.'

'If we could control Time – we could travel in Time,' said the man from MI5, 'and this isn't *Doctor Who*, you know, this is real life.'

Stephen Hawking was nodding. He reminded everyone of what he had often said – that if Time travel were possible in the future, we would have visitors from the future, visiting us, now, in our present and their past. As there were no visitors from the future, there could be no Time travel happening in the future.

'That's right!' said the man from MI5.

'That's not quite right . . .' said Regalia Mason.

As the scientists fell to arguing, Regalia Mason smiled to herself and looked at her watch. There would be another Time Tornado this evening, and then the arguments would stop. They would come to her, to Quanta, for help.

Deep underground, Silver and Micah and Gabriel had crawled along the tunnels and under the river. Micah's spies had found out about the meeting, and Micah had told Silver that they might discover some clue that would help them. He had been particularly interested in one of the advisors to the Committee who had been flown in from America. More he would not say.

The three had crept inside a secret passage that Micah said had been built for the first Astronomer Royal to use to visit his mistress on the other side of the River Thames.

'What's a mistress?' asked Silver.

Micah hesitated. 'A mistress be the woman you love even though you not be married to her . . . The whole of London be digged with such Lady Lanes, so that a man may travel in secret to his mistress. Some be deep, some be shallow, some be creeping for miles through the gloom of the pit, some be connecting two houses that rubs next to one another, and all lit by love.'

There was a crash above them as Sir Bertie dropped his coffee cup on to the floor.

In the confusion in the room of I'msosorry . . . let-mehelpyou . . . slippedthroughmyfingers . . . sokindthank-you . . . dearme Micah hastened Silver and Gabriel to a wide opening in the room itself. Silver realised they had come up inside the fireplace.

'Many believed Sir John Flamsteed, the first Astronomer

Royal, be an alchemist,' said Micah, 'and that he could disappear into the fire. In truth he disappeared into the fireplace.'

Micah and Gabriel were further back than Silver. They could hear but not see what was happening. Silver was able to peep through the ornamental guard that sat in front of the fireplace that nobody used nowadays, either because of central heating or because the Astronomer Royal no longer kept a mistress.

'Your proposal startled me,' Sir Bertie was saying, still mopping up the coffee from his papers.

'My proposal is a practical one. That old saying *Time is Money* is true enough. I am here to buy Time. If Quanta invests the necessary billions in the research your scientists need to stabilise time, Quanta will want a return on that investment. Any "discoveries" will belong to us. Any surplus Time will belong to us. If I am buying Time today, I want to be able to sell it tomorrow – if you understand me.'

'I do not,' said Sir Bertie.

'Then I will be plain. I believe that what is happening to Time gives us a unique opportunity to control Time. We will be the ones who decide on the lengths of the seasons – if we want summer all year, we shall have summer all year; if we prefer our enemies to live in winter all year, they shall. If some countries are short of Time – if some people are short of Time – we will sell them Time from people who have too much Time on their hands. But all this trade in Time must be controlled by Quanta.'

'You cannot trade in Time,' said Sir Bertie.

'Why not?' smiled Regalia Mason. 'We trade in everything else.'

Silver leaned back into the fireplace and whispered to Micah, 'Who is she?'

'I fear I do know,' said Micah, 'but I cannot be sure until I see her face.'

At that moment Regalia Mason got up from the table and walked towards the fireplace. Silver thought she would die of fright, but she kept absolutely still. At the very second when Regalia Mason would have been looking straight at her, a voice called from the room.

'Dr Mason – a word in private, please.'

Regalia Mason turned round. Silver shrank into the depths of the fireplace. Micah had glimpsed the woman he thought he knew. His face was serious.

'If he be the devil, she be the serpent.'

'What? Who?'

'If Abel Darkwater be the devil, then she be the serpent. Her true name is Maria Prophetessa – One becomes Two, Two becomes Three, and out of the Three comes the Four that is One.'

'What?' said Silver.

'That woman be in Jamaica, when I be in Jamaica, and they say her voodoo magic comes from the pyramids of Egypt. And when I boarded ship homewards, she be there, kept to herself in a closed cabin, and I seen her visit Abel Darkwater in Bedlam many times. She it was who began the

Experiments.'

'What experiments?' said Silver, whose head was spinning, either from too much information or not enough air.

'Come,' said Micah urgently. 'If you fear him, fear her more. Come away!'

TIME PASSES

S ilver and Gabriel were friends.

Back in the Chamber, Micah let them run and play as much as they wanted, and he did not ask Gabriel to find food or help with the daily jobs.

He had not said to Gabriel how disturbed he was by their visit to Abel Darkwater's house, and then to the meeting in Greenwich. He wanted to protect Silver but he could not allow Abel Darkwater and Regalia Mason to destroy the safe home of the Throwbacks, and he feared for his clan and his kind, as well as for Silver.

But if Abel Darkwater found the Timekeeper . . .

Deep in his thoughts, Micah hardly spoke to Silver, trusting Gabriel to take care of her.

Gabriel began to teach Silver how to find her way through the labyrinths, and where to come Upground. They told each other stories about their lives, and Silver promised Gabriel that whatever happened, one day she would take him to Tanglewreck.

'I should be glad to see the place that you love,' said Gabriel. 'Nothing matters but those things that matter, Micah says.'

And Silver thought she understood.

In the timeless, ageless space of the Throwbacks, Silver felt happy again, happier than she had been for years. She remembered that with her parents and Buddleia at Tanglewreck, every day had stretched into every day, and she had been free, just like this. She started to sleep on her back, instead of curled up in a ball. She had no sense of how much time was passing – perhaps all of it. Perhaps none.

One day, finding Micah on his own in the Chamber, smoking his pipe, she asked him what he had meant by the 'Experiments'. His face grew dark.

'They be alchemists – him and Maria Prophetessa.'

'That's the beautiful woman called Regalia Mason?'

'Yea.'

'Is an alchemist a sort of magician?'

'Yea, in sort.'

And Micah explained how hundreds of years ago, science and magic were nearly the same thing. Nobody studied physics or chemistry, they studied mathematics, or astronomy, and they studied alchemy. Astronomers were also astrologers, who predicted what would happen by measuring the movement of the stars. Even Isaac Newton, who studied mathematics, and discovered gravity, was an astrologer.

'And Isaac Newton, he be a member of a secret society called Tempus Fugit.'

'Time Flies!' said Silver. 'Abel Darkwater's shop!'

'Yea,' said Micah. 'Many of the alchemists spent all their

lives labouring to turn metal into gold, but some, like Isaac Newton, and Abel Darkwater, and Maria Prophetessa, and a very powerful magician called John Dee, they laboured to make Time.'

'You can't make Time,' said Silver, thinking, even as she said it, how grown-ups were always saying they had to make time, usually for their children.

''Tis why he be alive and not dead in the earth,' said Micah.

'But you are all alive too,' said Silver.

'Yea,' said Micah. 'He experimented on us in the lunatic asylum in ways that would curdle your heart, but when we escaped we discovered that we be not dying as Updwellers do. Have you not noticed something about Abel Darkwater?'

Silver thought about his marble eyes, his round body, his shadowy face . . .

'He be like us who don't want the light. If our kind do go in the light, as Updwellers do, we die. Abel Darkwater is cleverer than we; he don't die in the light, but he can't be in the light for long. The dark slows death down, like hibernation. Like animals who sleep all winter.'

'What else slows it down?' asked Silver.

'Cold,' said Micah. 'You put a piece of meat in your cold safes – fridges, you call them. Yea, in the cold safe it does not decay. In the sun it decays.'

'Dark and cold,' said Silver.

'Yea,' said Micah. 'Dark and cold. Come.'

Micah hoisted Silver up on to the warm shaggy back of a

bog pony, and led her through a short maze of tunnels.

Silver hung on to the pony's thick mane, and felt his warmth on her fingers. Now she understood why Abel Darkwater's house was so cold. It wasn't because it was an old house like Tanglewreck; it was to keep him alive. That was why he had no electric lights, and that was why Mrs Rokabye had been complaining so much about the cold – she had complained a lot, even for her. Silver didn't feel the cold much. They had hardly any heat or electricity at Tanglewreck because their parents couldn't afford it. Only Mrs Rokabye had electric fires and electric blankets, and even an electric headscarf that she wore in the winter.

'Behold!' said Micah.

They had come to a round corral where half a dozen cattle were contentedly munching hay. The temperature was freezing, and a haze of cold hung over the cows.

Silver shivered and wrapped her legs round the pony. She looked up and saw that the opaque natural light and the steaming cold were coming from a perfectly round sheet of what looked like frosted glass. But it was perhaps fifty metres in diameter.

'In thine own world that be an ice-skating pond,' said Micah. 'A great marvel, for it remains frozen the whole of the year, and through your four seasons.'

'It's an ice-rink,' said Silver.

'We depend on it for our cattle. These cattle be bred by Abel Darkwater in 1805. We keep them in calf for milk, and we eat the calves for meat.'

'When will they die?' asked Silver.

'I know not. None of us knows when we shall die. But that is true of thine own world too.'

Silver and Micah made their way back to the Chamber.

'Why are you still afraid of Abel Darkwater?' said Silver.

'For the chains and the beatings and the blood-lettings and the faintings, and the dissections and anatomies he performed, and the great cold he kept us in, and the darkness where we dwelled before we be made different by him and her, and that he was my Master. He could destroy us still. He does not destroy us for reasons of his own, but I know them not.'

'Why does he want the Timekeeper?'

Micah stopped as he was walking. 'Abel Darkwater never must find the Timekeeper. If truly you know where it be . . .'

'I don't know where it be, I mean, where it is,' said Silver.

'He must not become Lord of the Universe, for that is his wish and his many lifetimes' work,' said Micah, his face grave.

'How can we stop him?' asked Silver.

'He cannot do it without the clock.'

'But he says I will lead him to the clock!'

Micah was silent. 'It may be that you must dwell with us for the remainder of your days.'

Silver gasped at this. 'What, and never see Tanglewreck again?'

'It may be. If you be the Keeper of the Clock, it be your duty to keep it safe.'

'But I DON'T KNOW WHERE IT IS!'
'That may be the means of keeping it safe,' said Micah.

Micah was troubled. He had been in close council with Eden and Balthazar, but none could decide whether Silver should stay or go. Finally Micah had decided that Eden must cast the Oracle and read the runes.

'She learned it from a witch imprisoned in Bedlam – a true witch of ancient line. The Oracle will speak.'

'When?' asked Silver.

'This day,' said Micah.

That day, if day it was, and impossible to tell, Silver thought about everything Micah had said. What if she had to stay here with the Throwbacks? Live underground for the rest of her life? But the house had promised her that she would return. Yes, but one day, and one day might be a very long time away. And what would happen to Tanglewreck if she never went back? Would Mrs Rokabye inherit it if Silver just disappeared? Mrs Rokabye would never love it. She didn't even dust it.

But if she didn't stay, then she would have to confront Abel Darkwater again, and she was frightened of him, and Sniveller, and what they might do.

All these thoughts and more were crowding in Silver's head when Gabriel appeared with a sack in his hand. She suddenly wondered how old he was. He looked about thirteen.

But Gabriel didn't know how old he was. The Throwbacks never celebrated birthdays, nor did they follow a calendar or a clock, like Updwellers. Gabriel had been born underground, he knew that, and he was not old enough to have children of his own.

'Don't you remember anything from when you were a baby?' asked Silver.

'Yea, I remember great horses with manes round their feet, pulling wagons.'

'And what about cars and stuff?'

'Nay, not till I was grown nearly as high as a barrel.'

'Well, what did people wear when you were a baby?'

'They wore black clothes and tall hats and the ladies wore skirts like bells.'

Silver thought about this. Gabriel was just a boy, like she was just a girl, but he was talking about a hundred years ago, or maybe more. She had seen pictures of Queen Victoria and people in the nineteenth century, but it was impossible for Gabriel to be so old and so young.

'I must feed Goliath now,' said Gabriel. 'Come with me, thou?'

He smiled and held out his hand. Silver took it shyly, feeling how different was the strong square palm to her own small soft hand. He made her feel safe, this boy, with his careful slow ways and the sense she had that he was always looking to see if she was safe.

As they went down the maze of passages, Gabriel had begun to sing in his strange high-pitched voice. Soon the tunnel began to shake, and when they entered the Feeding Room, where all the animal feed was kept, Goliath was already there, blinking at them mildly through his small eyes.

'I love thee, Goliath,' said Gabriel. 'When I was a baby you did rescue me from the Devils.'

Gabriel opened a wooded pen and started throwing in what looked like molasses cake. Goliath trotted in and began eating contentedly. He was much bigger than an elephant and much stronger too. Silver was a little bit afraid of him, but Gabriel was busy running round his body and clipping out knots and tangles from his thick coat.

'Mammoths are supposed to be extinct,' said Silver.

'He is the only one,' said Gabriel. 'He would be lonely without me.'

'When did he come here?'

Gabriel sat down, as all the Throwbacks did when they were about to tell a story. He began . . .

'There was a time before the Throwbacks ever were, called the Great Frost. The River Thames sheeted over like a new land, and the water was so thick-and-fast froze that for a full winter-time, four moons, men and women and their children lived on top of the water, in wooden buildings and in tents, and lit fires that were hot as hell but not hot enough to burn the frozen furnace beneath. And it was a furnace beneath, for under the ice, shapes and apparitions of the dead could be seen.

'It must have been by an accident of Time that Micah tells us of, yea, that the Mammoth had been preserved deep deep in the river for longer than any man knew, but the ice-winter brought him slowly slowly to the surface, and a crowd of gentlemen had him dug out in his ice-case and displayed there on the river in all his silent sleeping wintry might.

'Then, when no one expected it to happen and by chance and by fate, the thaw began one night, and houses and ships and lives were pulled down through the ice into the waters where they say life began. But here life ended and many were lost.

'The Mammoth in his ice-case began to thaw too, he did, but he did not sink back into the mud where he had lain since the days of Boadicea, great queen of Britain. He awoke with a mighty trumpet, and his massy legs carried him through the torrents of the river, and he hid in the labyrinths of its banks – sometimes seen, as Time melted the years, but he was a superstition and a dream.

'Then we came, and we found him, and we saved him.

'There were two men who had begun to dig deep underground – Brunel, one was called, and Bazalgette, the other was called – and they dug pipes and sewers and drains and conduits and passages deep in the earth, and Goliath was seen by them, and they wanted him for their zoo, and they pursued him. But we saved him, and Time went on, and the men died, and others came, but in the new time there was no such thing as a Woolly Mammoth; he was a superstition and a dream.'

Silver looked at the beast and at the boy and suddenly she

felt better. She felt that she could stay here with this strange boy who had become her friend. Tanglewreck and the Timekeeper seemed very far away. Maybe she didn't have to be brave at all. Maybe someone else would be brave instead.

Somewhere in the tunnels, a horn sounded.

'Hark,' said Gabriel. 'The Council is done. We must go to hear what they have debated.'

'They've been reading the runes,' said Silver. 'I'm a bit worried about that. I don't think I know what a rune is.'

Goliath bent his shaggy head so that Gabriel could pat him between the eyes, then, leaving him eating as slowly as he liked to do, Gabriel took Silver's hand and they ran back down the passages and into the Chamber.

HOLES!

As Thugger regained consciousness he had the sense of someone stroking his hair, very agitated, and saying sorry all the time.

It was Fisty.

'Didn't mean to conk you out, Mister Thugger. I was fighting for me life, after all that rabbit business.'

'What rabbit business?' said Thugger, feeling the bump on his head.

'We've been tricked by a rabbit – terrible mean beast, it is, with big staring eyes. It tied me up, but I got one arm free and that's what I hit you with.'

'You were born stupid and you will die stupid,' said Thugger.

'Elvis is dead already,' said Fisty sadly, picking up his dog's ear with his one free hand.

'He can't be dead, cos he was never alive,' said Thugger.

'He was to me,' said Fisty sadly, staring at Elvis's rigid metal body stretched out on the floor.

'Boo hoo,' said Thugger. 'And when we've cried over your non-existent dead dog, how are we going to get ourselves out of 'ere?'

'We can't. The rabbit has spies everywhere.'

'I am not scared of a rabbit,' said Thugger.

'Wait till you see it – size of a pony, it is.'

'Gimme yer feet, I'll cut the twine and we'll find a way out. Come on, come on!'

When Fisty was free, he carefully put the remains of Elvis, including his ears, into the carrot sack and slung it over his shoulder. Then he followed Thugger round and round the cellar while they searched for a way out.

'What's this?' said Thugger, feeling a metal plate under his fingers. 'Shine my torch.'

The plate in the floor was rusty and worn, but very clearly written on it were the words

ELF KING

'Forget it,' said Fisty. 'I've done rabbits, I'm not doing elves.'

But Thugger had already lifted the plate and was shining his torch down the hole.

'There's a ladder here, and if I'm not daft, which I'm not, but you are, I can hear running water.'

'Water elves,' said Fisty. 'Bad news.'

'Come on, Superman, we're going down – you first.'

'No, no, no!'

'Yes, yes, yes!'

Terrified, Fisty slung his legs down the chute and felt his way down the slippy wooden ladder. For a fleeting moment he had a happy picture of himself back at home, eating an Indian takeaway and watching the boxing, with Elvis at his feet chewing a clockwork mouse.

It was not to be. He was in a hole, all right, and Thugger's legs were coming after him.

Down they went. Down and down. Above and above, watching watching, were the yellow sulphur eyes of Bigamist.

A TRIP TO TOWER BRIDGE

I t was a grim night in the Chamber.

Everyone was silent when Gabriel and Silver returned, and Silver guessed that they had made a decision. She felt a strange tight feeling in her head, like before an exam.

Eden came forward and gave the children lentils with stewed apples and onions to eat. As usual there was thick heavy bread with the dish, and milk to drink.

When they had finished, Micah asked Silver to come and sit by him near the fire. He was kind but grave.

'Silver, all be your friends here. I had thought to keep you here, so that the Timekeeper would be safe from Abel Darkwater, and you be safe too, but Eden has thrown the Oracle, and read the secrets therein, and now we know that you must find the Timekeeper, whether you will or no.'

'But what will I do with it when I find it?'

'That we do not know. The journey will unfold. Your destiny will unfold. But first you must begin.'

'The Oracle speaks true, Silver,' said Eden. 'Here, see the runes – look.'

Eden had drawn a circle on the ground and cast into it thick gold coins and beads that formed a pattern through the smoky lights set round it.

As Silver squinted through the smoke she saw a face forming out of the pattern of coins and beads. She drew in her breath. The face was hers, her face. She looked round wildly at the others. Eden was nodding.

'You be the Child with the Golden Face.'

'But who is she? I mean, if she's me, who is she? I mean, who am I?'

'You be the one who must keep the clock. You be the one who holds Time.'

'I don't understand,' said Silver, very unhappy.

'You are a Timekeeper.'

'But that's the clock!'

'The clock belongs to you. It must find its rightful place.' Micah paused, and, with some hesitation and very slowly, he untied a rough jute bag and emptied out two tiny paintings – like the size of something from a locket.

'These be the last two paintings on the numbers of the Timekeeper,' said Micah. 'And this be your face.'

'Where did you get these?' asked Silver, turning them over in her hands – one was a road winding through the stars, and the other was a tiny child holding a clock.

'The night I stowed the clock for safekeeping at thine own house, I carried these two away with me – I know not why. And I hid them down the centuries, even from Abel Darkwater – I know not how. I vowed never to show them to a soul. But show them to you I do, because they are your own.'

He put them back in the bag and gave the bag to Silver.

'I could stay here. I'd like to stay here,' said Silver desperately.

Micah shook his head.

'Shall we go with her?' said Gabriel.

Again Micah shook his head slowly and sadly. 'Abel Darkwater shall destroy us if we journey with you. There are great powers at work. Abel Darkwater desires the Timekeeper above all things, yea, above life itself, and Maria Prophetessa will set out to defeat him, as she plotted to do in ages past. We cannot battle with these two by any means we possess. Only we can pray that they be defeated both together. Know you well that if we leave our home for too long, we shall die.'

'But what about me?' said Silver.

'You shall journey to the Sands of Time.'

'What? Why?'

'The Oracle points there. It may be that the Timekeeper be hidden there.'

'But my daddy had it on the train.'

'It may be that thy father be there also.'

Silver's heart leapt.

'The prophecy speaks of the Sands of Time, and a hundred hundred and more years gone, when I won the clock at dice, this map be given to me also, and it is of the Sands of Time.'

'Where are they?'

'I know not, but we can feel the trembles in the Earth, as animals do, and this very night there will be a great disturbance. You will go to Tower Bridge above the River Thames and when the moment comes you must trust your fate.'

Micah took out an ancient map in a leather folder. He passed it to Silver.

'I'm not scared,' said Silver, who was. Then she said, 'Do I have to go?'

'Yea.'

'Micah . . .' said Eden, her voice full of doubt. She was sending Micah a Mind Message, something she didn't want Silver to hear. Micah nodded reluctantly.

'Silver,' he said. 'The yea or the nay is for you to choose. You need not go. You be free to stay here, free to return to your own place, free to begin the quest that only you can complete. What be your answer?'

Silver looked into his kind troubled eyes. She had a few questions.

'Do I have to go without Gabriel?'

'Beyond the bridge, he may not go. At the bridge, you must travel alone.'

'When must I go?'

'This very moment. If you will.'

Silver looked down at the map. It was just squiggles. Her eyes were blurred with tears. She had never been any good at geography.

She remembered when she had sat in the high attic room at Tanglewreck, and although she had asked her beloved house to tell her what to do, in her heart she had known the

192

answer herself. It is easier when someone else can give you the answer, but when it comes to the really important things, no one else can.

She looked around the Chamber. Suddenly everyone had gone.

Silver began to pack some food into her bag. Then she put on her own shoes and her duffle coat. She stood up very straight, her little bag packed.

'Yes,' she said. 'Yes.'

Suddenly, out of nowhere, Micah was beside her again. He hugged her hard, and then he took her hand. He was pressing something into her palm.

'You be not learned in telepathy and cannot send Mind Messages as do we, but hold this in thy small hands and say my name and I shall hear.'

It was the medallion he wore around his neck with his name on it. She nodded, too tearful to speak. Micah stepped back.

'Three things have I given thee; the map, this medallion and the jewelled faces of the clock. The Timekeeper must thou find alone.'

Silver nodded, too upset to speak. Gabriel came out of the shadows leading two bog ponies. He gave Silver a leg up, and Micah slapped the back of her pony with the flat of his hand, and the little animal started forward.

'Farewell, Child of Time!'

Riding slowly, Silver and Gabriel travelled without speaking through the passages and tunnels, for what might have been an hour, or might have been a day, until Gabriel halted and slid off his pony.

'Here we be, Silver. I will take thee into the light, though I may not stay.'

Gabriel pushed back a wooden hatch and gave Silver a leg up on to a platform into what looked like a generator shed. She could hear cars whizzing along the road somewhere near.

Gabriel swung himself by her. 'We must pass through this door into the Tower.'

'What tower?'

'The Tower of London. There be a secret passage from the Tower of London to the watchman's room on the bridge.'

Gabriel led the way through a low oak door into a stone corridor. Dark figures stood in the shadows. Silver hesitated.

'They be but armour,' explained Gabriel, urging her on. 'This be where they keep their armour and their weapons.'

Silver knew that all places like museums and castles keep a lot of their treasures hidden away in the cellars.

'We must not take anything,' said Gabriel, 'that is the rule.'

Silver had stopped by a very small suit of armour that must have been made for a child. She badly wanted to put it on. It might protect her.

'Make haste,' said Gabriel, already ahead of her in the gloom.

Quickly Silver snatched up the pair of chain-mail gloves

lined in leather and fur, and put them in her duffle coat pocket. There was a small double-headed axe hanging on the wall near the armour, and, glancing guiltily at Gabriel's retreating form, she shoved it into her duffle bag, and ran on past the maces and the pikestaffs and the balls on their chains, and the crossbows, and the swords, and caught up with Gabriel, who looked at her with a question in his eyes.

Cabbage, thought Silver, *cabbage, cabbage cabbage*.

The rules were all very well, but she had nothing and no one to look after her, only her own wits and what she could steal.

'*Roger Rover's grandchild indeed!*'

'What?' said Silver, who was sure she had heard a voice, and once again, as she had done in the tunnel that had taken her to the Throwbacks, she looked round with the uneasy feeling that she was being followed.

'Look, there be the Crown jewels,' said Gabriel, trying to cheer her up, and sure enough, on red plush and ermine, locked in a glass box, was the Crown of England, that had been worn by so many kings and queens throughout history.

How strange, thought Silver, *that you can wear Time on your head*.

Pearls the size of a baby's head – that was what Roger Rover had given to Queen Elizabeth the First, and here was one left, in a special case of Elizabethan treasures.

As Silver looked at it through the darkened glass, she was sure she saw a face, yes, a face, a reflection, a man with a neat red beard. She spun round. There was no one behind her.

She looked again at the case. The pearl was opaque.

The castle was closed to visitors that day, and so Gabriel and Silver were able to make their journey like mice round the outskirts of the room.

'Evil eye,' said Gabriel, pointing upwards at the CCTV cameras. Deftly, he took a cloth weighted with lead at the corners and threw it over the face of the camera as they crossed the floor in front of it to another door.

'Beefeaters,' said Gabriel, pointing downwards at the men in red guarding the Tower. 'And ravens. When the ravens no longer fly to the Tower, England will fall.'

Steadily, Gabriel led them on, dipping underground again, and emerging through a vent shaft to a rusty disued ladder.

'This leads us unto the bridge,' he said.

'How do you know these ways?' asked Silver.

'We know all the ways,' said Gabriel simply.

Tower Bridge stands high above the Thames. It is the only bridge over the Thames that can open to let through tall ships. Each half of the bridge is raised on a great winch, and the tall-masted ships sail on.

Abel Darkwater knew exactly where Silver was because he was following her progress with his Detector. He had a sock left behind by Silver, and he put this sock into the drawer of his Detector, and let the machine track down her imprint of atoms as she moved through the world.

'We are all made of atoms,' he said to Mrs Rokabye, 'and

what are atoms but empty space and points of light? The alchemists understood this as fire, and learned that the fiery body can be consumed and made again, like the phoenix from the ashes. Oh yes, we can all be consumed and made again.'

Mrs Rokabye had no idea what Abel Darkwater was talking about and she didn't care. She had a plan of her own, and now she was in league with Sniveller. They would soon outwit Abel Darkwater with his nonsense about atoms and fiery bodies, and then they would have the Timekeeper themselves, and sell it to the highest bidder.

Regalia Mason, the highest bidder of them all, was sitting quietly in her suite at the Savoy Hotel, overlooking the River Thames. Her white fur coat was on the bed. She wore her white lab coat over her white Armani dress, and she was busy tapping numbers into her computer. She too knew exactly where Silver was, because she was tracking her with GPS satellite.

'A great improvement on the days of the crystal ball,' she said, to no one in particular, and to anyone who might be listening.

As Gabriel and Silver climbed out on to the very top of Tower Bridge, Silver was amazed to see the cars zooming underneath her in miniature, and to hear the fierce roar of the city all about her. So many people, so many lives, and the river running through them all, as it always had.

She turned to Gabriel, and saw that he was terrified. He

was too high up. There was too much light, and it was too warm for him under the lamps that lit their tower. She had never seen him afraid. Now he was afraid.

'I must go down quicker than a dropped stone.'

'Don't leave me, Gabriel. Please.'

'I have come too far. I must say goodbye. Take food and blankets for you.' He dropped his bag on to the platform where they stood. Silver picked it up, or tried to. 'It's too heavy for me, Gabriel. You'll have to take it back.'

'Time be a cold place.'

'You don't care about the cold.'

'Updwellers care to be warm.'

'I've got my duffle coat. I'll be all right.'

It was nearly dark. The car lights, yellow at the front, and red at the rear, lit up the road under the bridge. Gabriel put his hands over his eyes. He was squinting.

'What should I do now, Gabriel? Here on the bridge?'

'Micah says you must wait.'

'Please wait with me.'

He was hesitating, his fear fighting with his love for her, for he too had been solitary and lonely and a little different from the others, and then Silver had come, and he felt he knew her.

'Gabriel . . .'

She put her arms round him. They stayed like that, very close and very quiet, for what seemed like no time at all, and for ever, when suddenly the whole bridge began to shake like a giant held it in both hands.

Silver fell flat on the floor of the platform. She couldn't get up. It was as though a weight was pressing on her body. She raised her head and looked down the river.

The sky had gone completely black. The cars were at a standstill. There was a clap like thunder. Then the rain came, rain so wet that she was soaked in seconds, rain so sharp that it punctured her clothes and stung her skin.

Gabriel was clinging to the ladder. She shouted to him, but he couldn't hear her above the smashing sound of the rain.

Silver was looking upriver, towards Big Ben. She was aware that the clock had stopped, its creamy faces bright and bland and motionless.

She felt seasick in her stomach. She felt like she was lurching, sliding, and then she realised that the bridge underneath her was opening, and that she and Gabriel were rocking high above it.

'Hold! Hold,' yelled Gabriel, but Silver's hands were small and soft, and the machinery that operated the bridge was heavy and blind. If she did not swing out now, she would be crushed.

She remembered the chain-mail gloves. She put them on and clung with all her might. Underneath her, the cars that were tipping off the opening bridge should have fallen into the river, but they didn't; they hung in Time for a moment and they disappeared. Completely disappeared.

Soon the bridge was empty. The bridge was open.

There! Coming towards her now, pennants flying, sails fat with a following wind, oars rising and falling from the water in time to a drumbeat, men waving from the decks, the prow high and painted, boys hanging from the rigging, and, in the crow's nest, an old man with a trumpet.

The ship is coming through now, surrounded by a flotilla of small rowing boats. Crowds line the banks of the river. The buildings are low, hugger-mugger, crouched in the mud, leaning over the water, some supported on tree trunks rammed into the river. Washing is strung between the houses, and a man slitting a pig's throat runs the river red. He looks up when he hears the shouting. *Yes, the ship is coming!* He leaves the pig on his jetty and yells as hard as he can, slicing the air with his knife, 'JOLLY ROGER, JOLLY ROGER.'

At the ship's wheel, dressed in furs and pearls, is the bearded man that Silver knows so well from portraits and from dreams. Roger Rover is sailing up the River Thames, his ship sunk to its portholes with treasure.

As the ship passes directly under the bridge, the very top of the topmost sail is glowing gold. The gold light spills down the sail, like dye, and then the sail is all gold, and then the gold floods across the deck and over the ship, and as the ship sails through, she begins to waver and shimmer.

The shimmering golden ship is spreading like a wave. It is hard to say now exactly where the ship is, or where the ship isn't, because the ship seems to be everywhere and nowhere. The gold light is intense.

Silver looks at herself. Is she dissolving? She looks at Gabriel, holding his blue coat over his head with one square hand to keep away from the light.

She looks down at the ship, or what is left of it, and one thing she sees: Roger Rover's eyes fixed on her.

Then she does something she never meant to do. She lets go, simple as that. She lets go into the stream of golden light.

'SILVER!' It is Gabriel's voice, far away. 'SILVER!'

But now she is definitely dissolving. She has a vague sense of her arms and legs, but not in their usual place. She thinks, *I'll collect them later*. She laughs. Ridiculous. Arms are arms and legs are legs. But not here, in this spinning dissolving place. It should be painful, but it isn't, not painful at all. It's like drifting off to sleep except that she is wide awake.

'SILVER!' Gabriel's voice again, loud and high. She tries to answer but she doesn't know where her mouth is and so no words come out.

The Throwbacks can mind-read, I'll send him a Mind Message, like Micah said. This thought comes to her as though someone has posted it through a slot in her head. Yes, a Mind Message. 'Here I am, Gabriel. HERE I AM.'

A stout pair of arms wraps round her, like she's being rescued at sea. Suddenly she can feel her own arms and legs again. She can feel the edges of her body. She's not dissolving, she's Silver, and she's four feet ten inches tall and she weighs forty kilos, and Gabriel is carrying her and their belongings to what looks like a checkpoint on an empty road. There are guards and barriers and coming towards them is a man in a Security Suit toting a gun and walking a double-headed dog.

'Where are we?' said Silver.

'I know not,' said Gabriel. 'You leapt into the air and you hung there like a bird hovers, like a bird of prey, like a falcon over a field, and I called you, and you turned to me, and I could not leave you alone, so I leapt too, into the swirling air full of voices.'

'I didn't hear any voices,' said Silver.

'You called to me and I found you.'

'I thought you wouldn't come with me!'

'I am with you.'

Abel Darkwater was packing a small leather bag. He was wearing his old tweed suit as usual, but over the top of the suit, he fastened a fur-lined dark wool cloak. He had some tools, a crystal ball, his Detector, a spherical glass jar called an alembic, a Primus stove, and a sharp knife.

He consulted his gold pocket watch. Yes, it was time to go.

Regalia Mason's GPS satellite link had jammed the second the Time Tornado struck Tower Bridge. She had closed her computer, stepped out on to her balcony over the river and put on her long-distance surveillance glasses; something her firm had developed for the Pentagon.

She could see Tower Bridge clearly, and she could see Silver and Gabriel on the bar above it. How predictable everyone was! Predictable that the child and her idiot friend would imagine Time as an adventure they could win. Predictable Abel Darkwater, setting out to look for a clock. She could have told you all this would happen without a crystal ball. She laughed. Science had done away with so much magic and mumbo-jumbo. Abel Darkwater invented his quaint devices, like the Age-Gauge, but a carbon-reader could have told him the age of a tree or a slice of limestone. Biometric data meant that anyone, anywhere, could be tracked by using a silicon chip, a satellite and a computer. There was no need for Detectors and Searchers, and the rest of Darkwater's toybox.

In the old days she too had passed her hands over the crystal ball and stuck pins into poppets, and sweated over a cauldron to cause a bronze head to speak. All unnecessary now. She was the most powerful woman in the world, and not by magic. She was a scientist.

These thoughts were like clouds floating across her mind as she watched the bridge. No doubt the Time Tornado would sweep the child Silver away, and Abel Darkwater would go after her, and torment her and threaten her, and then all that was left was for she, Regalia Mason, to make sure that the Timekeeper was never found. She had a right to lose it. After all, it had belonged to her once . . .

She smiled.

'For though we cannot make our sun
Stand still, yet we can make him run.'

Then suddenly she saw the child Silver leap of her own free will from the bridge and into the light ripples.

Regalia Mason was filled with fury. The child must not be allowed to take control. By leaping into Time, the wretched child had already begun to control it. Now she would arrive at the Checkpoint. Well, she must not get any further.

Regalia Mason went into her room and opened her quantum computer. It was the only one in existence. Quantum computing was still decades away, and teleporting was just a science-fiction-movie dream, but Regalia Mason had already gone further than that.

On the screen was the sad face of a woman.

'Send your twin Castor to me at once,' said Regalia Mason.

Very soon there was a knock at the door of her room, and a beautiful young man entered, identical in face to his sister on the computer screen.

He was trembling, his head down.

'Kiss me,' said Regalia Mason.

The young man Castor kissed her, and Regalia Mason vanished, to appear on the other side of the Universe as an exact copy of herself.

Meanwhile Silver and Gabriel had found themselves somewhere very odd indeed. A very tall policeman with a double-headed dog was walking angrily towards them. Above them, in the sky, were three moons.

'I don't think we're in London any more,' said Silver.

THE EINSTEIN LINE

S ilver and Gabriel were sitting in a long low hut surrounded by a lot of angry shouting people.

'I've got my visa, I can travel!'

'Can't you see that I'm on business here?'

'My husband has already gone – we're just joining him.'

'This is simply not acceptable in the modern world.'

The problem was simple. Everyone in the hut wanted to travel back in Time, but the Time Police wouldn't let them. Time travel was forbidden. Well, almost forbidden.

Which meant that Silver and Gabriel had broken the rules.

The policeman with the double-headed dog asked them all kinds of questions about where they had come from, and Silver tried to explain about the Time Tornado blowing them off the bridge.

'Blow-ins, are you?' he said. 'That's what they all say.'

'Is this the future – where we are now, I mean?' asked Silver.

'Not as far as I'm concerned,' said the policeman. 'This is Now – 2:45 p.m. precisely – and I am on duty for another six hours. If it was the future, I would already be at home.'

'But is it the future for me?'

'Not exactly, because you have no future. You will be deported back to your own Time, once all the paperwork has been done, and if the paperwork can't be done, you will be Atomised.'

'Atomised? What does that mean?'

'It means you will be No More.'

'You can't kill us. We're children, and we haven't done anything wrong.'

'That's what they all say. Now you come along with me.'

Gabriel and Silver followed the policeman to the long low hut on the inside of the checkpoint. The hut and the checkpoint were ugly, but the sky was deep black and shining with big stars. In the East were three crescent moons.

'Are we still on Planet Earth?' asked Silver.

The policeman shook his head. 'This is Philippi, on the other side of the Milky Way to Earth, but connected by the Star Road. You travelled along the Star Road, through Time, and landed here. Everyone always does.'

'Everyone?'

'Even the Pope.'

Silver knew all about Popes because her own family had been Catholics for hundreds of years, though her father never went to church. She wondered why the Popes wanted to go Time travelling.

'When they die they come here,' said the policeman. 'Nobody knows why. Millions of people die every year and we never see them again, but for some reason the Popes somersault down the Star Road and end up here. Eventually we built this for them.'

He pulled back a curtain and showed Silver and Gabriel a full-size replica of the Vatican in Rome. The Popes were busy going up and down blessing people.

'It's a bit of a tourist attraction,' said the policeman, 'and when we get crowded out with people here – and if you think this is busy, you should see it in the summer – well, when we get really busy, the Popes help out. They do Mass and blessings and things.'

'How many Popes have you got?' asked Silver.

'All of them. The last Pope died in 2333, but we've got a full set. Three of them are women.'

'Are the Popes dead or alive?'

'Ah, well,' said the policeman, 'that's what you don't understand because you live in the past. Dead and alive are to do with Time, aren't they? The Popes die, yes they do, and they think they've gone to Heaven, because they always expected Heaven to be like one big Vatican City, and they always expected it to be full of other Popes, even the wicked ones. So here they all are, and because they have travelled the Star Road they are outside of Time now. There is no Time here.'

'None?'

'None at all. We have clocks so that we can divide the day, and we even have day and night, but this is the Einstein Line. Time is steady here, not future, not past, just the present. Stay here and you won't get any older, ever. That's why people come – it's not just for the Time travel, it's a bit of a health spa.'

'It doesn't look much like a nice place for a holiday.'

'Not right here, stupid! This is a military zone, but a bit further on, behind St Peter's, it's very nice indeed.'

'Well, I wouldn't come here,' said Silver. 'I like the seaside for a holiday.'

'Plenty of seaside here. We've got the Sands of Time here.'

'Where?' said Silver, pricking up her ears.

'Just a star's throw away. Now stop asking questions.'

'I'm only asking questions because you are answering them,' said Silver.

'Well, now I'm going to ask you some questions. What year have you come from?'

'2009,' said Silver, making up a date.

'District?'

'London.'

'And what about him, your pal, the funny-looking one?'

'Do you laugh at me?' said Gabriel, and there was something in his voice that made even an eight-foot-tall policeman pause.

'Gabriel is a Throwback,' said Silver, 'and I am a Pirate.'

'A Throwback and a Pirate, eh? You'd better go straight to Quarantine, without passing Go or collecting a thousand Astros.'

'Do you still play Monopoly?' asked Silver.

'Course we do!' said the policeman. 'Everyone plays

Monopoly, even the Popes. Now come on.'

Silver and Gabriel got up to follow the policeman when a beautiful woman swept into the room wearing a white fox fur. The officers stood to attention.

Regalia Mason whispered in the ear of the senior officer with the double-headed dog, and he laughed, and nodded and gestured towards a back room. Suddenly Silver and Gabriel were picked up bodily, and taken into the back room like a pair of parcels.

'You don't know me,' said Regalia Mason.

(*Oh yes, we do*, thought Silver, but she didn't say anything and she tried practising her Mind Messages to tell Gabriel to keep quiet.)

Regalia Mason was smiling. 'I am here to help you. I am going to accompany you back to your own time. You see, you were caught in the Time Tornado, and it must be upsetting for you. Never mind. Although Time travel is strictly forbidden, some of us are less bound by the rules than others.'

She laughed like icicles breaking.

'Where are we?' said Silver.

'You are on the Einstein Line.'

'That's what the policeman said, but I didn't believe him.'

'The police sometimes tell the truth,' said Regalia Mason.

Then Regalia Mason explained that the Einstein Line was a Time boundary; no matter what part of the future you lived in, this line was as far back in Time as anyone could travel.

'There are people here who want to go back to the 1960s,

or the 1560s, and that is not allowed. You may have noticed that in your world there are no visitors from the future. Some scientists take that to mean that Time travel hasn't happened – but of course it has happened, it's just that we don't let it happen before it was invented.'

'What?' said Silver, completely confused.

Regalia Mason sighed. 'Time travel has been a scientific possibility since Einstein discovered some interesting things about curved space and the speed of light, at the beginning of the twentieth century, but not until the twenty-fourth century did Time travel become a reality. So if you live in the twenty-seventh century, for example, you are allowed to go back as far as Time travel allows – to the twenty-fourth century – but no further back. It is strictly forbidden.'

'Who forbids it? Is it God?' asked Silver.

'God does not exist any more. The Quantum controls Time.'

'Well, what is the Quantum?' asked Silver stubbornly.

'That will be too hard for you to understand; you are only young, and you live in the past. In your world there are Governments, Parliaments, the Central Bank, the Law, the Military, Presidents, even Kings and Queens, even God. In the future, all those things, all those institutions, are taken over by the Quantum. It's much simpler for everyone.'

Silver was thinking hard. At Greenwich, hidden behind the fireplace, she had heard Regalia Mason talk about her company in America called Quanta – so what did Quanta have to do with the Quantum?

'It's very kind of you to take us home,' said Silver, 'but can't we stay for a few days and look around, as we've come so far? The policemen said there were some sands just down the road. Can we go there?'

Regalia Mason's eyes flashed cold fire. 'I am sorry to disappoint you, but you see you cannot go anywhere from here. You have not been through Quarantine.'

'Quarantine? What, like a dog when you come back from abroad?'

'More or less,' said Regalia Mason. 'In the future all diseases from the past have been wiped out. Think how awful it would be if some of those diseases were to return.'

'I haven't got any diseases! I haven't even sneezed since last September.'

'We mustn't take any chances, must we? Now wait here while I organise things. I'll send in some lemonade and chocolate cake.'

Regalia Mason smiled her white-and-snow smile and left the room.

Silver wondered if all not-to-be-trusted grown-ups handed out lemonade and chocolate cake? It was what Abel Darkwater had given her. Well, she wasn't going to make the same mistake as Tinkerbell.

'Don't eat whatever she gives us!' she said to Gabriel, as a guard came in with a tray.

Gabriel sniffed the food. He had a nose as keen as a mole's.

'It be drug food,' he said. 'I smell it on the cake.'

'We've got to escape before she comes back,' said Silver. 'Do something, Gabriel!'

'Me?'

'Can't you dig a hole or something?'

As Regalia Mason walked tall above the milling crowds at Checkpoint Zero, only one thing preoccupied her; the future is not fixed. Time forks. Every possibility is always present, though only one outcome is chosen. But Regalia Mason was a Time traveller. She had visited the future, and she knew that the Quantum controlled the Universe. All she was doing now was making sure that the future happened as it should.

Abel Darkwater she did not consider a threat, although she knew full well what he wanted. He was not a danger, but he was capable of slowing things down. It was unlikely that he could alter the course of events, but his meddling might cause a hesitation in Time, and that might be enough to upset Regalia Mason's plans in the twenty-first century. It was essential that the Time Tornadoes be frightening enough to persuade all Western governments to cooperate with her company, Quanta. Once Quanta began to take control of Time – *at the world's request*, of course – the future was history.

Foolish to let a little child get in the way . . .

Preoccupied as she was with these thoughts, she failed to notice the arrival of Abel Darkwater at Checkpoint Zero. She was not the only one who failed to notice; he walked straight

214

through the police and their dogs, invisible in his woollen cloak, and went towards St Peter's, where he knew one of the Popes personally.

He was just in time for Mass.

Preoccupied as she was, she did not realise that Gabriel had noticed a trapdoor in the floor of the backroom where they were waiting for Regalia Mason to return.

'It be a drop and a tunnel, but narrow as hope.' He lowered his small strong body down. 'Will you come after me, and follow me, and I will make it open?'

Silver peered down. It was worm-size. Weren't there things in space called worm-holes? Holes that connected one part of Time to another? Where would they end up?

'I'm scared, Gabriel,' she said. 'Maybe we should just let her send us home. You're not meant to be here, anyway. We're only kids – everyone here is eight feet tall. And now she's here as well, I bet Abel Darkwater is on his way. We should go home.'

Silver went to the window; it was barred. She went to the door and opened it slightly; a guard stood on the outside, gun over his shoulder. Oh, why had she ever got herself into this? She wished she was back at Tanglewreck. She even wished she was back at Tanglewreck with Mrs Rokabye.

As she stood, hesitating and miserable, Gabriel said quietly, 'Remember what you have come to do.'

Suddenly, in her mind, like she was watching a video, she saw an image of Abel Darkwater, and how he had clubbed

215

Micah with his truncheon, and how Gabriel had leapt off the bridge to save her, when he could have left her on her own for ever.

They could all have left her alone for ever. They didn't even know her but they had cared about her. Her eyes filled with tears.

She didn't understand a thing about the Timekeeper, but she couldn't give up now – for Gabriel and for Micah, and for Eden, and the Throwbacks, she had to try her best. And for her father too . . . they had all tried their best for her.

She stood up straight, took a deep breath, and turned round to Gabriel . . .

Who

had

gone

down

a hole.

The bright lights and fresh air were making him feel ill, though he had not said anything to Silver. He was determined to take his chance underground, and to Silver's astonishment he began to do something she had never seen him do before.

He was standing in the hole, his shoulders and head at floor level. He clasped his hands across his chest, so that his elbows stuck out on either side, and he started to turn, slowly at first, then faster and faster. He was making himself into a human corkscrew.

Earth came flying out of the hole round Silver's feet as Gabriel drilled himself deeper and deeper. She heard him calling her, and then she heard Regalia Mason's voice, flirting with the guards.

She jumped after Gabriel, holding her nose.

No way out but through . . .

AUDIENCE WITH THE POPE

A bel Darkwater was talking to Pope Gregory XIII.
    'Ah, how long is it since we saw each other last?'

'My son, there is no Time here, and no clock to measure it by. We are in Eternity now.'

Abel Darkwater knew that they were at Checkpoint Zero on the Einstein Line, but he knew too that the Popes liked to believe in Eternity.

And this particular Pope had no regard for Time – in 1582 he had chopped ten days out of the calendar in order to align the all-important feast of Easter with its appointed date. The Papal Bull read, 'Let it be done that after the fourth of October, the following day shall be the fifteenth. Amen.'

Anyone who refused to follow this new calendar was branded a heretic. For a long time – in fact, 170 years – this included every person in England.

Abel Darkwater knew that a man like this, who wanted Time on his own terms, was a man he could make a bargain with.

'We may be in Eternity,' began Abel Darkwater, 'but Time is still moving forward in the rest of the Universe, and many things have happened to displease you. There is no God and there is no Church.'

'I could have you burned at the stake for saying such things, Son of Satan.'

'I have been burned at the stake,' said Abel Darkwater mildly. 'It was unpleasant but I am prepared to forget about it today.'

'What do you want, foolish man?'

'If I said to you that we could reverse Time, that we could plan a Universe where the Church was again all-powerful, and the Pope as the Head of the Church, the most powerful man of them all, what would you say to me?'

The Pope looked round out of his hooded eyes. There was no one listening.

'I know enough to know that in the twenty-fourth century the Holy Roman Church collapses and the Vatican becomes a Museum.'

'And do you know that what you describe begins in the twenty-first century when a company called Quanta learns how to control Time?' said Abel Darkwater.

'Quanta? You are talking about the Quantum?' asked the Pope.

'As it is called now and afterwards, oh yes, but the Quantum is all-powerful. Quanta was not all-powerful. Quanta was a multi-national corporation, an important bully, but not all-powerful, oh no.'

'What are you offering me, son of man?' said the Pope in a whisper.

'A chance to turn back the clock!' replied Darkwater triumphantly.

'How?

'There is only one way to turn back the clock, and that is by finding the clock itself – the Timekeeper. Oh yes, surely you remember the Timekeeper?'

The Pope leaned back in his purple chair, his long nose resting against his long ringed fingers. Abel Darkwater's round eyes were like two dark-lit orbs hypnotising him. His mind was moving back through red robes and purple corridors. Yes, he remembered, yes, he remembered, he remembered, and his memories swirled like smoke across a mirror . . .

Ficino, a boy with burning eyes running through the streets of Rome.

Heretical talk of an after-life without Heaven or Hell.

A green lion with its paws cut off.

A wolf caught in a jar.

The arrest of Maria Prophetessa.

The torture chamber. The rack. The pin and screw.

His private chambers at the Vatican. The heavy dark furniture, the fruit on the table, the long windows open to the evening, the faint sound of the choirboys singing a Te Deum. A new machine for smashing a man's hand under torture. His prayer book, jewelled and worn. A decanter of wine.

The smoky memories cleared. He was through the mirror now. He was back in his own past.

He poured the wine. He drank. He was waiting.

Gabriel and Silver came choking up out of the well, and lay down flat on their faces. As Silver opened her eyes, she saw an orange rolling towards her. She put out her hand, took it, pulled off the peel, and gave half to Gabriel.

The sun was shining. The day was boiling hot. They were in a walled courtyard garden where beautiful fruit trees, oranges and lemons, were growing in pots. They could hear a choir singing a little way off. Above them was a wide stone window opening on to a small balcony. The window was open. The voices of two men could be heard coming from the room.

'Where are we?' whispered Silver.

'I know not,' said Gabriel. 'I digged and digged and then I felt me pulled as if by a wind, it was like a wind.'

Hungry and thirsty and dusty, they ate two more oranges each, and looked around. The garden had peaches growing against the wall, and a winged cherub spouted water in a raised lead fountain. The garden was beautiful and deserted.

'There's a ladder,' said Silver. 'We could climb over the wall.'

There was a gardener's ladder with a wide bottom and a triangle top for propping into the fruit trees. Gabriel went to drag it over to the wall, when Silver heard a commotion and beckoned him back to hide.

Through the little door into the garden came two men dressed in strange uniforms. A woman walked proudly between them.

'It's her!' gasped Silver.

It was, unmistakably her, though very different. Regalia Mason, her hair as black as it would be blonde. Her eyes with their same fierce and proud stare.

She spoke haughtily in a language Silver didn't understand.

''Tis Italian,' said Gabriel. 'My mother Eden be Italian, you do recall. These men be leading the woman to the Pope!'

'The Pope!' said Silver. 'Then this must be the Vatican, like on the Einstein Line, but we've gone back in Time. Miles back in Time! Look at their shoes and clothes and stuff. They look like some of the people in the paintings on the wall at Tanglewreck. What shall we do?'

'I know not. Wait – see what they do.'

One of the guards took out a horn and blew it. A face appeared at the open window. It was a man dressed in red; red robes and a red skullcap, with a big silver cross hanging round his neck.

'A cardinal!' whispered Gabriel.

'Let the captive be brought forward. His Holiness commands it.'

The guards took Regalia Mason through a tiny locked door. Silver and Gabriel heard them lock it noisily again on the inside.

Gabriel looked round quickly, then darted over to the ladder. He propped the ladder against the wall, climbed up it, and over on to the balcony.

No! thought Silver, longing to call him back and knowing

she couldn't. There was only one thing she could do, and so she ran across the flagstones, and climbed up after him.

Kneeling side by side, they peered in.

The room was dark, even though the day was bright and the sun was hot.

They were directly behind the massy carved chair of the Pope himself. On the wall opposite him was a mirror flanked with gold candlesticks. The candles were lit, in spite of the sun. They could see the shadowed face of the Pope in the mirror, which meant that if they were not careful . . .

Suddenly the door opened, and in came Regalia Mason, her wrists bound behind her back. The Pope raised his hand. She was released. He raised his hand again, and the guards left the room, bowing and walking backwards. The red cardinal sat in a corner ready to take notes.

The Pope spoke. 'So, Maria Prophetessa. We find that you still pursue your sorcery.'

'I am an alchemist, not a street magician.'

The Pope nodded, his fingers tapping his lips. 'What marvel have you brought me to buy your freedom?'

'I have brought you Time itself.'

He watched her open the bag. He half expected the Universe would fall out, rolled up like a ball, hidden in its own thoughts. Had not St Augustine said that before Time began, the Universe had hidden in its own thoughts, waiting?

He understood that; each of us is a tiny universe, waiting.

He waited. From the bag she drew out a timepiece, bigger than a table clock but less grand than a papal clock. Angels decorated its double face. The twenty-four segments of the hours were etched with pictures. She said that each segment was an hour and that each hour was a century. The clock began with the birth of Christ, and it would run until the End of Time.

On the stroke of midnight on the last day of the twenty-fourth century, so the prophecy ran, Time would cease for ever.

The clock now stood in the sixteenth century, at 1582. Pope Gregory turned it over in his hands while she talked.

He smiled when he saw the pictures; he knew what they were, invented over two hundred years earlier for family friends of his, the Visconti of Milano. They were known as the Tarot cards. Some called them a harmless card game, some said they were much more; something occult and forbidden.

The zero hour showed the picture of a carnival Fool in tattered clothes, his little dog jumping beside him, as he stepped cheerfully off the edge of a cliff.

The first hour showed the Magician, Lord of the Universe.

The second hour showed the High Priestess, sitting between her pillars, Keeper of the Mysteries.

The third hour showed the Empress, Mother of the World.

The fourth hour showed the Emperor, worldly ruler of this realm.

The fifth hour showed the Pope himself, hooded and veiled, all-powerful between Heaven and Earth.

The sixth hour showed the Lovers – three of them. He sometimes called this picture the Eternal Triangle.

The seventh hour showed the Chariot Driver driving his Chariot, pulled by black and white sphinxes; worldly success and secret knowledge.

The eighth hour showed a woman taming a lion.

The ninth hour showed the Hermit, lantern in hand.

The tenth hour showed Dame Fortune turning her wheel.

The eleventh hour showed Justice, sword and scales hanging by her.

The twelfth hour, which was the zero hour, returned to the Fool.

The Pope turned the clock to its reverse face and scrutinised what he saw.

At the thirteenth hour was a man dangled upside down, one leg crossed over the other.

The fourteenth hour showed an angel, one foot on sea and one on shore, pouring green liquid from one gold cup to another.

The fifteenth hour showed the Devil.

At the sixteenth hour, a tower struck by lightning exploded.

The seventeenth hour showed a naked star-maiden by her pool pouring golden water.

The eighteenth hour bayed the Moon, silver and mysterious over a deep pool.

The nineteenth hour showed the Sun.

The twentieth hour showed Judgement: an angel with a trumpet.

The twenty-first hour showed the World, spinning and glorious, and complete.

And here the Pope frowned and paused, because his cards were only twenty-two – three rows of seven according to the sacred numbers, and the zero of the Fool. What were these other images he saw now? These final two?

Maria Prophetessa was smiling.

Cut in silver and gold were two images of the future. One was a road winding through the stars. The other was a child holding a clock.

Out on the balcony, Silver felt for the bag with the two pictures in it. Yes, it was still there, but how could they be in two places at the same time? *But this isn't the same Time*, she thought to herself.

Pope Gregory looked carefully at the picture of the child and the clock. The clock was the clock he held in his hands. And the child?

'The Timekeeper,' said Maria Prophetessa.

The Pope poured them both wine. He reminded the woman he could have her burned and tortured.

'For keeping a clock?' She smiled again, her smile cold in the heat of the Italian summer evening. She was not afraid of him. He was slightly afraid of her, even though she was a woman and therefore inferior.

'God has decreed the hours and the days,' he said. 'We have evidence that you do not follow our new calendar.'

'Not so,' said Maria Prophetessa. 'Much of magic was worked in the ten days that you took away. We call them now our secret days – locked out of Time, but powerful still.'

'You will be burned for this,' said the Pope.

He was about to call for the guards, but his gaze fell on the strange beauty of the clock, and he felt himself compelled to know more of it. He tapped his long hawk nose with his fingers.

'What do you say is the purpose of this clock, this Timekeeper?'

Maria Prophetessa paused as the evening shadows fell in bars across the window, and then she began to speak.

'Long ago on the banks of the Nile, the holy priests of the great god Ra ordained that there should be twelve hours of daytime and twelve hours of night.

'Ra, falcon-headed, Ruler of the Sun, punted his boat across the sky every day, and at night sailed through the Underworld, until it was time for him to be reborn at daybreak.

'The worshippers of Ra understood the ancient mysteries of the Universe, and to them was revealed a prophecy that the dying god would be reborn at the End of Time.

'This god would be the new ruler of the Universe.

'The great dynasties of Egypt passed into the Sands of Time, and the sphinx's head was buried in the dust. Moses, the Israelite, brought a new god out of Egypt, made not of gold, nor in the image of an animal, but in the image of Man. This God Yahweh had a son, Jesus, whose birth we saw in a star.

'The pattern of the Heavens is clear. Twenty-four centuries will pass until the End of Time.'

'And then?' said the Pope, watching her.

'The god will be reborn and Time will belong to him.'

'But you say that Time will no longer exist.'

'Time will exist no more as we have known it.'

'This is a mystery,' said the Pope.

Maria Prophetessa inclined her head.

'And the child? Who is the child in the twenty-fourth symbol?' said the Pope.

'She is the Child with the Golden Face,' said Maria Prophetessa.

'And what is the meaning of that?' asked the Pope.

'I do not know. Not all can be revealed.'

'You do not know, or you will not say?'

'The child is a mystery, like the clock,' said Maria Prophetessa.

The Pope said, 'You are not a believer.'

'I do not believe what you believe, that is all the difference between us, but I am a believer.'

'You are a heretic.' The Pope banged his fist on the table.

'I do not believe what you believe,' she said again.

'You have been arrested on suspicion of sorcery and heresy, and in your defence, you offer me a clock?' The Pope was snarling like a wolf.

'I am offering you the secret of Time!'

'How did you come by this clock?' demanded the Pope.

Maria Prophetessa was silent.

Then the Pope did a terrible thing. He took the clock and hurled it at the wall, where it broke into pieces.

'Curses on you to the limits of the Heavens!' shouted Maria Prophetessa, on her hands and knees trying to capture the beheaded angels, pendulum rods, tiny cogs, jewelled numbers.

The Pope laughed at her. 'I care nothing for your sorcery, woman, and I care nothing for your toys. The clock is destroyed, and your raving prophecies with it. The Church of God will last until the End of Time and the End of Time will be that day when God takes His flock to His Heaven, and Hell is shut for ever on your weeping.'

Maria Prophetessa lunged forward to grab at the wounded fragments of the clock, and, as she reached past the Pope's chair, she looked out on to the balcony and into the faces of Silver and Gabriel.

There was a second's pause, and then she twisted a vial from round her neck and flung it straight at them, crying, 'Away with you, away with you, it is not the time!'

The Pope looked round, surprised, but saw nothing,

because Silver and Gabriel had vanished.

He rang the bell, and the guards came and dragged away Maria Prophetessa, screaming oaths and curses as she went.

Then the Pope bent down and carefully collected all the pieces of the clock and put them into the bag and put the bag into his drawer, and locked it.

Abel Darkwater was leaning forward, watching the Pope intently. He had half-hypnotised him, and his memories were cast behind him on the wall.

As the Pope returned to full consciousness, Darkwater was saying, 'You failed. You did not destroy the Timekeeper.'

'The pieces were stolen from me.'

'And taken to Peru, where a new emerald was cut, to replace the one you kept to wear in your ring.'

The Pope shrugged his shoulders.

'And it came by way of a pirate ship to England in the reign of Elizabeth the First.'

'She was a heretic,' said the Pope. 'We excommunicated her.'

'And then its history is hidden until it was found again in Jamaica in 1762 by an apprentice to a clockmaker called Harrison.'

'And where is it now?'

'That is the question,' said Abel Darkwater.

For many minutes the Pope and Darkwater were silent. A

serving nun came and brought them wine.

'All could be altered, oh yes, if I had the Timekeeper again. If I had it, we could thread our way fine as a needle back through the fabric of Time, and what has happened need not happen.'

'What has happened has happened,' said the Pope.

'Indeed it has, oh yes, but it need not.'

'What are you saying?'

'I am saying,' said Abel Darkwater patiently, 'that the last of the hours of the clock are the ones that matter to us. In the twenty-first century, where I am living at present, there begins for the first time in Time, if you will pardon the expression, disturbances, rents, tears, in Time's fabric, which, if properly understood, allow us a moment to change history, I mean, to choose our future. Your old enemy is your enemy still. Would you be defeated by her?'

'Maria Prophetessa?'

'How she winds through Time!' said Abel Darkwater. 'Her name now is Regalia Mason, and it is she, oh yes, it is she, who stands at the head of the company called Quanta, which, if we do nothing . . .'

'Will become the Quantum,' said the Pope, his eyes flashing like his emerald ring.

'The Quantum,' repeated Abel Darkwater. 'Ruler of the Universe, a new god indeed.'

'And if we act now?' said the Pope.

'Victory will be ours.'

'And Maria Prophetessa?'

'She will be destroyed.'

The two men smiled at one another – the smile of a crocodile and the smile of a wolf.

BIG RED BUS

For the second time in how many minutes, hours, days, months, years, were Silver and Gabriel lying face down in the dust?

They had no idea how much time had passed or where they were now.

'She threw something at us,' said Silver, trying to get up.

'The something she threw, threw us,' said Gabriel, rubbing his bruises. 'Be you hurt?'

Silver shook her head and looked round. 'Gabriel! We must be back on Philippi, there are three moons!'

'This be a wasteland,' said Gabriel, slowly looking around.

They were at the edge of a scrubby field piled high with scrap metal: cars, washing machines, cookers, filing cabinets and bikes with their wheels off. As they walked through the heaps, some smouldering, some cold, Gabriel was filling the baggy pockets of his blue coat with hooks and nuts, wires and clips.

'What are you doing?' asked Silver.

'Throwbacks put to use all that we find,' he said simply.

'Did you understand what Regalia Mason, I mean Maria Prophetessa, was saying?'

'Yea,' said Gabriel.

'So, what was she saying? And anyway, the Pope broke the clock.'

'She spake all of the prophecy and the clock,' said Gabriel. 'I do not think the clock is broke for ever. Remember Micah my father found it many years after, in Jamaica.'

'But it was broken then,' said Silver.

'It may be that you will mend it,' said Gabriel.

He did not say more. What he had seen and heard had frightened him, not for himself but for Silver, and he had made a silent vow that he would protect her at any cost, even his own life. While he was thinking these thoughts, Silver took his hand.

'Look,' said Silver. 'That's weird, that's really weird.'

About half a mile away, but clearly visible in the distance, was a big red London bus. Small figures were running round it. As Gabriel and Silver stood still, watching, they didn't see a group of four men closing in on them. The men wore long coats and bobble hats and their faces were rough and unshaven. Two of them carried baseball bats. Suddenly Gabriel sensed them and he grabbed Silver's hand.

'Run Silver, run!'

They ran towards the bus, the men following. Gabriel and Silver ran as fast as they could – or as fast as Silver could – but the men were faster, and they were catching up.

'Help!' shouted Silver. 'Help!'

The figures at the bus heard and turned, and with a great roar one of them started running straight towards Silver and

Gabriel and the men. The men slowed, hesitated, then jogged to a halt, swinging their bats from hand to hand. Stones started showering over Silver's head. The kids from the bus were hurling stones at the men.

'GET LOST YOU LOT, YEAH?' the boy at the head of the kids was yelling at the men. Then he waved at Silver and Gabriel. 'Come on, come on! Faster, man!'

The men slowly turned tail, mocking the kids, and threatening them, but at last heading back to the scrapheaps, while the black boy stood his ground. The kids surrounded Silver and Gabriel.

'Thanks!' said Silver. 'Who are they?'

'Scrappers,' said the boy. 'Real evil. Lives on the heaps, yeah? They always out on the rob.'

The young black boy was looking curiously at Gabriel: his ears, his face, his clothes, his hands.

'Do you laugh at me?' said Gabriel.

'No, man, no, no way!' said the boy, losing his swagger. The boy wasn't scared of the Scrappers, but he was a bit scared of Gabriel. He smiled and opened his arms to move everyone forward.

Silver and Gabriel began to walk towards the bus with the kids. All the kids were wearing tattered and patched school uniform, except for a pair of twins who hadn't joined in with the others, and were swinging on the pole on the open deck of the bus. They were both wearing identical white dresses, so clean they shone. Silver wondered how anyone could keep so clean out here in all the dust and scrap.

'Where you from?' asked the tall black boy, obviously the leader.

'London,' said Silver.

'Yeah, like us. We was on that bus. We was goin' to school and then we was here. Just like POW! There in London. Then here . . .'

'You're the kids on the bus!' said Silver excitedly. 'You came in the first Time Tornado! You were on the telly – well you weren't, cos you had all disappeared, but everyone heard about it.'

'Cool, we were on telly!' said one of the girls.

'Oh don't be stupid about stupid telly, I want to go home. I want my dog.' The girl next to her started crying.

Another went to comfort her, saying to Silver, 'We get food and stuff, it's all right, but we don't know what's happening – are there aliens on Earth?'

'No,' said Silver. 'There are Time Tornadoes.'

And she told the kids everything that had happened.

While they were all talking, a bell rang, and a woman came out from a far building.

'Sally and Kelly! Inside now, please!'

The twins in the white dresses broke away from the group, and, holding hands, walked across the scrubby back lot towards the steel buildings at the other side. The buildings looked like the small low huts you got in car parks and places, but they were made of steel.

'What's happening?' asked Silver.

'Dunno.' The boy shook his head. 'Every day the twins go

to the hospital for check-ups or something, and they have to wear those white nano-dresses.'

'What's a nano-dress?' said Silver.

'It don't get dirty whateva you do, and it keeps you warm whateva the wevva. The people who lives here wears nano-suits and dresses all the time – they don't have to wash 'em 'n' stuff. They got nano-chips in the material. Like smart cards 'n' computer chips, but real tiny, yeah?'

'We don't know anything about this place,' said Silver. 'Will you take us round with you?

'Yeah, we can show you all the stuff – like the Vatican, which is dead stupid cos it's full of Popes.'

'I'm a Catholic, so shut up,' said one of the girls.

'Yeah, but you only supposed to get one Pope at a time, right? This place has all of 'em. Everywhere you look, like wow, another Pope.'

'Be we on Philippi?' said Gabriel.

'Yeah, Einstein Line, Checkpoint Zero.'

'Then we be back where we were.'

'Why, where you been?'

'Rome, I think,' said Silver.

'In 1582,' said Gabriel.

'Cool!' said the boy. 'My name's Toby.'

'Gabriel,' said Gabriel, making a little half bow.

'Silver,' said Silver, smiling.

Toby shared out the day's food the kids had been given, so that there was enough for Silver and Gabriel. They had sausages and hard-boiled eggs and apple pie and orange juice.

Toby said he would show them round. 'It's a bit like Disneyland here. Kind of a theme park? I'll show you.'

Silver and Gabriel and the kids set off in a noisy tribe to walk round the streets, which weren't really streets, but were groups of buildings, and squares, and then empty open spaces with rubbish all over them.

Ragged men were sorting through the rubbish.

'More Scrappers,' said Toby. 'Like dossers in London, no job or any stuff. They sells scrap. These ones is OK, not so savage like, yeah, but them wild ones out on the rubbish dumps, you gotta be real watchful.'

'What's that doing here?' said Silver, staring up at a tall tower.

'Yeah, Leaning Tower of Pizza.'

'Not Pizza – Pisa,' said Silver, who wasn't as bad at geography as she thought.

Around the base of the tower was an assortment of vintage cars: MG, Pontiac, Rolls-Royce, Model T Ford, Thunderbird, Big Healy, Bugatti, Porsche, all with FOR SALE signs propped on the windscreens.

'If we could hotwire one, we could escape,' said Toby.

Gabriel was very interested in the cars. He told Toby about the Enfields.

'Cool!' said Toby. 'Can you wire one of these up to go?'

Gabriel nodded. He could make anything go.

'Tonight, then!' said Toby, who had decided to forget about Gabriel's funny ears and strange clothes. Maybe this wasn't the place to behave like anything was strange.

'How do these petrol wagons come here?' asked Gabriel.

'Huh? You mean the cars? It all come here first, man – the Scrappers told me,' said Toby. 'You know like how stuff and kids disappear and nobody knows where they gone, or why they never comin' back? Yeah, right, well, is because they get time-warped and they come here. Whateva it is from the past or the future comes down the Star Road and it gets ticketed at Checkpoint Zero. Then it goes off for sale some place else. All the dealers come here to get stuff cheap. We sold our satchels and Walkmans and mobile phones, even our money. They got a coin shop, the lot.'

'What about people? What happens to the people who come here?' said Silver.

'Dunno, really. We just waitin' to be Deported, but we in a queue or whateva.'

They had come round a corner to a neat Parisian apartment block, with a big neon sign on the roof that said POL. The other half of the POL had broken off.

'Parrots, maybe,' said Toby. 'My grandma in Barbados had a parrot called Pol, or Polly. Or maybe Pol is Police, dunno. Here's like the posh part of town. The police chief lives here and the scientists. This building just dropped in from Paris one day, the Scrappers said.'

'It must have been a Time Tornado,' said Silver.

Silver wondered if Regalia Mason had an apartment in the Pol. She described her to Toby. Had he ever seen her? He shook his head. He hadn't seen anyone like that.

A fat concierge came out of the main door of the Pol and shouted at the kids to go away. 'Allez! Dépêchez-vous! Je travaille! Je déteste les jeunes!' Then she started mopping down the marble steps.

'She speaks that Frog stuff so we don't get it,' said Toby. 'I think she came here with the building.'

They went on, past small neat rows of terraced houses, and wooden clapboard buildings from the American Mid West, and a disused factory that said SUNLIGHT SOAP.

In a siding, on tracks going nowhere, were locomotive trains, steam trains and diesel trains, their abandoned carriages home to refugees, who stood outside, cooking and staring.

'You gotta be careful here,' said Toby. 'Kids go missin'. Kids get sold. These can't hurt us cos we've been tagged – yeah,' and he showed them his orange triangle, 'but you not been tagged yet. How come?'

'We'll be tagged later,' said Silver warily. 'There's a queue. We only came last night.'

Toby nodded. He seemed satisfied. The other kids straggling around weren't interested. Toby was the leader.

Right in front of them was a big white stone building with columns and fountains and a paved area with benches and guards with guns walking up and down, but not threatening anyone who was just sitting or eating their lunch. A couple of the Popes in robes and hats were chatting to a man in a white coat so white that it reflected the morning light. Silver screwed up her eyes.

'What's this place then, Toby?'

'The hospital. Bethlehem Hospital.'

'What?' said Gabriel, really taken aback. 'Bedlam?'

'Not Bedlam or whateva, BETHLEHEM, like in Jesus 'n' Christmas 'n' stuff.'

'It is the same thing,' said Gabriel, walking ahead and looking fixedly at the hated and fearful place of his nightmares and his father's nightmares. He thought this place had long since been destroyed.

Silver said, 'Is this a hospital for sick people, like in England?'

'Yeah, I guess, and where they screen you when you arrive. We come here to check for diseases. You get wicked food and it's not like a horrible hospital in London. I was in one once when I broke my leg. It was disgustin', like slop to eat, and dirty, and everyone yellin' all hours, days and nights. This is like a hotel.'

'Can we go in?' said Silver.

Toby shook his head. 'No way. This is like free space out here. Like a meeting place. But you can't go in. Sally and Kelly come here every day, but when we ask what happens they says nothing happens. They just get their DNA mapped – y'know, DNA?'

Silver nodded. The guard was looking at them. Gabriel was conspicuous in his strange clothes. He was agitated and upset too. He clearly wanted them all to move on, but Silver was staring at the gleaming white hospital.

Then Silver saw her, Regalia Mason, coming down the

steps of the hospital.

'Let's go,' she said to Toby, already moving away.

It was too late. Regalia Mason had seen Gabriel. In less than a second he was surrounded.

'Wozappinin?' said Toby, frightened.

'Go!' said Silver. 'Just go!'

Something in her voice made Toby obey. He whistled at the kids and they vanished like mice. Silver ran straight over to where Gabriel stood surrounded.

'Let him go!' she said, trying to pull the huge guards away.

'No need for violence,' said Regalia Mason. 'They won't hurt him.'

'It's me you want, not him,' said Silver.

Regalia Mason laughed. 'I only want what is best for both of you. When you disappeared last week, we were naturally very worried about you.'

'Last week?'

'Time flies, doesn't it?' said Regalia Mason.

'Tempus Fugit,' said Silver, before she could stop herself.

'Yes . . .' said Regalia Mason, 'and that is why we should have a little talk, you and I. Will you come and and sit down with me? I know a very nice cafe nearby.'

'What about Gabriel?'

'I will make a deal with you, Silver. If you will come and talk to me, I will make sure that Gabriel is kept safe and not Deported immediately. We will have to pretend to go through the formalities – so he will be taken away – but I promise you he will not be Deported without you. Do you agree?'

'I don't believe you,' said Silver.

'I always tell the truth,' said Regalia Mason. 'Gabriel will not be sent back to London without you. I give you my word.' She motioned to one of the guards.

'Take this boy away, but treat him as we did Count Palmieri. You understand? Count Palmieri.'

Turning to Silver she said, 'He was an important Italian aristocrat we wanted to look after, but here, on the Einstein Line, we must obey the rules, or be seen to obey them, at least. Now come along, won't you?'

Silver ran over to Gabriel. The guards let her, though.

'It's just pretend,' she whispered. 'You'll be safe.'

Gabriel smiled and nodded. 'Don't fear for me, Silver. Never forget what you must do. Never forget why you are here.'

And the funny thing was that Silver had forgotten. She hadn't thought of the Timekeeper all day long. She shook herself like someone trying to remember. Regalia Mason's eyes were watching her.

'I won't forget,' said Silver to Gabriel.

Gabriel watched her walk away with Regalia Mason.

He did not know if he would ever see Silver again.

'Micah.' He was sending a Mind Message. 'Micah . . .'

THE STAR ROAD

The Caffè Ora was behind St Peter's church.

Silver was hungry and she was glad to eat the toasted ciabatta that Regalia Mason ordered for her. All her life, Silver thought vaguely between bites, she had never had enough to eat.

Regalia Mason was not eating.

'Why is everybody here so tall?' asked Silver, looking at the waiter. Like the guards, the waiter was at least eight feet high.

'The people who live and work on the Einstein Line are known as Les Marginaux. They are outcasts, dropouts, refugees, protesters, and they have been forced to live rough. Living rough in Space is different to living rough on Earth. Earth has gravity, but many of the Space colonies do not. When humans live without gravity for too long, their bodies begin to come apart. They stretch.

'These are the lucky ones who had medical treatment before they stretched too much. But, as you see, they are still taller than is usual.'

'Why do they have to live rough?'

'They don't. No one does. The Quantum offers everyone a house and a job.'

'Then why have they run away?'

'There are always those who don't know what is best for them. The future has changed a lot of things, Silver, but it hasn't changed human nature.'

Silver nodded, and thought about human nature; her only examples were her parents and Buddleia – good, and Mrs Rokabye and Abel Darkwater – very bad. And the Throwbacks and Gabriel, but were they human? And Regalia Mason . . .

Silver looked at her directly, then she asked, 'Are you going to kill me?'

Regalia Mason laughed, but for the first time in a long time, she felt uncomfortable. 'Perhaps we should be honest with each other. Shall we?'

Silver nodded.

'All right. You are here because you are looking for the Timekeeper.'

Silver didn't answer.

'But if you find the Timekeeper, what are you going to do with it?'

'I don't know, but I don't want Abel Darkwater to have it.'

'That is a wise decision. In which case you had better take my advice and go home, because you will lead him to the Timekeeper, whether or not you want to, and he is a very powerful man.'

'What will happen if he finds it?'

'He will alter history.'

'What will happen if you find it?'

'I do not need it.'

Silver was thinking back to the Maria Prophetessa she had seen in Rome. She had to keep reminding herself that this woman who seemed so reasonable and kind was also the one Micah had called both the phoenix and the serpent. She had a strange feeling of being warm and tired. She didn't want to think hard at all. She had to think hard. Under the table she pulled Micah's medallion out of her pocket and rubbed it between her fingers. Her mind cleared again.

'Then why is it important to you? I know it is important to you . . .'

Regalia Mason smiled and shrugged her shoulders.

'It isn't important to me as long as it stays exactly where it is.'

'Do you know where it is?'

'Of course.'

'Then . . .'

'Then all you have to do is go home.'

'My mum and dad died because of the Timekeeper.'

'I am sorry.'

'And it's something to do with our house, with Tanglewreck, and it's something to do with me.'

Regalia Mason was watching Silver intently. The child was no fool; and she was better than that, she had something in her that money couldn't buy and fear couldn't paralyse. She would grow up. What would she become? Regalia Mason had intended to wipe her memory and have her Deported. That would be enough to thwart Abel Darkwater, but, if this child really was the Child with the Golden Face, might the Quantum find in her an enemy it had never expected? Unlikely, very unlikely. The Quantum was all powerful . . . but . . . the future is forked . . . what might happen . . . what does happen . . .

'Why don't we go for a walk?' said Regalia Mason.

They set off together down a long avenue lined with trees. Brightly coloured birds sang in the branches.

'Will you keep your promise about Gabriel?' said Silver.

'I promise I will not kill Gabriel and I promise I will not have him Deported,' said Regalia Mason. 'I promise I will tell you the truth.'

Silver nodded. She had put Micah's medallion away, and the sun was making her warm and sleepy again.

'The road goes on far and far,' said Silver.

'This is the Star Road. Few from your time have seen it.'

Instinctively Silver felt in her pocket for the two pictures Micah had given her. The road winding through the stars – yes, the picture was this road. This road was the picture.

And Regalia Mason began to tell Silver the story of what had happened after the Time Tornadoes in the twenty-first century, and how Time travel began, and how the Star Road was discovered.

'Go back to the day when you were on Tower Bridge. What did you see?'

'I saw Roger Rover sailing up the Thames in his treasure ship.'

'What do you think happened to the hundreds of people walking up and down Shad Thames that day, or driving across the bridge?'

'I don't know because I jumped into the Time Tornado as it came towards me. I saw the river rearing up in gold, and I thought, "If I don't jump now, I'll be swept away."'

'And you jumped.'

'Yes.'

'The ones who were swept away were whirled through Time, and they will never be able to return to their own time. Some have already been Atomised. Others will have to adapt to life here on the Einstein Line. We cannot Deport them back to their own time, because their relatives and friends, the British Government, the whole world, knows that Time has begun to destabilise, and any returning refugees would be scanned for information about the future.'

'But you just said that I can go home!'

'That is because no one knows you are here, and because once your memory malfunction has been completed by us, you will never remember that you have been here.' Regalia Mason smiled her cold smile.

'But you said that people come here from the past any- way,' argued Silver.

'There have always been Time travel accidents,' said Regalia Mason. 'Perhaps you have heard of the Bermuda Triangle, a strange stretch of water where sailors and their ships have disappeared completely. Or have you heard of a ship called the *Marie Celeste*, found floating without a sign of passengers or crew? There is a mountain in Australia called Hanging Rock, where a group of school children and their teacher vanished without trace. And there are thousands of men and women and children who have simply walked into a Time Warp, and landed light years away from home.'

'But now it's different,' said Silver.

'Yes, very different, and that is why I came to London to offer help. At Quanta we have special skills, and in the twenty-first century, we were gradually able to stabilise Time again. Without us, what do you think would have happened?'

Silver didn't know.

'Space and Time are connected,' said Regalia Mason. 'We can only really talk of Space–Time, not one without the other. If Time had continued to heave, the world itself might have folded up. We might have disappeared again into the tiny point of light that we were when Time began.'

Silver nodded again, even sleepier than before. It all made sense when Regalia explained it. It was only Abel Darkwater who was upsetting everything. Suddenly she heard Micah's voice, as though he were standing right next to her: *'Fear her much more than you fear him. She is the phoenix of old, the one who dies and is reborn.'*

Silver opened her eyes wide, and looked round. Regalia Mason was watching her closely.

'What is the matter, Silver?'

'Oh, nothing. I just heard something, that's all.'

'You are tired,' said Regalia Mason gently, 'very tired.' She took Silver's hand.

Silver and Regalia Mason were walking steadily along the Star Road. All the buildings were far behind. Fields stretched on either side of the road. The air was heavy with the sound of insects. It was like the day in the garden in Rome . . .

'Where does this road take us?'

'This road winds through the past and the future, through worlds dead and new-born. It is a trade road and a traveller's road, and something else too – it is part of the journey.'

'What journey is that?'

'You will discover.'

Silver never wanted to stop walking. She felt light and free under the sky of pale suns and visible stars. She wished she could just walk and walk until she came to the day when she was grown up, and then no one would be able to ask her where she was going, and she would come to the last mile of the Star Road, and disappear.

It didn't matter about the Timekeeper. Everything would be all right.

Regalia Mason squeezed her hand. Did she read her thoughts?

The road wavered in the sun. A heat haze shimmered up ahead.

'That's your wave function that you can see, shimmering

there,' whispered Regalia Mason. 'You think you are bound by your body, but in reality your body is only an outline. Every sub-atomic particle that you are sends out a wave – through Space and Time. Your wave function is the pattern that you are, spread through the Universe, and if you knew how to do it, you could concentrate yourself in any place and any time.'

Silver had the dissolving feeling she had when she jumped into the Time Tornado. She could feel herself moving away from herself. She wanted to let it happen; it was like drifting off to sleep and beginning to dream.

This time Gabriel's arms were not there to steady her. This time there was no one to call her name. She had a thought that it was much much easier to dissolve into this wave pattern than it was to re-form as herself, or as any other possibility. It was easier to sleep than to wake, and she was very very tired.

'Where's Gabriel?' she asked suddenly. 'You promised –'

'He is where you will never find him.'

Regalia Mason let go of Silver's hand, and the little girl fell down by the roadside.

Night came. White stars and three moons.

A BLACK HOLE

Gabriel had been driven back to Checkpoint Zero.

The guards had bundled him out of the van and pushed him towards a corrugated iron shed. '"Palmieri", don't forget,' said one of the guards, laughing. He shoved a piece of paper in front of Gabriel. 'This is your pass to get you out of here whenever you want to go. Just like Palmieri. Keep it safe!' They all burst out laughing again.

'Do you laugh at me?' said Gabriel.

There was silence. The guards looked uncomfortable, then angry. They had all been recruited from the Scrappers, and because they had been treated so badly all their lives, all they liked to do was to make other people feel worse than themselves.

'Beat him up,' said one of the guards.

'No, don't bother,' said another. 'He's free to go whenever he likes, after all.' There was another burst of laughter. 'Just get in there, you little weirdo, will you?'

'What be here?' asked Gabriel, looking at the shed.

'Go and see for yerself,' said the guard, 'and when you've had a good look around, you're free to go!'

They yanked open the shed door. A terrible searing wind

blew out, and the guards had to struggle against it to stand up to it. With all their might, they threw Gabriel into the shed. The shed had no floor. Gabriel fell and fell, falling down the wind, and into a blacked-out world. With a terrible thump he landed on something very soft, something that half choked him as he tried to get up.

'Who is it come here?' said a Voice, in a whisper that was sharper and higher than the rush of wind around him.

'One like us,' said another Voice. 'It must be.'

'Pull him up!'

'No, let him slip!'

Gabriel had ears that could hear everything; he had been born and bred underground and his ears were keen as an animal's that lives in a burrow.

He had eyes that could see in the dark too, but in all his life he had never seen darkness like this. It was thick as a hood. He held up his hand in front of his face. Nothing.

He reasoned that whatever lived underground here had ears and no eyes.

Better keep quiet.

'Does he know what time it is?' There was the Voice again. 'I want to know what time it is.'

'He's lost his twin. He'll never see her again. Poor sonny! Ha ha ha.'

Gabriel didn't like the sound of this. He had to get out. He tried to pull himself up, and found that he couldn't move. At least, he couldn't move upwards. He could move down-

264

wards, and that was where the force of the wind wanted him to go; downwards.

'Let's get him!'

Gabriel panicked, terrified. Memories of being chased, memories of being beaten, memories of running with Goliath through the dark low tunnels, the Devils shouting from behind, their glowing bodies red, their faces blank and cruel. He wouldn't be sent to Bedlam. He wouldn't be chained like his father.

Frantically he dug his square spade hands into the soft stuff to try and get a grip, and that is how they found him. Two lassos grasped his hands. Two more lassos grasped his feet, and he was being pulled down, suffocating, into the soft blackness.

'Gotcha now, sonny! Ha ha ha! Let's feel what he is.'

There was a horrible wet slithering sound as Gabriel was felt all over.

'Two arms, yes, two legs, yes, head, hands and feet, and, AND, funny ears. Ha ha ha.'

'Do you laugh at me?' said Gabriel.

There was a silence. There was no answer. Gabriel heard rapid whispering. Anger made him bold.

'You feel what I be, now I feel what you be,' he said, plunging forward and touching the nearest shape.

It was horrible. The shape was long and thin, but not flat. The shape was round and pulpy, like warm spaghetti, like a fat worm, and its longness and thinness never seemed to end. Gabriel was coiling the body like a rope over his arm.

'Where be thine end?' he said, his boldness gone.

'No end,' said the Voice. 'Soon enough it will happen to you, sonny. This is what happens here. You are not sucked down enough yet. But you will be by night, ha ha ha.'

Night? How could anything be darker than this?

'What be this place?'

'Black Hole.'

'That be its name? Black Hole?'

'Did they throw you down here like the rest?'

Gabriel told them about the shed, but the Voices knew nothing of that. They said they had been thrown down the hospital chute after the Time Transfusions.

'Hospital?' said Gabriel. 'Bedlam Hospital?'

'The hospital is called Bethlehem,' said the Voice.

'We've got the Time,' said the other Voice. 'We've got the Time, ha ha ha – that's what their doctors say – but they haven't got the Time, WE got it, and they take it off us and sell it to other people, and then they throw us down here. Half of us, anyway. We're all twins. One twin escapes, the other gets thrown down here, sonny. Your twin has escaped, ha ha ha.'

Gabriel was glad Silver had escaped, even if she wasn't his twin.

The Voices told him quickly and harshly about life in the hospital. The hospital only took twins, and for six months they treated you well, and fed you and looked after you, and made you healthy and strong, and then they started the experiments.

266

So many people in the world were short of time, and that's what the hospital took – Time. The best years were carefully removed and transfused in discrete packets of a year each, to whoever could pay for them.

The twins aged rapidly. Forty-nine years was the maximum taken from any one body, but, by using twins, the hospital had discovered that they could take ninety-eight compatible years and sell them as a healthy screened package to families, or to companies who wanted to extend the working life of their top executives.

Transfusions were taken at thirteen years old.

'Orphans,' said the Voice. 'Orphans or mothers who will sell their children. You get good money for selling your children.'

'What be your fate?' asked Gabriel.

'When they've finished the experiments, and they don't always work, you get sick and old. A boy of thirteen looks sixty when they've finished, and he can't walk. Sometimes they take too many years off him, and he dies straight away – the nurses take extra for illegal sale. You can get cut-price Time off the Time Touts, but a lot of it is no good. They don't give you a guarantee and you can't complain to anyone if you pay the money and the stuff is rubbish.

'Well, even if they stick to the rules, and they only take what the law allows, the boy soon gets sick anyway, and the weak ones they throw down here. There's no Time in a Black Hole, sonny, no Time at all. Time stops, and it stops because there's so much gravity down here that it pulls everything in with it, even light. Even light can't escape this place. No Time, no light, just what they call the Stretch.'

'The stretch?' Gabriel was nervous.

'Gravity down here will stretch you like spaghetti. That's what we are now – human spaghetti.'

'Let me go,' pleaded Gabriel.

'Can't do that, sonny. No one leaves a Black Hole because no one can travel faster than the speed of light, and that's what you'd need to do to get out. You'll be sucked down, and you'll start to be spaghetti. Ha ha ha.'

The speed of light. Gabriel didn't know much about light, because he lived underground, and he had never heard of light having a speed. He was a good runner though.

'How fast must light travel?'

'300,000 kilometres a second. Beat that – ha ha ha.'

Gabriel's heart sank. It was as if he was already giving in to the gravity of the Black Hole and being pulled down and down.

'They were bright stars once, these Black Holes,' said the Voice. 'Think of that.'

'Why do they imprison you here?' said Gabriel.

'Only one of us,' answered the Voice. 'The other is for the experiment. You see, if there's no Time down here, and there isn't, we can't actually die. We should be crushed to death by the force of gravity, but that hasn't happened, we just stretch and stretch and stretch. My feet are a thousand miles away, easy. While we live in limbo here, our twin can't die either. Who knows why not? Then they use us for more of their experiments.'

'What are their experiments? Tell me,' said Gabriel.

'Can't tell you, sonny. Know about the Time Transfusions, don't know about the rest – teleporting, they say, but why you need twins for that, I don't know. Just know that here we are without light, without Time, slowly stretching through this dark dead star.' The Voice fell silent.

Gabriel felt the wind tugging at him, and the sensation of being pulled outwards and downwards. He couldn't hold on with his strong hands, because there was nothing around him but blackness.

He tried to hold on with his mind. He would send Silver a Mind Message. She wasn't very good at reading them, but if he could only reach her as he had when they were both spinning through the Time Tornado. He had felt a cord connecting them then, and he had only ever felt that with his own kind.

He concentrated. 'Silver, Silver . . .' But he sensed a cloudiness, a vagueness, not her bright smile or her clear eyes. He tried to imagine her, but it was like looking at a photograph that is fading. 'Silver, Silver.' He closed his eyes, even though it was so dark, and he made his picture of her stronger. Now she was coming into outline a little bit. He realised with fear that she too must be in danger.

'Never know,' said the Voice. 'Never know where she is now, sonny.'

'I shall know!' he shouted, above the wind that was increasing.

'Too late, you're slipping already. Can't you feel it?'

He could feel it. He could feel his sturdy compact body moving away from itself. He was being broken up by the huge force of gravity in the Black Hole. Well, all right. If this was the end, he would use all his last will and strength to hold on to Silver. He would be like Goliath and dig his legs firm and make his muscles work for him one last time. He would wake Silver from her sleep. He would shape her again and she would remember who she was.

The wind was on his body. The Voices had gone. He was alone.

Deep under the earth, in London, on the Thames, the Throwbacks were sitting in a circle holding hands.

'Steady him,' said Micah. 'He is in Hell. Steady him.'

No one spoke. A wind began to rise in the Chamber. The wind whipped up the pots and pans and blew them against the walls. The ponies whinnied and shivered, and Goliath could be heard roaring in his tunnel.

'Hold against the wind,' shouted Micah. 'It is the wind at the End of Time, it is the wind of the Dead, it is the wind of Nothingness and Void, hold hold!'

With all their might they grasped each other and remained seated as they were, using every ounce of their power to hold Gabriel in their sights.

And Gabriel in his turn held Silver in his sights. He did not think of himself at all, he thought of her only, and he drew a silver line round her body and when it wavered he strengthened it, and when she faded he blew his own breath through the raging wind, as though he were breathing life back into her.

His mind was going dark. He dared not move at all for fear of slipping down the soft scree into the windy formless emptiness below.

He had one chance perhaps to hold on for longer. Fiddling in his pockets he took out the wire and clips he had scavenged from the scrap heaps, and he bound his feet to his waist, and then wrapped his arms round his chest. If he could make himself as compact as possible, he would be harder to break up.

'Help me, Micah,' he said. 'Help us both.'

On the Star Road, the little girl lay in a heap. No one took any notice of her or tried to help her as they passed up and down. She was another of the outcasts. It was common for refugees to die by the road. The Van would come and take her body away tonight or tomorrow.

It was cold on the road. The child was numb and quiet, like a sleeping thing in the snow. Then, faintly, so faintly, like a piano heard in the distance, the child's spreading and dissolving mind heard a note it recognised from another place, another life.

'*Hold*,' said the note.

The note came again, stronger, the same, distinct this time.

'*Hold.*'

Or was it just the wind in the trees?

INTERNATIONAL RESCUE

Something warm and furry was licking her face.

She dreamed she was at Tanglewreck and her parents were alive, and the whole world was safe.

What was this warm and furry thing? She didn't want to open her eyes. Still it persisted, licking her like she was a pat of butter. She felt like butter. Melted butter, except to be that she would have to be warm, and she wasn't warm; she was freezing. Freezing melted butter. Stupid!

She opened her eyes. There was a ginger cat about an inch away from her face.

'Who are you?' she said.

'Who are you?' said a voice that didn't belong to the cat.

'I'm . . .' and she stopped because she didn't know. There was Tanglewreck, her beloved house, but . . .

'Memory malfunction, maybe?' said a woman's voice.

'I don't think so. She's dissolved into her wave function. We have to pinpoint her back in the here and now. Come on, come on, little sister. We're watching you, we're talking to you. You are here with us.'

Two women were bending over her.

'We want to get you inside. Will you come with us?'

The child nodded and staggered up using their arms to help her. The cat rubbed against her jeans.

'We want to get you away before the Van comes. Hurry up if you can. Just over there to the Caffè Ora.'

The child knew that name. She furrowed her brow.

They hurried across the road. A round man in a woollen cloak was watching from the shadows. No one noticed him.

The Caffè Ora was closed and the blinds were tight across the windows, but inside the tables were packed with people sitting and talking.

The child blinked against the light and felt faint.

'Sit down,' said one of the women. 'My name is Ora, I run the cafe.' She put her hand on the other woman's shoulder and smiled. 'This is Serena. Everyone here is a friend. Now, come on, concentrate on something you know really well. What is it?

A house, a moat, a room in the attic, a long ragged drive . . .

'Tanglewreck,' shouted the child. 'That's where I live.'

'Is that a planet or city?' said Ora.

'It's my house. My own house, well, apart from Mrs . . .' But she couldn't remember the name.

'That's good,' said Ora approvingly. 'Everyone here wants to help you. We're all looking at you, and we all want to know your name.'

The people at the tables started clapping and cheering. The child felt shy. She wished . . . HE were here . . . what was his name? His name, his name . . .

'Where's Gabriel?' said the child wildly. 'He's my friend. He's small but strong, he wears a blue coat, and he has a pale face and jet-black hair. We came here in a Time Tornado and Regalia Mason found me and left me on the Star Road. I have to find my friend Gabriel, and the . . .'

She stopped. Were these really friends or enemies? What was happening? Why had she forgotten her own name?

'My name is Silver,' she said.

Ora sighed with relief. 'You nearly died out there. If the Van had found you, you would be dead by now.'

'What's the van?'

'The Van takes left-over people to be used up elsewhere.'

'What happened to me?'

'You were dissolving into all of your possibilities — that's what a wave function is. At a sub-atomic level, your particles are spread throughout Space and Time. You're everywhere and nowhere. At the crude level of ordinary life, you need to be someone to exist, or you need to exist to be someone, whatever you prefer.'

Silver nodded.

'It happens a lot on the Star Road. It's easy to forget who you are. That's what was happening to you. You were drifting through all your possible states of existence. When we came, we took a measurement –'

'You measured me?' asked Silver, really confused.

'In a way. But not with a tape measure. By observing you, we determined your position in the Universe. We brought you back from everywhere to somewhere.'

'Give the girl some pasta!' said one of the men at the table.

'John's right,' said Serena. 'She needs food before she gets the science!'

Ora brought her a steaming plate of pasta and Silver wolfed it down. Between mouthfuls she said, 'I was here just before, in your cafe. This afternoon, I think. Regalia Mason brought me here.'

Nobody knew the name or the description, so Silver carried on talking. 'She's got a company called Quanta, but I think it's called the Quantum here.'

'What do you know about the Quantum?' said Ora.

'Where I come from, in London, in the twenty-first century, something is going wrong with Time. There are demonstrations in the streets, and the Government doesn't know what to do. Regalia Mason owns a company called Quanta. They're in America, and only they can fix Time, which is why nobody in the future is allowed to interfere with the past. If they do, she says there will be no future and no past. Time will implode and everything will disappear.'

Ora nodded. 'I'll tell you something, Silver. Many of us here in this room tonight have risked our lives, and those who are not here have lost their lives, trying to travel back in Time to change what was happening then, so we can change what is happening now. We have all failed. Where you are, in London, in the twenty-first century, is the time and place where the future is set for hundreds, perhaps thousands of years to come. You have no idea of the importance of the time you are living in.'

Silver thought back to the meeting of the Committee at Greenwich, and how Regalia Mason had told all those clever scientists and important people in the British Government that her company would be the one to control the new research into Time.

'But what is the Quantum?' she asked.

The people in the room were silent, looking at each other. Ora spoke.

'At the highest level – no one knows. There are ministers, officials, functionaries, police, soldiers, offices, TV stations, everything you can think of, but no one knows who, or what, is at the centre.'

I do, thought Silver, and she was afraid.

'Here, on the Einstein Line, there's a Resistance Movement. We try and help people who are victims of the Quantum, and we infiltrate Quantum organisations with our spies. People arrive on the Einstein Line from all times and all parts of the Universe. We give them shelter, and in return, they give us information. If we help you to get back to your own time, will you take a message for us?'

'Yes,' said Silver, 'but I need to find my friend before I go back, and . . .'

She was about to say that she needed to find the Timekeeper too, but something warned her that these people would not understand.

'We will help you to find your friend. If the Time Police deport you, they will re-circuit your brain neurons, and you won't be able to remember anything about where you have been. If we arrange your travel, you will remember all of this, and you will be able to take a message to one of our workers in London.'

Silver had thought of something. 'If this is the future and you know what happened in the twenty-first century, why don't you know who controls the Quantum? It must be in the history books about Regalia Mason, and her company Quanta, and the Time Tornadoes.'

'History is unreliable,' said Ora simply. 'The Quantum has re-written history. The rest has been erased.'

Silver thought to herself, *That's why they don't know anything about Regalia Mason. She doesn't want them to know anything. She wants to be invisible.*

And Silver realised that even she was somehow keeping Regalia Mason's secret. There was so much that could not be said. Anyway, why would they believe her?

Ora took Silver into a little back room and started to make up a bed for her. The room was mainly a storeroom for the cafe, but Ora said that the Resistance often tried to help out travellers who had nowhere to stay.

'It's dangerous to sleep on the roadside – the Van comes along and picks you up, and then you wind up in the hospital for tests. And then – well, who knows?' She said this in the voice of someone who knows too well.

There was a cat box in the room. It said CAT BOX on it,

but when Silver lifted the lid and looked inside, she saw that the ginger cat was dead. She called to Ora, and hung back, a little bit frightened by the stiff dead body of the warm furry cat that had licked her awake.

Ora laughed. 'That's just Dinger. The most famous animal experiment in history. He's got his own website and fanclub, like Bambi or Shere Khan, or Dumbo, except he's a real cat and not a cartoon.'

'But he's dead!' said Silver. 'And he was alive!'

'He's dead now, he'll be alive again later.'

'How?'

'He exists in the sum of all possible states. It's his wave function.'

'How can a cat be dead and alive at the same time?'

Ora sighed. 'It's like this. The wave function of the cat exists in all possible states – dead, alive, eating, sleeping, running, washing. You see, atoms and other small particles, the basic stuff that we are made of, well, that basic stuff can simultaneously exist in more than one state at once – just like when you were dissolving on the Star Road.

'Only when an observation is made – call it a measurement, or an observation, whatever you like – well, only then do these tiny bits of you and the cat definitely enter one state or another. The cat used to be shut in a closed box and threatened with a vial of poison that would be triggered by the atomic decay of a radioactive substance. Until the box was opened, no one could know whether Dinger was alive or dead – and as the single atom that triggered the poison could be both decayed and not decayed at the same time, so too could the cat be dead and not dead at the same time. You can't know till you open the box.'

'But he's dead now!' said Silver.

'And when you open the box again, he'll be alive. He's a quantum cat.'

Silver looked at the dead body. 'Have I poisoned him?'

'No! That was all years ago – 1935, actually – when the guy called Schrödinger did the experiment on the cat. Dinger doesn't have to go through all that any more – but once a quantum cat, always a quantum cat. He just comes and goes through his wave functions.'

'Where did you get him?' asked Silver.

'I bought him from Quantum Pets. It's a place for collectors. He was very expensive – but he doesn't eat much.'

'Well, he won't if he's dead,' said Silver.

Ora was fussing around with the bed. She put the overhead light out, leaving Silver with just a small bedside bulb.

'You won't forget about my friend Gabriel, will you?' asked Silver.

Ora smiled. 'I know someone who knows someone who will know. That's how it is here. We'll find out for you if we can. Now go to sleep.'

Ora went out, leaving Silver with Dinger the cat. Hesitatingly, she touched his fur. His eyes were open and glassy. He was definitely dead.

She closed his box and got into bed.

ELVES!

Thugger and Fisty had crawled bent-double through the low passages that led away from the cellars. Thugger was sure that if they followed the water trail they would reach a culvert somewhere in the grounds of the house, and then they could run as fast as their criminal legs would carry them back to their van.

Fisty was frightened. He had never been good at doing more than one thing at a time, which made him useful for smashing down doors or robbing old ladies, but now he was nothing but fear, and he trembled as he scurried along with dead Elvis in the sack over his shoulder.

'Come on, come on, think pizza and chips, think "Match of the Day",' said Thugger, by way of encouragement.

But Fisty couldn't think. Not even on a good day could Fisty think, and this wasn't a good day.

As they continued, Thugger noticed swan's feathers floating on the water. Swans didn't live underground, so that must mean that the watercourse ran into a river or a lake somewhere. He picked up a swan's feather and held it for good luck.

Not long after this, his eyes that had grown used to the

dark noticed a light ahead of them, getting stronger all the time; a bright light, like daylight. He was right! They were going to escape. Dragging Fisty by the sleeve, he stumbled and ran and ran and stumbled, and yes, there they were, in a panelled room with light cascading through the red and green illuminated windows, and a man with a beard was dipping his knife into a spit-cooked swan.

'Villains!' shouted the man. 'What are you doing in my house?'

Thugger thought fast – humility might be better than a fight. The man looked strong and his knife was keen.

'Beg yer pardon, guvnor, we's lost. Just show us the way to the door and we'll be on our way.'

'There is no door,' answered the man. 'The door was sealed long since by my enemies.'

'Are you the Elf King?' asked Fisty, shaking so much that he could hardly form the words.

'I am Lord of this Manor. And who might you be?'

'Thugger and Fisty,' answered Thugger.

'Servants of the Crown?'

'We're here on behalf of Abel Darkwater.'

It was the wrong thing to say. The trim man stepped forward, pulled a rapier from above the fireplace, and moved towards them.

'Darkwater! That gentleman has swindled me out of a clock and deprived me of my liberty. Put up your swords!'

Thugger took out his cosh. With one swift step forward, the neat small red-bearded man had cut it in half. The flexing point of his sword pinned Thugger to the wall. Fisty whimpered.

'Answer well and you will be spared. What monarch rules the land?'

Thugger thought he had better answer. 'Queen Elizabeth.'

Redbeard nodded and seemed pleased. 'Then not as much time has passed as I feared. I may yet recover my liberty and my property. What is your business from Darkwater?'

'He wants the clock,' blurted out Fisty.

'The knave has the clock! It was my ransom, but my ransom has been paid and still I languish here.'

'He didn't say nothing about a ransom, but he don't have the clock thing and that's for sure. He sent us here to find it, when everyone had gone out.'

'Gone out? There are twenty indoor servants and ten members of my household at Tanglewreck, to say nothing of the stable boys and gardeners and water carriers and farm men. Where have they gone out to? Are the wars raging?'

'Not on this island, sir.'

'Well, well, and that is good, and your tone is civil wherewithal. Now, tell me all you understand of the whereabouts of your master Darkwater, and let me see if I may not buy your services for a better price.'

'But are you the Elf King?' repeated Fisty stubbornly, for, like dead Elvis, he could never let go a bone once he had it between his slow and stupid jaws.

'What on God's blood are you talking about, you foolish cowman?'

'I'm not a cowboy,' said Fisty. 'Look, it's written 'ere, on the way down to your place 'ere. It says ELF KING.'

He lifted the big rusty culvert lid out of his bag. Thugger put his head in his hands. *Once a moron always a moron*, he thought to himself. Now the gent with the red beard was going to get really angry and probably skewer them both like a couple of chicken kebabs.

Redbeard had stepped forward and was looking at the rusty circle of metal. Then he took a napkin and dusted it off and started to laugh and laugh.

'What's funny?' said Fisty, who never got a joke till it had been explained to him fifteen times.

'I am obliged to you, sir – I have not laughed so much for many a year.'

Thugger got up out of curiosity and went to see for himself. He started to laugh. 'ELF KING, eh, Fisty? ELF KING?'

The rusty heavy culvert lid said

SELF LOCKING PLATE

'Yeah, well,' said Fisty. 'Yeah, well, and I don't believe in elfs, never did . . .'

The man with the red beard was wiping his eyes with his napkin. He slapped them both heartily on the back.

'Sit down, gentlemen both! Sit down! Sir Roger Rover invites you to dine.'

TRUE LIES

S ilver slept long and deeply and she did not dream.

She woke at dawn, which here on the Einstein Line was not one dawn, but three, because Philippi had three moons and three suns.

The three suns rose on the three horizons and made a triangle of pink clean light. The Star Road stretched in the distance.

She found her duffle coat and felt in the pockets. The chain-mail gloves were still there, and the little double-headed axe she had stolen from the Tower of London. True, she had lost the diamond pin, but she had Micah's map, his medallion, and the two pictures from the face of the Timekeeper. She pulled them out of their little jute bag and looked at them. They would help her remember what she had to do.

At the Caffè Ora, the breakfast business was bustling. When Ora saw Silver was awake, she gave her toast and eggs and orange juice. The cat Dinger was sitting up washing his face with his paws.

'He's alive!'

'I told you that last night . . .'

'Yes ... did you find out anything about my friend Gabriel?'

Ora's face was grave. She looked away and started stroking the cat. Silver felt her heart beating too fast.

'What's happened?'

'It's too late, Silver.'

'What do you mean? Where is he?'

'He's lost. There's a place . . . oh, it's not a place as you understand it – it's more an absence of place, a void.'

'What place?'

'It's hard to explain –'

'I WANT TO KNOW!' Silver was shaking with fear and anger. Ora went to touch her, but Silver pulled away. 'Just explain.'

Ora nodded. 'All right. Well, our galaxy is called the Milky Way. At the centre of the Milky Way is something called a Black Hole. You can't see it, because it has no light, but you can sense it, because of the force it exerts. If anyone falls into a Black Hole they don't come out again.'

'Why not?'

'Light travels at 300,000 kilometres a second, yes?'

Silver nodded. She knew that.

'And nothing can travel faster than the speed of light, you know that?'

Silver nodded again. Ora looked down at her hands and continued.

'So, a Black Hole is black because even light can't travel fast enough to escape the force of gravity in there. You need to get some speed up to escape gravity. Even to get out of Earth's gravity, a rocket needs to travel at 25,000 miles an hour. Your friend would have to travel faster than light to get himself out of the Hole he's in.'

'Is he dead?'

'No one knows what happens inside a Black Hole.'

'But we have to find out! We have to help him!'

'We can't, Silver. No one can.'

'Well, where is this Black Hole?'

'They took him back to Checkpoint Zero. There's a way into the Hole by the Atomic Fence. Once you are in the Hole, there is no way out.'

Someone shouted for Ora from the bar, and she had to leave Silver on her own. Silver sat down and tried to think clearly.

Gabriel couldn't be dead – and if he was dead it was her fault. She had brought him on this journey, when he had been happy with his clan and his kind, living underground.

She concentrated hard and tried to send him a Mind Message. She called his name – 'GABRIEL!' She felt the thought go out, but into darkness and silence, no, not silence, into a wind. She sent the message again – 'GABRIEL!'

He couldn't hear her.

She was filled with anger at Regalia Mason. No, he had not been Deported. No, she personally had not harmed Gabriel, but Gabriel had been harmed. She had told Silver the truth and lied all the way through the truth, like when someone poisons the water supply.

There was a tapping on the window. It was Toby.

'Found you!! Bin lookin' for you all places! You disappeared afta the hospital. You in trouble, yeah? Where's Gabriel?'

'He's in a Black Hole.'

'Wot?'

'I don't know. They took him back to Checkpoint Zero.'

'We – the kids 'n' me – all goin' there today to be scanned 'n' stuff. We bein' Deported, yeah.'

'Today?'

'Yeah, weird, but after you went off, then some police came and asked about you, but we said we just seen you wanderin' about. My mum told me never to tell the police nothin'.'

'When are you leaving, then?' asked Silver.

'Dunno – today, that's all they say.'

'Can I come with you?'

'Why?'

'I have to get back inside Checkpoint Zero.'

Silver felt sure that Gabriel was still alive. She took out the medallion Micah had given her, and closed her eyes and concentrated as hard as she could.

'Micah! It's Silver. If you can hear me, please help Gabriel. I'm coming to find him. Tell him that I'm coming to find him.'

Deep under the earth on Earth, Micah heard Silver as he sat cross-legged in his trance. He tightened his hold on Gabriel; he was using his last strength. They both were.

SPEED OF LIGHT

At Checkpoint Zero Silver and Toby and the kids got out of the van that had picked them all up from the bus, including Silver. They had been sent straight to the guard at the gate. The guard took one look at them, checked his list and waved them through.

'You're the kids from the bus, right?'

'Right,' said Toby. 'You all knows us. We're all here.'

'I can't keep up,' said the guard. 'This is a crazy day. They're sending everyone through at double speed. Go down to the white building and get yourself scanned. You're for Deporting at two o'clock.'

'How do you send people back to their own time?' asked Silver innocently.

'Top secret,' said the guard, tapping his nose. 'Now get on with it, and don't you go near that red building. You just go to the Waiting Room. The white building.'

The Checkpoint was very busy, and the guards were all arguing with at least six people at once – plus there was the Deportation . . .

They were heading for the Waiting Room when Silver noticed a line of children walking two by two towards the red huts. She stopped and stared. They were all twins.

Suddenly a guard came over to the kids, singled out Sally and Kelly, and pointed to the line moving towards the red hut. Meekly, and holding hands, the twins went across. The guards ushered them into the hut, then bolted the doors from the outside, checking briefly through the spy-hole before they walked away.

'Toby!' said Silver. 'Come on!'

They broke away from the group, dawdled by some containers until the guards were looking the other way, then ran over to the red hut and looked inside.

The twins inside were all dressed identically, like Sally and Kelly. They had been given a packed lunch, which they were eating quietly.

Silver and Toby went round the side of the long red hut, and saw two more huts, marked ARRIVALS and DEPARTURES.

Through the spy-hole, she could see that ARRIVALS had a lone African man sitting gloomily inside.

DEPARTURES was very different. The hut was full of men, women and children of all ages and nationalities. As Silver was standing on tiptoe, peeping through the spy-hole, she heard one of the guards shouting at her, 'Hey, you, what do you think you're doing?'

The guard was tall and angry. Toby stepped forward, looking cocky and sorry all at the same time. He was used to dealing with the guards.

'We all bein' Deported today, man. We just lookin' around, y'know?'

'Name?'

Toby gave his name and gave Silver's name as one of the other kids from the bus. The guard scanned down his palm organiser.

'This place is chaos. Come on, back to the neuro-unit. You haven't been Wiped yet.'

'Wiped?'

'We don't want you telling everyone where you've been, do we?'

The guard prodded Silver and Toby across the camp towards a group of white hospital vans with BETHLEHEM HOSPITAL written on them. Orderlies in white gowns and gloves were passing in and out.

'Here's another two for you. The bus kids. Toby Summers and Esther Waters,' said the guard.

The orderly nodded and checked his own hand-held organiser. 'May as well just send them now. Take them straight down to the AF.'

'What's the AF?' asked Silver.

'Atomic Fence, nosy,' said the guard, then he turned back to the orderly. 'But they haven't been Wiped.'

The orderly looked embarrassed. 'We've got an extra unit down at the AF. There's a lot of work on today. Red Alert day. We'll Wipe them at the AF.'

The guard nodded and flipped shut his computer. He marched Silver and Toby down the camp, towards the Atomic Fence. Sure enough, there was another Bethlehem Hospital van parked there. People were milling around, joking about getting home and telling their friends.

'Not that they'll ever believe us,' said one woman. 'Men eight feet tall with double-headed dogs, would *you* believe it?'

There was laughter. Then somebody said, 'We won't remember a thing – they Wipe us before we leave.'

'Not me,' said the woman. 'I remember everything.'

Silver was feeling uneasy. 'Toby, watch out for the kids coming down here. I'm going to look in the van.'

Silver saw the back door was open, and two men in green operating theatre suits and masks were helping a woman and a little boy up the steps. But there was another door on the side of the van. She went straight to it, opened it quietly, and folded herself inside.

She stopped still. It wasn't a van at all; it was a portal.

One side, the side she had entered, looked like a mobile medical unit. But the other side didn't have a side. It opened on to the vast starry sky of the Universe.

Silver heard footsteps. She hid behind an oxygen cylinder. Good thing she was small. An orderly appeared from the back of the unit, with the nice-faced young woman holding her little boy by the hand.

'Will we land on Earth where we got lost?' she asked the orderly. 'I mean, I haven't any money or anything, or a phone.'

'You won't need anything,' said the orderly. 'Tags, please.' The woman knelt down and held out her little boy's wrist, with its tiny tag. The orderly held his ring against it, and the tag came off. Then he did the same for the woman.

'We were just on the beach,' she said. 'When the wave came, we were knocked unconscious, and when we opened our eyes, we were here, weren't we, Michael?'

Michael nodded happily. 'I've been to Space,' he said. 'I wish we could take home one of the double-headed dogs.'

The orderly smiled faintly.

'Will this hurt?' asked the woman.

'You won't feel a thing,' said the orderly. 'Step forward, please.'

The woman looked out at the endless stars. 'What, just go?'

The orderly nodded.

'But what happens? I thought we'd go in a rocket or something.'

'No need for that these days. We can teleport you.'

'That's exciting, yes, it is.' The woman was frightened but she didn't want to scare her little boy. She held his hand more tightly. 'Big breath, Michael,' she said. 'One, two, three . . .'

They jumped. They jumped into the silent floating world on worlds, and, for a moment, they hung there together, like two surprised angels, and then there was an intense burst of sparks, pale and strange, and they vanished for ever.

Suddenly Silver realised what was happening. These people weren't being Deported. They were being Atomised.

She looked around her hiding place, desperate for anything she could use to cause confusion, and then she saw an Emergency button behind a glass window, like on trains. There was a coded keypad to open it, but Silver took out her axe, smashed through the glass in one clean strike, and plunged the blade right into the button.

Immediately a wailing siren sounded so loudly that she covered her ears as she dropped back behind the cylinder. The orderly leapt up and out of the van.

Silver jumped out the way she had come in and ran to Toby among the milling panicking crowd. Guards were arriving.

'Hide in the crowd,' said Silver. 'Wait for our chance. You have to get to the kids.'

A guard came past them. He leaned down to Silver and whispered, 'I work for the Resistance. Follow me.'

Without a word they fell in line behind him.

'Ora knew you would come here,' said the guard. 'I'm going to get Toby and the other kids away. Come on.'

'I've got to find Gabriel,' said Silver stubbornly.

'You'll never find him,' said the guard. 'Now come on, there isn't much time. Usually they Deport. Today they're Atomising. Security. Red Alert. No prisoners. *Atomising*. Understand?'

Silver nodded. Regalia Mason must be nervous. She wondered why.

'Look out, man!' said Toby. 'The kids is comin' down this way right now!'

The guard set off quickly, Toby following him at a run. Silver took her chance to dart off the other way, back into the milling confusion.

Her mind was racing. She was at the Atomic Fence. The

302

entrance to the Black Hole was here somewhere.

'Micah,' she said out loud, 'show me where to go.'

She closed her eyes and concentrated on the medallion in her hand. She saw Micah's face. When she opened her eyes again, she was looking directly at a big rough shed. The shed was unmarked; no guard, no barrier, but she knew this was it. Slowly, as though she were the last person alive, she walked towards the silent door.

Gabriel was almost done now. The ledge that held him was giving way as Micah's own strength faded. He lay flat, quiet, his face in the dirt, aware of long loops of flesh lassoing him down.

There were three pictures in his mind. Three pictures that told him he still had a mind; that he was Gabriel.

The first was Micah, eyes closed, hands outstretched, every sinew trembling as he struggled to hold the boy he loved. The second was Goliath, his strong body bent under the boy, trying to push back gravity, as he had once bent his huge head and pushed out of his ice prison.

The third was Silver, so serious in her face, never laughing at him even for a second, but smiling at him for what felt like his whole life. He had known her for ever. Somewhere. Not here.

He smiled in return.

'GABRIEL!'

What? Could he hear her? His name again, and her face very close to his, but she couldn't be here. With pain and struggle, because one of his shoulders had dislocated, he raised himself up, risking the ledge, which sank a little more under the movement.

'JUMP UP!'

What? He couldn't do that. He couldn't jump up; he could only spin down.

'COME ON, GABRIEL. I'M JUST HERE. NEAR.'

Silver had opened the door, and she felt the wind roaring through the End of Time. She didn't step forward. She knew there was no floor, nothing at all, she knew this was where he was. She lay down on her tummy and she put her hand down into the Black Hole.

As she lay there, imagining light spinning at such speed through the Universe, she saw in her mind, very clearly, the first time she had met Gabriel, on the banks of the Thames, and he had saved her. Something had passed between them, and from then on, something always did, some understanding, some recognition. Love, it was – yes, love. Instantly love. And she saw a light-beam racing away through Time, and then she saw love like a rope thrown out – as bright as a light-beam, as fast as light – a rope across Time.

In the Black Hole, Gabriel's mind began to clear. It was Silver calling him. He sat up. He stood up. He was on his feet, though his feet seemed miles away.

'JUMP, GABRIEL – I CAN REACH YOU.'

The ledge was crumbling. Underground, light years away, Micah fainted and Goliath roared. A great wind swept through the Chamber. Swept across Gabriel. It was now, now, or . . .

He jumped. He jumped with all his remaining strength, and what happened, happened. He did not fall back. He rose up, spinning through the black air, the warm lassos around his body loosening, the sound of Voices, babble of Voices. *THE BODY CAN'T ESCAPE.*

But he was escaping. He was travelling faster than light, because he was travelling at the speed of love.

THE WALWORTH HOLE

Mrs Rokabye was enjoying life at Tempus Fugit since Abel Darkwater had fastened his cloak and left. Every morning Sniveller made her breakfast in bed, and every evening they plotted their plan.

Mrs Rokabye thought of her plan with a capital P. It was a Plan. It was a Masterplan. Soon she would be living in a brand new Executive Home on a gated estate near Manchester. It was all she wanted; it wasn't much, but if she had to destabilise the Universe to get it, then she would.

Sniveller was less sure of Mrs Rokabye's Plan, but he was prepared to help her because he longed to escape from Abel Darkwater's service. He had worked for him for over three hundred years, without a day off.

It was night, and the two of them were sitting in Abel Darkwater's drawing room by a roaring fire. Sniveller had what looked like a set of Scrabble letters on the table in front of him, and he was rapidly spelling out words with them.

EINSTEIN LINE. BOTH NO. YES.

This meant nothing to Mrs Rokabye.

'The Control tells me that Silver and her friend the Throwback are at the Einstein Line, that they are not to-gether, and that Silver is moving towards the Timekeeper.'

'Who exactly are you talking to?' asked Mrs Rokabye, who had assumed they were alone in the room.

'My Control. His name is Saul and he tells me all.'

'Does it always rhyme?'

'No it doesn't, but I do.'

'Well, ask Saul how we get to the Einstein Line.'

'I don't have to ask him, I knows the way myself. A map is better than a slap.'

'Then we must go to the Washing Line, wherever that is, and rescue Silver as soon as she has rescued the Timekeeper. When will that be? Ask him.'

Sniveller muttered something under his breath, and his fingers flew over the letters, forming the word SOON.

Soon! Mrs Rokabye was excited. At long last the wretched child was going to do something useful and make Mrs Rokabye rich.

'Put on your shoes, Sniveller – we must set off at once.'

'It's gone eight o'clock,' objected Sniveller.

'Everyone in this house is obsessed with Time,' said Mrs Rokabye, unreasonably, as that was why she was here.

'If I puts on my shoes after eight o'clock I will run away. Never run away in the day. Flight at night.'

'You didn't run away when we went to see *The Lion King*.'

'I was on a lead,' explained Sniveller. 'Invisible to your eyes, but a lead nonetheless.'

'But you don't want to run away from ME, do you?' asked Mrs Rokabye, batting her few eyelashes.

In truth Sniveller didn't want to run away from Mrs

Rokabye because he had quite fallen for her. Yes, in his own way he loved her, even though she was a foot taller than him, with a face sharp as a saw.

But he knew that if he put on his shoes he would run and run and never come back. That's what happened if you had been in Bedlam for too long.

Mrs Rokabye was already putting on her hat and coat. She went downstairs to the little kitchen and filled her coat pockets with tins of sardines, packets of salted peanuts, and teabags. Then she borrowed a very long scarf from the coat rack, and whistled up the stairs for Sniveller.

He appeared in his greatcoat, feet bare.

'Ready steady, don't think twice, but treat me nice.'

'Are we going by taxi?' asked Mrs Rokabye hopefully.

'A short stroll then straight down the Hole.'

Mrs Rokabye's suspicions were aroused.

'What hole?'

'The Walworth Hole. It's the quickest way to the Einstein Line.'

'Just where is the Einstein Line?' asked Mrs Rokabye, who had been vaguely thinking about Morecambe Bay.

'It's on the other side of the Milky Way, in our solar system, and three hundred years off. I swear the Walworth Hole is the knack of there and back.'

Disquieted but resigned, Mrs Rokabye walked the necessary miles to Walworth. In a dark and gloomy side street, Sniveller glanced round, then pulled a jemmy wrench from his greatcoat, and levered up a paving stone.

Underneath was a cast-iron grille made in the eighteenth century. This he pulled aside with both hands, then, fiddling in his coat once more, fished out two miner's helmets with lamps. He offered one to Mrs Rokabye, and strapped the other on his own bald head.

'Down the Town!' he said cheerfully.

Mrs Rokabye looked into the hole. There was no ladder, no rope, no stairs, no lift.

'What do you expect me to do?'

'Where there's no stair, it's both feet in the air. Jump!'

'JUMP???????!!!!!!!!!!!!'

Sniveller recalled that ladies are the fairer sex, and faint-hearted, and in need of encouragement and support. He had never been married but he knew his manners. Bowing slightly, he arranged himself at the edge of the black yawning gap, with the flourish of an Olympic diver.

'Dear lady, away I go, and don't be slow.'

Without hesitation, Sniveller leapt down the Walworth Hole.

Mrs Rokabye waited for the scream and the crash. She waited and she waited and after five minutes she reasoned that Sniveller could not be dead. She considered her options; she could go back to Spitalfields, but she didn't know the way and she didn't have a key to the house. She could go back to Tanglewreck, but there were two dead men there already, and besides she didn't have a train ticket.

What did she have? Sardines, peanuts and teabags. They

wouldn't last long in this cold cruel world. She felt the pin in her pocket. She could sell that, but she had to be careful, someone might think she had stolen it – which she had done.

Very well, then. So be it. Chin up. Best foot forward. Stiff upper lip.

She fastened the miner's helmet over the top of her hat, and tied the borrowed scarf all the way round her, to stop her coat flapping open. She had read somewhere that parachutists are always streamlined.

Stuffing her handkerchief in her mouth to stop herself screaming, Mrs Rokabye jumped.

There she goes, speeding faster and faster through infinite blackness. She seemed to be dropping through the weight of the world. She had a sense of nothing around her but open air, except that it was closed air, with a texture to it, like cloth – yes, she felt as though she was falling through cloth.

Then she felt herself start to spin. She was no longer hurtling downwards, she was spinning round and round like a corkscrew, and she was getting dizzy. She could hear voices. She closed her eyes.

Her last thought as the freezing air numbed her into unconsciousness was of Bigamist. Would she ever see her beloved rabbit again?

BETHLEHEM HOSPITAL

A t the Caffè Ora, Gabriel was lying on a camp bed under a thick blanket. Ora called a doctor, who clicked the dislocated shoulder back into place, and bound up the cuts and bruises that covered poor Gabriel's body.

Silver, Toby, Ora, Serena, everyone wanted to know what had happened to Gabriel in the Black Hole, but he was too weak to speak, and somewhere in his exhausted mind, he wasn't sure that he wanted to tell them. Troubled and sore, he drifted off to sleep, with Dinger the cat curled up at his feet.

Ora was holding an emergency meeting. No one had had any idea that the Deportees were being Atomised.

Try as she might, Silver couldn't make anyone listen to her story about Abel Darkwater and Regalia Mason.

'Look,' said Ora, patting Silver gently, but not really listening to her, 'this place is full of people who think they can find the magic numbers of eternal life, or eternal youth, or whatever they want. It's full of people who have nothing and who are trying to be something. A man who thinks he's a magician is no big deal here. There's a special Hocus-Pocus Focus Group for those who are anti-science.'

'But the Timekeeper –'

'Yes, and the Holy Grail, and the Lost City of Atlantis.'

'But Regalia Mason is the Quantum, and she's here.'

Ora shook her head. 'The Quantum isn't one person. It's everything, it's everywhere. We know that, Silver, we have our Intelligence out there.'

Silver shook her head. 'Well, they weren't intelligent enough to save Gabriel. And nobody knew about the people being Atomised.'

Ora frowned.

'And I want to know about the twins,' said Silver. 'I saw loads of twins at Checkpoint Zero. I mean, pairs and pairs of them, like Noah's Ark or something.'

'Yeah,' said Toby. 'Sally 'n' Kelly'z still in there. Wazappinin?'

'The twins have been taken to the hospital. I have an excellent contact there who tells me both girls are safe and well.'

'What goes on at the hospital?' asked Silver.

Ora sighed and sat down, exhausted. She had been up all night. 'Silver, I can't answer you now. You have to leave this to us now. This is very serious. This is an emergency. Go in with Gabriel, both of you, and as soon as I can, I'll explain, OK?'

Silver shrugged. She knew better than to argue with grown-ups. You had to wait until they forgot about you and then get on with things.

The other kids from the bus were playing board games and eating bowls of steaming pasta. Toby and Silver took their plates and went into the little back room where Silver slept.

Gabriel was sleeping soundly with a sprawled-sideways Dinger.

'Man, that cat's well dead,' said Toby, poking Dinger with his foot.

'Yeah, I thought that when I first came here, but he's a scientific cat. He was used in a famous animal experiment by someone called Dr Schrödinger – that's why he's called Dinger. He's alive and dead at the same time.'

'No, that ain't so!' said Toby. 'Can't be done, man.'

'It's his wave function,' said Silver. 'He tunes in and out of Universes. He's just tuned in to a Universe where he's dead, that's all, but he'll tune in to us again later, and he'll be fine.'

Toby did not look too happy to be sitting next to a dead cat, but he had no choice.

'Wot now?' he said.

'I've got to go to the Sands of Time.'

'Yeah?'

'There's something there I need to find – that's why I'm here really. We didn't really come by accident.'

'You think I'm stupid? I know that.'

'Yeah.'

There was a silence. Then Toby said, 'But I gotta get the twins out, y'know?'

'Yeah. I think so too, and I should help you. You helped me. Let's go together.'

'It's dangerous out there.'

'Yeah, but so is a Black Hole, and so is being Atomised. It's all dangerous here – what could be worse than Bethlehem Hospital?'

As she said these words, Gabriel sat bolt upright in his

bed, his bandage slipping from his head.

'Fools and fiends there are and no others. It rises to the north of the City of London, isolated, majestic and imperious, brooded over by the water-tower and the chimney, unmistakable and daunting.'

Silver threw her arms round his neck. 'Not Bedlam, Gabriel, you're never going back there. This is a modern open white hospital in a square.'

'It is the same place,' said Gabriel.

He calmed down and wiped his forehead. 'You saved me.'

The cat Dinger stirred and stretched.

'I'm coming with you,' said Gabriel.

Late that night, when it was completely dark, Gabriel, Silver and Toby got up and got dressed without putting the light on, and went to the window. No one was around.

They climbed out quickly and slunk like night-animals round the edges of the buildings, until they came to the hospital courtyard, floodlit and patrolled.

Gabriel was crouched down, and he began to tremble. Silver put her arms round him. 'This isn't the place you remember. Don't worry.'

'Round the back,' whispered Toby, 'to the kitchens. They deliver food 'n' stuff at night. We can get in that way.'

On all fours, like cats, they slunk round to the brightly lit kitchen entrance, and, sure enough, the big doors were wide open, and some of the Scrappers were unloading pallets on to a little train that ran on its own tracks into the hospital.

'It used to be robots here,' said Toby, 'but humans is cheaper.'

'Can we get out the same way?' asked Silver.

'Till dawn-time. When the third of the three suns rises, thazzit. Slam.'

'And what do you think you want, you little snoopers?' said a voice as nasty and high as a dead rat. One of the Scrappers had come up behind them. Toby took a swing at him and winded him in the stomach.

'You little thug . . .' His friend came forward and grabbed Toby, who twisted and turned and fought back as hard as he could. Gabriel lunged from his crouched position, straight at the legs of the man who had Toby, and brought him crashing down. The boys and the men started some serious fighting, even though Gabriel had one arm in a sling. In the heat of the fight Silver was forgotten.

She hesitated. Then she dodged away and into the darkness behind the kitchens. As the train came round she jumped into a carriage, and hid herself under a sack of flour.

The train ran silently into the hospital and stopped smoothly. Silver waited, but no one came to unload the trucks. Cautiously, she raised her head and looked round. No one was there, but she could hear two pairs of footsteps. She jumped out and ran up a flight of stone stairs that she hoped might lead somewhere. The door at the top was locked with a fingerprint scanner.

She waited and listened. 'Get those bananas in the lift,

OK? They're wanted in the kitchens for breakfast.'

She peered down. Yes, she could see the lift. If she could get in, she could go higher, maybe take the lift further.

Two Scrappers started unloading the first few sacks into the open door of the lift. After three sacks, one of them stopped and offered his mate a swig at a bottle.

'Don't kill yorsel fur this lot,' he said, and his mate nodded, and they turned away.

Silver took her chance and ran across behind the little train, and hid in the lift, crouched small as small behind the three sacks of bananas. After a while the Scrappers resumed their work, and at last, at long last, one of them pushed the buttons on the lift, and travelled, humming a tune, up towards the kitchens, with the bananas as required, and Silver as not required.

She felt the heat as soon as the doors opened on the stainless-steel-polished kitchen. Men in hats and aprons were making jokes she didn't understand about bananas, but while they were busy with their banter, Silver reached out and pushed the button that said OPERATING FLOOR. The lift closed and glided upwards, and before anyone could start investigating, Silver was out and away.

She had done it. She was in Bethlehem Hospital.

Swing doors. Polish. Electrical hum. Low lights. Corridors. Trolleys. Door opens. White coat. Door closes. Conversation. Can't hear. Beeping. A blue line on a white screen. Beeping. Antiseptic smell. Clatter of tin on tin. Tray of swabs. Someone's coming. Hide. Beeping. CCTV. Fear. Someone's coming.

Silver hid behind bags of used sheets. Orderlies were changing the bedding. The ward was empty. On the door it said BOYS 8–12, but there was no one there.

Why would you have a hospital with no one in it?

At home she had heard on the news that hospitals were always in crisis because there were too many sick people and not enough beds. Here a whole ward of – she counted, twenty-two beds – was empty. Did that mean that all the boys aged between eight and twelve on Philippi were healthy and well?

At the end of the ward was another door. This one said GIRLS 8–12, and it was empty too. The whole floor was deserted. This was the operating floor, but there was no one here to be operated on.

Then Silver remembered the lines of twins she had seen at Checkpoint Zero that day. She had seen the girls going into the red hut, and when she looked in the hut, the boys were there too. Were they from the hospital? Were they going to be Atomised because they were so sick? They hadn't looked sick.

She wandered on in the quality of a dream. A deserted hospital, endless silent corridors, herself alone, and no sound except . . .

Then she heard it, unmistakable, like on a loudspeaker; a heart beating.

Lub dup, lub dup, lub dup, lub dup.

Silver followed the beating heart.

She came to a pair of double doors with mesh safety glass in the small observation windows. The noise of the heart was loud enough now to hurt her ears.

She pushed lightly against one of the doors. It opened. She was in a spotless room where two big horizontal cylinders – like giant cigar tubes – were placed side by side connected by wires. Monitor screens that she didn't understand lined the room, each showing a different moving coloured line. She guessed from the peaks and troughs of one of the screens that it was a heart monitor, but she didn't know what the others were showing.

On top of each of the cylinders was a big clock. It was the clocks she could hear ticking like heartbeats, and she remembered that day in Abel Darkwater's study.

Everything in the study was ticking, even the two of them, their hearts beating like human clocks.

She was very frightened but she tiptoed up to one of the cylinders and looked through the glass panel. There was one of the twins! Silver didn't know which one because they were identical.

Kelly, or Sally, was lying peacefully inside. Silver watched her, and saw something very strange start to happen; the girl began to age.

Faint lines appeared on her face. Her skin grew redder and coarser. The lines deepened, her hair thinned and turned grey. Her skin wrinkled. She was old.

Hardly able to stop herself crying out, Silver went round

to the other cylinder and looked inside.

The woman lying there was beautiful but not young, or rather she was getting younger every second. Her skin began to smooth out. Her cheeks plumped. The crow's feet under her eyes disappeared and the lines on each side of her mouth vanished. Her hair was thick and blonde and her face was radiant.

She was in the prime of life and she was Regalia Mason.

SPOOKY ACTION AT
A DISTANCE

Toby and Gabriel had got free of the Scrappers, but the two of them had been separated. Toby had smashed a crate over the bully twisting Gabriel's dislocated shoulder, and then, seeing more Scrappers arriving, he had run for it, shouting at Gabriel to do the same. Gabriel scrambled up and limped off. He had only one thought in his mind; to find Silver.

'Help me, Micah,' he whispered. 'This be Bedlam and I am fearful.'

In the Chamber Micah heard him. 'Bedlam . . .' he said to himself. 'Not gone, still with us.' In his mind he pictured the way that Gabriel must find. How well he knew it!

Gabriel breathed deeply to try and ease the pain in his shoulder. He had never been comfortable above ground, but since his time in the Black Hole, fresh air and light seemed sweet to him.

He stood in front of the hospital, but he did not see a place to heal the sick, he saw the place he remembered: massive, brutal, barred.

The way in . . . He closed his eyes and Micah's picture cleared in his mind. If he walked to the side of the fashionable main drive where the ladies came to marvel at the madmen, he would find the grille opened by Micah on the night of his escape in 1774. He would find the tunnel dug with wooden spoons and bleeding fingers, and he would squirm through its crumbling depths until he forced his body up into a narrow cell for the Confinement of Raving Lunaticks.

His heart was beating fast. What if they were waiting for him at the other end? The White Lead Man with his poisonous stare and filthy ointments? Abel Darkwater himself, leather truncheon and straightjacket?

Micah had not hesitated. He must not hesitate.

He lifted the grille and plunged down into the mire.

Silver knew that she had to move away from the cylinder before Regalia Mason opened her eyes. She had to move now, this passing moment, this ticking second, this final click of the clock.

Why then did she stand staring into that face?

Down went Gabriel, bending with difficulty in the tunnel. It must have collapsed. He had to crawl. He had to wriggle. The air was foul. Pestilence and rot. He found a food tin with the inmate's name scratched on it – Beulah. He used it to catch some green water trickling down the side of the tunnel. He was thirsty. They were always thirsty. The water was only piped into the hospital for two hours a day and the wells outside were kept locked.

He was coming to some rough-made steps. Not far now.

Silver couldn't make her body move. She felt as though her body belonged to someone else. She tried to lift her arm. She tried to move her foot. She willed them to move and nothing happened. She could not even turn her head away from that face. She could not even close her eyes . . .

Gabriel was through. Yes, here was the way into the room. He swung up. The room was lit by a single flare, and in the corner shadows he could just make out a hunched and desperate shape, its arms and legs shackled.

'Who art thou?' he whispered.

'King of England,' said the man.

Gabriel looked down at the poor fellow, lost and wretched. He took out a tool from his pocket and undid the shackles. The King of England rubbed his ankles and wrists. He smiled. Gabriel gave him two chocolate bars, and he tore at them with his long teeth, a bar in each hand.

'Go down there,' said Gabriel, 'and leave this place.'

Gabriel went to the heavy door and opened it with a quick turn of one of his delicate metal jemmies that Micah had made for him. He locked it behind him again to avoid any suspicion, and crept on through the gloomy halls of Bedlam.

Regalia Mason opened her eyes and smiled at Silver.

She pressed certain buttons in the cylinder, and the heart-beat noise began to die away. Then the monitor screens went blank and the cylinder lid slid open. Shaking her head,

Regalia Mason sat up and swung sideways, her long legs and bare feet lightly hitting the floor, and then she walked and stretched, and glanced briefly into the second cylinder.

'You're a murderer!' said Silver.

'You have a vivid imagination,' said Regalia Mason, 'and a very clear idea of right and wrong. So did I at your age, many many years ago, but things change. Besides, the girl isn't dead.'

'What have you done to her?' said Silver, who still couldn't move.

'You could say I am living on borrowed time.'

'Let me go! I can't move!'

Regalia Mason went over to a switch and pulled it. 'I am not Abel Darkwater,' she said, 'and I haven't put a spell on you.' Silver moved again.

'You were standing on a magnet,' said Regalia Mason. 'This is science, not magic, just like the twins. Now come with me.'

The two of them walked out of the Zone and into what looked like an ordinary kitchen in an ordinary world. There was a big table and white plates, and a fat loaf of bread next to a round creamy cheese. Regalia Mason cut some cheese, stuffed it in her mouth, and started making scrambled eggs.

'Protein is essential after a Time Transfusion,' she said, talking with her mouth full. Silver had the wild thought that no one would ever believe that this beautiful barefooted blonde woman, eating bread and cheese and cooking eggs, was the most powerful being in the Universe. No one was ever going to believe her. Regalia Mason would never be caught.

'Caught by whom?' she said, reading Silver's mind. 'Just who do you think is going to make a better job of it? Abel Darkwater and his friend the Pope? Would you like them to be in charge of a whole Universe?'

'No,' said Silver.

'Or your friend Mrs Rokabye?'

This was such a ridiculous idea that Silver laughed, even though this was no laughing moment. Imagine Mrs Rokabye and Bigamist ruling the Universe! Regalia Mason laughed too, and tossed Silver a piece of bread and butter. For a second – not even that, a nano-second – Regalia Mason felt something like sadness and something like happiness, and then she was herself again.

'Let me tell you now, Silver, that where you live, on Earth, in the twenty-first century, Time Transfusions will be successful, thanks to billions of dollars of Quanta research. Wasted Time will be a thing of the past. Parents will have more Time to spend with their children, children will live longer happier lives. There will be no need to rush and race. There will be enough Time.'

'But you make people die.'

'Quanta has been instrumental in reducing the world's surplus population.'

Silver tried to keep her mind clear. Whenever she was with Regalia Mason, she found it hard to think clearly. She concentrated.

'And you tried to kill Gabriel. You broke your promise to me.'

'I promised you I would not have him Deported. I promised you I would not kill him. Is he dead?'

'No! I saved him.'

'Exactly, and that was remarkable. Science says that nothing can escape a Black Hole – but one of the pleasures of being a scientist is to prove science wrong.'

'And you left me to die on the Star Road.'

'I left you to find your own way – it was a little test.'

That sounded like school to Silver, and in the days before Mrs Rokabye, when she still went to school, she had never been any good at tests. She had to concentrate. She felt Micah's medallion in her pocket.

Gabriel was approaching the great room at Bedlam. That room, where the gallery ran around the upper part for observation, and where the Warders walked, truncheons in hand, one from the North Wing, one from the South Wing, meeting midway, bowing briefly and walking on.

Two fireplaces lit the room but never warmed it. Men and women, half-stripped, shivering, huddled as near to the fire as they could, and clutched each other for warmth and comfort. Twice a day many of the inmates were taken to a freezing cold tank of water, thrown in, and dragged out with a pole, like drowning dogs, and left to drip dry as best they could before being crammed into icy unchanged beds.

The room had a few pieces of furniture – benches and rickety chairs and tiny milking stools. Straw was scattered across the floor. Some preferred to sleep here than to mix with the bodies and the lice of the dormitories.

All manner of madness was loose in Bedlam. There were more kings here than there had ever been countries to rule over, and more Popes than sinners. The deluded, the counterfeit, the broken-hearted, the broken-winged, the savage, the pitiful, the chatterers, the silent, the violent and the cowed were all here in this mighty madhouse, this warning to the wise never to surrender their wits to the ways of fools.

And there were others too – ones like Gabriel and his clan and his kind, whose minds were free and whose bodies were shackled. These were the ones chained around the edges of the room, some trying to read scraps of books by the dismal light of dripping tallow candles.

Some of these men and women had been cruelly decorated with painted wooden wings that flapped uselessly on their shoulders.

Gabriel was angry, and wherever he could, he used his tools to unlock the cuffs and manacles, and to gently lift off the wings. These he broke up and threw on to the fires, so that at least for tonight the room would be warm.

He passed on, not knowing where he was going.

'Twins can be doubly useful in Time Transfusions,' said Regalia Mason, 'but they are particularly useful for teleporting – you know what that is?'

'Like *Star Trek*?' said Silver. 'You disappear in one place and arrive somewhere else?'

'Right,' said Regalia Mason, 'but at present it is very

difficult unless you have a pair of twins to help you.'

'I don't get it,' said Silver.

'It's called Entanglement,' said Regalia Mason, now eating fried eggs. 'Take a pair of particles – you know, bits of atoms – put them miles away, even light years apart, and they still share information. Entangled particles act as though they are a single object; what happens to one of the pair automatically affects the other. Remember Silver, that you, me, everything in the Universe came from a single explosion, so the atoms in our bodies are linked with every atom in Space and Time. The Universe is not local and isolated, it is a cosmic web. Have you heard of a scientist called Einstein?'

'Einstein said that $e = MC^2$,' said Silver.

'Very good, that's right, but although Einstein discovered what we call Relativity – and most important of all, that Time itself is relative – Einstein hated the idea of a cosmic web. He called these links, these connections, this Entanglement, "spooky action at a distance" because he was never comfortable with the implications of quantum mechanics.'

'Umm, what are the implications?' said Silver.

'One of them is teleporting human beings.'

'I don't want to be teleported,' said Silver.

'What I tried to show you on the Star Road is that while you think of yourself as a particular person living in a particular time and inside a particular body, that is only a part of the story. What you are is information, Silver. Coded information. DNA is coded information. Every cell of your body is coded information and that information can move and change.'

'I know I'll grow up,' said Silver.

'Yes, and nobody has to teach your cells to grow – they know they have to do that, it is in their code – but some of the cells that were you yesterday are already dead, and some are brand new. The You that is You is not constant, it is always changing.'

Silver's head was spinning. She rubbed the medallion and concentrated.

'But why do you need twins?' she said doggedly.

Regalia Mason sighed. 'It has been known since the twentieth century that if you separate a pair of twins at birth, they will often grow up and do the same things at the same time, even though they have never met. The coding they share makes this happen.

'Teleportation needs three things – me, the person who wants to be teleported, and a pair of twins who are entangled. Bring me Sally and I scan all of my information into her, and she will instantly relay it to Kelly on the other side of the Universe. Kelly becomes an exact copy of me.'

'But –'

'Of course, you need a quantum computer, but I have one. I had the first one ever developed – top secret. We made it for the Pentagon.'

'But –'

'Here's what we do with the twins. We separate them and we station them where people – that is, certain people –

337

might need to travel. There are depots of twins all over the galaxy. When I was in London and I wanted to come here, I used one of our London twins paired with his Philippi twin. Instantly, I was here – information, you see, is the one thing that can travel faster than the speed of light.'

'And love,' said Silver.

'What?'

'Love can travel faster than the speed of light.'

Regalia Mason was silent.

Gabriel had seen Abel Darkwater walking ahead of him down the passage. Then Darkwater vanished, leaving his faint outline shimmering in the air. Gabriel put out his hand and touched the hated shape. It tingled slightly, but it was nothing. Empty space and points of light.

He ran on towards the big barred doors ahead.

'What happens to you and Sally and Kelly?'

'My original is destroyed,' said Regalia Mason. 'As yet we cannot be in two places at one time, at least not in our physical bodies. I pass through Sally and into Kelly. The particle mass that was Kelly becomes me.'

'And what happens to Sally and Kelly?'

'They no longer exist as they once did.'

'You kill them.'

'For such a lively child you are obsessed with death! There is no such thing as death as you describe it. Our states alter, that is all.'

'You're like a crocodile, you just gobble everything up. If I get eaten by a crocodile I become part of the crocodile but I'm not me any more.'

'Then you have understood an important lesson – it is better to eat than to be eaten.'

Regalia Mason finished her sixth fried egg and mopped up her plate.

'In fact, I am not the crocodile in your story. That is your friend Abel Darkwater. Crocodiles don't die until something kills them. They have a very low body temperature, and, strictly speaking, they do not grow old as we grow old, they just go on growing. Abel Darkwater has lived a long time, but by very different methods to my own. What a strange place the world is, eh, Silver?'

At that moment the hospital alarms started blaring through the kitchen and the corridors. Running feet. Shouting.

Regalia Mason flipped open the lid of her computer.

'Gabriel, the Throwback, has arrived. He has set off the alarms because he came in through the back door.'

'I came in through the kitchen,' said Silver.

'Did you now? Still, you came in through the present. Gabriel has come in through the past. Entering a building via the eighteenth century is bound to set off the alarm.'

'Don't let them hurt him. Please,' said Silver. 'I only just got him out of the Black Hole.'

The door opened and a dozen guards dragged Gabriel into the kitchen.

'Gabriel!' cried Silver in amazement, as well she might, for something very odd had happened to him. The boy she had known before the Black Hole had been about four feet six inches tall. He had been bent double and could hardly walk when they had rescued him, and they had crouched down on their run to the hospital, so she had not noticed the great change that had taken place. The boy standing before them was over six feet tall. The Black Hole had stretched him. He looked magnificent. He looked like a fallen angel.

She went up to him. 'You're tall as a tower,' she said.

He hadn't noticed. He had just noticed that everything he wore was tight and everything he did was a bit more of a squeeze. He had thought it was because he was injured.

'Leave us alone,' Regalia Mason ordered the guards. 'The boy is no threat. I will deal with him. Have you prepared the twins?'

The chief guard nodded, and he and his troop left the kitchen.

'Have some eggs,' said Regalia Mason, returning to her frying pan. 'I have to leave shortly.'

'We are in Bedlam, the dread place,' said Gabriel.

'Gabriel, calm down, please,' said Regalia Mason. 'You came here via the eighteenth century. I was just explaining to Silver that all states exist simultaneously but we can only tune in to one state at a time – well, usually that is the case. This is a modern hospital – Bethlehem Hospital, named I agree after your very own Bedlam, but for reasons I need not explain here. Your Bedlam still exists, although it was long ago pulled down in your world. But Gabriel, there is no need to visit it. Leave the past in its permanent home. Do not make that reality so strong that it tears down this one.'

Silver listened. Regalia Mason frightened her because she was very clever and almost kind sometimes, the way people who didn't care about you at all could be kind. And yet, none of the people who loved Gabriel had ever told him that he could be free of the fears his clan had dragged with them for more than three hundred years.

'I know what you do to them that lives in the Black Hole,' said Gabriel.

'I am not responsible for everything that happens,' replied Regalia Mason simply.

'Yes you are,' said Silver.

'Then the Quantum is God after all. Is that what you want?'

Clever, too clever. Silver was caught. She was angry. She must concentrate. The Timekeeper. That's what she had to remember.

'The Black Hole was an unfortunate mistake,' said Regalia Mason. 'We did not realise that when twins atomised, one spun upwards into the light, and one spun downwards into the dark. We should have realised, because it is exactly what happens to entangled particles in their non-human state. It did not happen because I am cruel and omnipotent, it happened because when science experiments, science makes mistakes. Some in your century will protest outside animal laboratories. Soon they will be protesters on the rim of the

Black Hole. But we were right to experiment, and the future will know that.'

'You throw the wasted people down there,' said Gabriel. 'They spoke to me. I heard them. You experimented on my father and his kind, and now you experiment on them.'

'And you are killing people on the Einstein Line. I saw the portal,' said Silver. 'You don't Deport them, you Atomise them.'

'We are in a State of Emergency,' said Regalia Mason. 'Security is at risk. At such times the normal procedures do not apply. We regret it.' She stood up. 'Time to go.'

'What are you going to do with us?' asked Silver.

'See you out.'

'Aren't you going to kill us too?'

'Do you have a death wish?'

'No,' said Silver, 'but you don't want me to find the Timekeeper, do you?'

Regalia Mason said nothing. She opened the doors, pressed a button, and ushered Gabriel and Silver ahead of her.

Ranks and ranks of soldiers now lined the corridors of the previously deserted hospital. Barefoot, still finishing a slice of bread and butter, Regalia Mason ignored the soldiers and walked carelessly ahead. She reached the main door. In the vast open courtyard, rows of men in dazzling white uniforms stood to attention.

It was nearly dawn, and two of the three suns of Philippi had risen on the horizon. The white uniforms of the soldiers were washed in sun-red.

Silver and Gabriel stood with her on the steps looking out. There were armed men as far as they could see, and no path through.

'Walk on,' said Regalia Mason. 'The order has been given. The men will part as you pass. You are free to do as you please.'

Silver reached for Gabriel's hand. He squeezed it, though he was frightened himself. They began to walk down the steps, and, as they did so, the red sea of soldiers parted, and the children walked through unharmed.

Silver heard Regalia Mason's low clear voice.

'Now you know what power is.'

A NEW DEVELOPMENT

Mrs Rokabye was surprised to find herself in the Vatican. All her life she had been a Baptist.

'I thought the Vatican was in Rome,' she said to Sniveller, who was dusting himself down.

'Once a Pope always a Pope. Rome yesterday, Philippi today. Ave Maria, pass the beer, as we used to say after church.'

'Where exactly are we?' demanded Mrs Rokabye, still bound from head to foot in her extra-long scarf.

'A planet called Philippi. A place called the Einstein Line.'

Mrs Rokabye could not understand how a hole in the ground in Walworth, south of the River Thames, had brought her out by the Vatican Post Office. And she could not understand why this Post Office, these Popes, and this Vatican were not in Rome but on somewhere called the Einstein Line. She had never been any good at science.

'Life is more mystery than history,' said Sniveller cheerfully.

'Will we be going back the same way that we came?' asked Mrs Rokabye anxiously.

'Never step in the same river twice.'

'What?'

'Cats hunt mice.'

Obviously Sniveller had suffered a blow to the head in the Walworth Hole.

'Could you tell me in plain English what you mean?' asked Mrs Rokabye.

'No,' said Sniveller.

'I'll buy a postcard then. Might as well.'

As Mrs Rokabye went into the Vatican Post Office, Sniveller noticed Abel Darkwater walking towards him talking to Pope Gregory XIII. Sniveller knew all of the Popes' faces off by heart. He had memorised them the way some people memorise football teams.

He shrank his little body behind the bulky frame of the Swiss Guard holding his pikestaff.

'I must leave for the Sands of Time today,' said Abel Darkwater, as they walked by the Swiss Guard.

'Perhaps I will come with you,' said Pope Gregory.

'The child will lead us to the Timekeeper very soon.'

'And then?'

'And then the Universe is ours.'

They passed on. Sniveller popped out from behind the guard just as Mrs Rokabye came out with her postcards.

'I don't know who I'm going to send them to. I haven't got any friends.'

'You've got me,' said Sniveller.

'Not much point in sending you a postcard saying, "Wish You Were Here", because you are here.'

'Very true,' said Sniveller, 'but neither of us will be here much longer because we are going hand in hand to the Sands of Time.'

'It's not down a hole, is it?'

'It is very nearby, if I recall, though I don't recall at all.'

Mrs Rokabye let out a yelp. 'There's something moving in my coat pocket!'

She put her hand in her pocket and smacked it up and down her thigh, as though she were trying to land a fish.

'It's the pin!' she said. 'It's moving! It's alive.' She pulled out the shining pin, which had a force so strong that it was turning Mrs Rokabye's whole body northwards. 'It's like a divining rod,' she said. 'Where is it pointing?'

Sniveller's eyes were popping out of his head. He knew exactly what Mrs Rokabye had in her hands, but he could hardly believe it.

''Tis the Hand!' he said. 'The Hand that points to the Sands!'

'This is no time for gibberish!' cried Mrs Rokabye. 'I am being dragged off my feet!' And so she was as the pin, gleaming and vibrating, pulled her North.

'Where did you get that?' demanded Sniveller.

'I found it in the wretched child's duffle coat.'

'It is the Hand of the Timekeeper!'

'No!'

'Oh yeses, no guesses.'

'I thought it was treasure,' said Mrs Rokabye, disappointed.

'Treasure indeed in our hour of need!'

'You mean this thing is trying to lead us to the Timekeeper?'

'Yes!'

'Well, I must have something to eat first,' said Mrs Rokabye. 'Too much excitement on an empty stomach can be fatal. Tell it, oh, tell it we'll set off in an hour, but quick, because it's pulling my arm out of its socket.'

And Sniveller muttered something in a strange language, and suddenly Mrs Rokabye's arm that was whirling round and round fell back beside her body.

'It is the Hour,' said Sniveller. 'It is the Moment.'

'I am glad to hear it,' said Mrs Rokabye, 'but where can I find a fillet of fish and a Rum Baba?'

She was pale, it is true, her face as watery and cratered as the moon. Sniveller felt all his gallant and manly instincts come to the fore. He took Mrs Rokabye's arm, and escorted her straight to the Caffè Ora.

Soon they were sitting at a table eating fried fish and spinach, with chocolate cake to follow. It was a proper meal out, with a glass of wine, and Mrs Rokabye was enjoying herself. Soon she would eat out like this every day, because soon she would be rich.

'Here's to the money!' she said, raising her glass.

'Here's to love!' said Sniveller. 'A kiss is better than a miss,' and he leaned over and puckered his lips.

Mrs Rokabye ignored him and filled her mouth with fish.

At that moment, a weary and perplexed Silver and a

limping Gabriel opened the door of the Caffè Ora. Silver walked out backwards and trod on Gabriel's foot.

'We'd better go in through the window,' she said. 'Sniveller is in there with Mrs Rokabye.'

WORMS!

Sir Roger Rover, Thugger and Fisty had finished eating the swan.

Only then did they notice the worm.

The worm was round and brown and it seemed to be staring at them, which was unlikely, because worms do not stare.

And yet, the worm seemed to be staring at them.

It was quite a large worm.

'It's like the Loch Ness Monster,' said Fisty.

'Yeah, and so is the Elf King,' said Thugger. 'Hee hee.'

'Well, I tell you, that worm is looking this way. It's trying to tell us something.'

While Thugger and Fisty were arguing about the intentions, or otherwise, of the worm, Roger Rover had gone to examine it. He had noticed this worm before, but his rooms were full of spiders and mice and the like, and worms were, well, just worms.

Only this one had dug a worm-hole.

Roger Rover tapped at the panelling where the worm was waving its head, and the knocking noise told him that the panel was hollow. Eagerly he prised it off the wall with his short stout dagger, and then he fell back, amazed.

'I swear on my grandma's knickers,' said Thugger, 'that I

never seen the like in all my born days!'

Behind the panel was a glowing hole stretching deeply back through the wall, and on and on. The hole was not only glowing – it was rotating, slowly, like a spinning top.

'It's making me dizzy just looking at it,' said Fisty.

'Gentlemen – this is our escape!' said Roger Rover excitedly.

'Oh no, oh no,' moaned Fisty. 'No more holes, drops, or tunnels, please.'

'I have been a prisoner for too long. I shall take my chance with Fate,' said Sir Roger grandly. 'It is no worse than the hold of a pirate ship, no worse than this place that has become my cell.'

And he stepped forward and disappeared.

'He's gone!' said Thugger.

'And we're still 'ere,' said Fisty.

'Come on, then – or do you want to spend the rest of your life in this place, like he did? Gawd knows how long he's been here. 'Bout four hundred years, I reckon.'

'I'm only twenty-six,' said Fisty miserably.

'I'm going,' said Thugger.

'No, no! Don't leave me!'

'Goodbye till we meet again.'

And Thugger stepped into the rotating hole, and vanished at once.

'Oh Elvis, I wish you was 'ere!' wept Fisty, cuddling what was left of his robodog. 'What shall I do?'

Poor Fisty could not make up his mind what to do,

because he didn't have a mind to make up. But that didn't matter, because the worm-hole was already filling the room, spreading like a wave towards him, and his last thought as it swept him away into its rotating centre, was that he could smell curry.

GREENWICH

At Greenwich, Regalia Mason was talking to the Prime Minister. The Observatory was surrounded by police and the military, trying to keep order. The streets were full of demonstrators. Ordinary people were afraid. Religious groups were happily predicting the End of Time.

Regalia Mason had appeared on the BBC news, and explained carefully and simply why Quanta offered the best solution to the present problems. When she talked about her company taking 'Shares in Time', most people thought vaguely about a villa in Spain for three weeks every year. Others were excited by the idea of time machines and worm-holes, and all the paraphernalia of *Star Trek*.

Regalia Mason had the backing of many of Britain's top scientists, who longed for the money to begin research into the mysteries of Time. Even those hostile to an American company heading the project had to admit that there seemed to be no other solution. If the Time Tornadoes and Time Traps were to end, special help was needed. Quanta could provide that help.

That morning the Prime Minister had agreed that Quanta would control any commercial interest in Time.

Privately, the Prime Minister did not believe that Time

could be traded like a commodity. Nor did he believe in Time travel, Time Transfusions or teleporting. His view was that Regalia Mason and her company wanted to believe that there would be some return on the billions they would have to invest. The rest was science-fiction.

Possibly the research would generate some lucrative by-products – just as nuclear power had been a by-product of the atomic bomb, and just as the microwave had been invented when a radio operator had accidentally passed his sausage or his peanut bar or his egg or whatever it was through the waves of his radio transmitter, and discovered to his amazement that his sausage or his peanut bar or his egg had cooked itself.

Well, let Quanta have its version of the microwave. What harm could it do?

'Shall we sign the Agreement today?' asked Regalia Mason, gorgeous in her white Armani.

'Tomorrow, I believe,' said the Prime Minister. 'The European Parliament will ratify the decision tonight – as you know there have been disturbances in France and in Russia too.'

'Yes, I have heard,' said Regalia Mason.

'And there are some strange unexplained events surrounding the recent hurricanes in New Orleans and Florida. People have disappeared.'

'People often disappear,' said Regalia Mason, mildly.

Micah, crouching behind the fireplace, heard all of this. His mind flew back to the dark days of Bedlam, when Abel Darkwater and Maria Prophetessa had worked through the night, night after night, on their 'Experiments'. They had vowed to unlock Time's secrets, and with it the power of the Universe.

Since Silver and Gabriel had gone away, there had been two more Time Tornadoes. Regalia Mason was about to get the power she wanted, and not by force. The world was going to give it to her.

THE SANDS OF TIME

Gabriel and Toby were fixing the bus.

'Thazzit!' shouted Toby, as the bus shuddered to life.

All the kids piled on. Gabriel and Silver ran back to get some supplies from the Caffè Ora.

Gabriel's Mind Message from Micah had told him that he and Silver had to get to the Sands of Time today, and he had been working on the bus all night.

Toby had insisted they took all the kids with them, because he was afraid something would happen to them if they stayed round Checkpoint Zero. Hiding sixteen kids was not easy.

'They're like my duty, y'know, Gabriel? We can't just leave 'em here to be Atomised or Fried or whatever.'

Silver nodded. She was deep in her own thoughts. She had a feeling that both Abel Darkwater and Regalia Mason knew exactly what she was doing, and exactly what she would do. Yet, she had to do it. Why had this strange quest fallen to her? What made her different to all the other people in the world?

Gabriel smiled at her. 'Shall you know something about silver?'

'About me?'

'About the metal that is thy name.'

Silver nodded. 'I was named after a pirate.'

'That may be so, but the metal silver reflects nine-tenths of its own light. They fear you because you are shining,' said Gabriel.

'Who fears me?' asked Silver.

'Regalia Mason, she fears you. Abel Darkwater, he fears you.'

'I don't think I'm the Child with the Golden Face – I'm silver not gold.'

'It is the shining that the prophecy means,' said Gabriel.

Silver was silent. 'But Gabriel – all I'm going to do is lead him to it. I can't fight him – neither can you. Micah said so. Even if we succeed, we fail. I mean, if we find the Timekeeper, we just end up finding it for Abel Darkwater.'

'Silver –'

'I know I've got to do it. It's just, oh, if this was a story, like *The Lord of the Rings*, I could throw the ring back into the fires of Mordor and that would be the end of it. But when I find the Timekeeper I don't know what to do – except that Abel Darkwater will probably kill us both and then become Lord of the Universe, like Regalia Mason said.'

'Do not trust her, Silver.'

Before Silver could answer, Toby was shouting and waving at them from the driver's cabin of the bus.

'Come on,' said Silver, getting to her feet. 'If I don't go now, I'll never go. But stay by me, Gabriel, whatever happens next. I can't do this on my own.'

They climbed on to the bus, Toby turning the huge steering wheel by leaning across it with his body. Every time he changed gear there was a horrible grinding noise. But they were moving. They were travelling down the Star Road.

The children sang, then they slept, then they ate all their food, then some of them were sick, then some of them wanted to get off, then some of them cried, then some of them had a fight, then all of them were quiet at last, dreaming of home as they looked out of the windows, dreaming of other worlds.

Silver had the tight knot in her stomach again. She had worked so hard to get this far and now she just wanted to run away. Gabriel said she mustn't trust Regalia Mason, but maybe Regalia Mason was right. Why was Silver interfering? Nothing would ever be perfect. Maybe the Quantum wasn't such a bad thing.

'Hey!' shouted Toby. 'A fairground!'

Silver was baffled. They were driving towards somewhere that looked like an ordinary seaside resort, with a beach and sea and donkeys and people strolling up and down. She pulled out the map Micah had given her and unfolded it. She leaned over to Gabriel, his long legs propped on the seat.

'The Sands of Time on this map Micah gave me are wild and strange and stretch for miles. There are no buildings marked. This is like Disneyland or somewhere. Do you think we're in the right place?'

Gabriel frowned and looked from the map to the scene outside the window, but Toby had stopped the bus right by the pier and he and the other kids had already roared off on to the beach.

'I don't understand,' said Silver. 'Nothing precious can be here. It's just candyfloss and rides.'

Gabriel thought for a minute, then he said, 'Like Bedlam hides behind Bethlehem Hospital.'

'What?'

'This be a painted show, a hiding place. Something lies behind what you can see.'

Silver closed her eyes. She thought about what had happened to her on the Star Road, when she had begun to dissolve. Could she dissolve the surface in front of her?

Deep underground, Micah was pouring over the map he had copied. He was sending Silver the true geography of the place.

'See it for what it be,' he said, over and over again, 'See it for what it be . . .'

Silver opened her eyes, and the pier and the rides and the candyfloss started to bend and distort like someone was pulling them out of shape. Then everything went quiet, like someone had switched off the sound. Then everything went black, like someone had pulled the plug. When the light came back, there was no seaside, no donkeys, no trams going up and down; there was a desert stretching into the distance. A soft wind blew through the sand dunes.

'Oh yes,' said Abel Darkwater, looking into his crystal ball. 'She has gone through.'

Regalia Mason read her computer screen with interest. The child had learned to shuffle realities – or at least she had learned that there is more than one reality.

She checked her own frequency. The reality she was in was vibrating quite slowly. Silver was about to enter a different reality that lay on a different wavelength. Regalia Mason prepared to re-set her own frequency, like tuning a radio, and then she too could enter another world. It was so simple; everybody knows that all the radio stations are playing at once, but we only tune in to one at a time. Why did they not understand that reality was just the same?

She made the necessary adjustments on her quantum computer. The time had come.

Silver looked back. She could see her own footsteps pad-marked across the sand, and Gabriel's next to hers. What was this place, where the sands seemed to roll like waves? Just walking made her feel seasick.

They walked, and they walked, and they walked, and they walked, and they walked and they walked and they walked and they walked.

Night came. Desert night, cold and pitiless. She shivered inside her coat and pushed her hands deep into the pockets. Gabriel was curled up asleep in his blue coat. How had her parents ever got the clock here? Could they be here too? Could they be still alive? Had they been taken in a Time Tornado, the clock with them?

If she could find them, they could all go home together, and live together again. She sat up, huddling her body against the wind that never ceased.

She was very thirsty. She felt weightless in her body again, like she had on the Star Road.

What was that ahead? A light! A shape! A shape she knew! The shape of a house in the distance. It was Tanglewreck!

She scrambled up and ran as fast as she could through the shifting sand. Her shoes and her socks were gritty with sand and her nose was full of sand.

But just ahead, there was the house, and she was nearly at the drive, and although she was stumbling, and her breath was coming in gasps, and her mouth was drier than death, she would get to the house, she would go in, and her mother and father would be there, and . . . and . . . the mirage vanished.

Silver sat down and cried hot tears that stung her face, dry and sore with the sand and the wind. Gabriel, who had woken up and found her gone, came running behind her, putting his arms round her, comforting her, telling her they must go on.

'I can't, Gabriel.'

'I will hold you up.'

'I thought I was home. I thought I was happy.' Silver was crying so much that she couldn't see. Gabriel wiped her eyes with the dirty sleeve of his old blue coat, and put out both his hands to help her up.

She got up and they walked on.

She fell, and they walked on.

They walked on.

There was nothing in the world but tears and blisters and thirst and sand. She no longer knew who she was or why. And Gabriel held her as Micah had held him in the Black Hole. If he could only hold her just a little longer.

'Help me, Micah,' he whispered, and Micah heard, and walked with them, if they had known it, every step of the sands.

It was nearly morning when Silver fell flat on her face, tripping over something that was not a mirage.

It was a round stone sticking out of the sand.

She scraped at it with her fingers. It was big under the sand, whatever it was. Gabriel was excited and started to dig through the sand with his palms like a mole's. He smiled at Silver, and she forgot her pain and tiredness and dug and dug alongside him, trying to use her hands as he did, palms square like a mole. He laughed at her efforts, they both laughed, and soon the sand was flying everywhere, and they had uncovered something marvellous and strange: first it was an ear, then it was an eye, then it was a head, then it was a crouched body.

It was the crouched body of a stone sphinx. In its chest was a door, and behind the door was a passage.

Down, they went, down and down, into darkness and silence.

Lit by a single flare to the entrance to a chamber was the statue of a man with the head of a falcon.

The temple of the great god Ra.

So strange, the crumbling silent walls of the sacred space, lit by low-burning cruses of oil set in niches hammered out of the rock.

So strange, the smell of dust and incense and bandages; the ceremony of the dead before the night-journey to the pyramids.

There was an altar covered in a rotting cloth. Silver touched it and it shivered like a spider's web and turned to dust.

There was a painting on the wall, its colours faded, its lines hardly visible, but she knew what it was as soon as she saw it; it was a drawing of the Timekeeper.

'It is the prophecy,' said Abel Darkwater, stepping out of the shadows behind her.

Silver twisted round in panic. What she saw made her more afraid still. Abel Darkwater was in the robes of the High Priest of Ra.

'What began in the pyramids of Egypt will be completed today.'

'Sorcery,' said a voice that sounded like a snake. Pope Gregory XIII was in the ante-chamber.

'Your own Moses was a sorcerer,' said Abel Darkwater to the Pope, and then he turned his round and orb-like stare on Silver.

'Silver, do you know what I am?'

She thought of a crocodile, cold and cunning in the waters of the Nile.

Abel Darkwater read her thoughts and laughed.

'Perhaps I am a Leviathan, but I am something else too; I am the last of the Arcana. The last of the alchemists. I and my kind have turned base metal into gold, but we have sought something else, of infinitely greater value. We have looked into the secrets of life itself.

'Tempus Fugit is dedicated to knowing the mystery of time. Time Past and Time Future will be in our control. There are so few of us left now, so very few, and we have waited so long . . . for . . . the . . . clock.'

'I haven't got it!' said Silver.

Abel Darkwater hardly seemed to hear her.

'It was not made in Egypt, and it was not made in Israel. It was not made in the times of Romans, nor by St Augustine, though he had the drawings. The prophecy began to unfold in the year 1375 in France, when the Timekeeper was commissioned as a curiosity by Charles V, who as you will recall, had a great interest in Time.'

Silver didn't recall.

'In those days, the Timekeeper was a pendulum clock with a double face, showing the hours of midnight until noon, and noon until midnight. It kept time well, and it kept its other secrets well; secrets known only to myself and the sorceress Maria Prophetessa . . .'

Regalia Mason! thought Silver.

'Indeed!' said Abel Darkwater, reading her mind again. 'But Maria Prophetessa she was in those days, and to me she will be so always – the mysterious priestess of the Nile, the dark advisor to the Jew Moses, the whispering confidante of Joan of Arc, the mistress of Charles V of France. Oh yes, Silver, without her the Timekeeper would never have been made; it was made for her, it belonged to her, until this man smashed it into a thousand pieces.'

Pope Gregory stepped from the shadows, unsmiling, proud, hawk-faced, dark-eyed. 'And I would do it again,' he said.

'And what would it profit you?' Abel Darkwater laughed. 'Once made the Timekeeper can be broken, but it cannot be destroyed until the End of Time itself. That is the prophecy.'

'I destroyed it,' said the Pope.

'Oh no, you did not!' said Abel Darkwater.

It was night in the Vatican. Maria Prophetessa had been locked up. Pope Gregory had gone to hear a Te Deum in thanksgiving for the massacre of eight hundred Protestant Huguenots. The Jesuit priest Christopher Clavius opened the door to the Pope's study with his own key. Inside, he took the pieces of the Timekeeper from the drawer and hurried away with them. He was not interested in the clock or its prophecy; he was interested in the fabulous wealth of its jewels and its lapis and gold face. There was a man he needed to bribe – an Englishman, a Catholic, a pirate, a spy. It was a useful combination.

Clavius slipped outside and made his way to where the red-bearded man was waiting. He gave him the bag.

'What's this you offer me? A broken clock?'

'Only add the worth of the jewels to see what I offer you.'

Roger Rover tested one or two between his finger and thumb. He was satisfied. 'I will do your spying for you.'

That night the Timekeeper left Rome.

'Roger Rover had the Timekeeper!' said Silver, her fear battling against her curiosity and surprise.

'Oh yes, and in his turn he gave it as a bribe to a very powerful man named John Dee, astronomer and alchemist to Queen Elizabeth the First. Dee knew that at last he had the Timekeeper in his hands – and he knew of the prophecy and of its power. It was John Dee who founded our society, Tempus Fugit, and he was my Master for a time.'

'Was Roger Rover an alchemist?'

Abel Darkwater laughed out loud. 'He was a sea-faring fool!'

'If you're so clever why couldn't you mend the clock yourself, and why didn't you keep it when you had it?'

Abel Darkwater moved forward as if to strike Silver in the face, but the Pope restrained his arm.

'Torture, yes, violence, no,' said the Pope.

Abel Darkwater nodded. 'It seems that the clock is true to its own power, Silver, but when I find it, you will give me that power. I have been searching for you for centuries.'

'I'm only eleven years old!' said Silver.

'You have died and been reborn many times,' said Abel Darkwater. 'Many times.' And Silver, who didn't understand this, shuddered and remembered that Micah had said this about Regalia Mason.

'But this time, oh no, you shall not slip away. Let us prepare the alembic.'

Silver didn't know what an alembic was, and she was regretting her angry outburst. She suddenly realised that Gabriel was nowhere to be seen. He must have hidden himself.

Abel Darkwater had lit a fire in front of the altar. He took out a thing like a glass bottle, with a narrow funnel neck and a wide bottom.

'Now,' said Abel Darkwater, 'look into my eyes, Silver, and you will find yourself moving across Time to the day when your parents had arranged to bring the Timekeeper to London – to bring the Timekeeper to me.'

Silver felt herself going dizzy, but she held her mind firm. She thought of Tanglewreck, put herself inside it for safekeeping.

Abel Darkwater frowned and tried again. He took her face in his small hands and made her look at him. How round his eyes were! What faint and yellow light came from them, like a fog wrapping round her. Tanglewreck was there in the fog, she could hardly see the house now, where was it? Where was she? She suddenly saw her father's face. His expression, his eyes. Her mind cleared. She had nothing to say.

Abel Darkwater's eyes were old and cold. She noticed how cold his hands were on her face.

'Very well,' he said.

He let her go and attached a glass tube to the alembic. He blew into the tube and the alembic began to expand like a balloon. It grew bigger and bigger until it was more than a metre across and a metre high. The narrow funnel flared open.

'Your Holiness, please,' said Abel Darkwater, and the Pope stepped forward, and picked Silver up from behind and pushed her into the alembic. As soon as she was inside, Abel Darkwater sealed the funnel with a lead stopper.

'One hour is the limit for torture of any kind,' said the Pope. 'We must be merciful.'

'One hour, then,' said Abel Darkwater. 'Is it getting hot in there, Silver?'

She watched their faces, distorted by the bubbles in the glass; faces lined with centuries of cunning and greed. She could hardly breathe.

'You will tell me, Silver. You will.'

But she couldn't tell him anything, because something or someone was stopping her.

Across the Sands of Time, on a dromedary, Regalia Mason was travelling to the temple of the great god Ra.

As the alembic slowly heated up towards the unendurable, Abel Darkwater told Silver more of the story.

'Oh yes, I stole the Timekeeper from my master John Dee, and fled with it from England's shore, taking it to the best clockmakers of Italy and France, but none could repair it. Only in time, in its own time, was the clock mended. In 1675 Robert Hooke gave it a double-face, one in the body, and one in the lid, and he replaced the pendulum with a spring mechanism. For the first time in more than a hundred years its heart began to beat again!

'Then I thought I had it, I thought it was mine, but two of the original pictures were missing, the most important pictures of all. The pictures of the prophecy.'

Abel Darkwater came forward, his face pushed up against the glass of the alembic. 'Do you have those pictures, Silver? Do you? Do you?'

Silver was listening through the fever of the heat. Her hand went slowly towards the jute bag – why not just give him the pictures now? She was delirious with the fire and her slow suffocation. Yes, she should give him what he wanted, then she would be free, then she would go home.

She tapped feebly on the glass. Abel Darkwater looked triumphant. Then, not knowing where she found the strength to fight him, she shook her head.

'Burn, then!' said Darkwater. 'I shall melt you like a candle over a fire.'

The Pope had taken out his hourglass and was computing

380

the allotted hour of torture.

As he toyed with it, a strong arm slammed itself like a lever under his throat and, as he choked and fainted, Abel Darkwater turned round to see Gabriel running towards the alembic.

'Stand still, you mongrel,' shouted Darkwater, and Gabriel's whole body jerked to a stop. Rooted to the spot by magic, he was unable to move his arms or legs. He turned his eyes desperately to Silver, who was now too weak with heat to make any sign.

Abel Darkwater took a rope from his pack and bound Gabriel tightly.

'You fool! As low and stupid as your father Micah. Shall I tell you something? If she dies, it is your father Micah's doing. He will be her murderer, not I. If he had sold me the Timekeeper in 1762, how many centuries of waiting could have been erased! How many lives might have been spared!'

He turned back to Silver. 'You are the child of the prophecy. You are the child, you must be sacrificed. You will tell me where the Timekeeper is, and even if you do not, your blood will lead me to it. I will draw your blood and divine you, as I did the falcons of the Nile.' Abel Darkwater pressed his face against the steaming jar. 'You will tell me or your blood will tell me.'

'She cannot tell you because she does not know.'

There was Regalia Mason, tall and magnificent in the entrance to the chamber. 'I am the one who knows.'

Abel Darkwater's face was filled with rage. 'You! Always

you! And yet this child's own father was bringing the watch to me. I drew it to me with centuries of patience. The Timekeeper was about to be mine!'

Regalia Mason stepped forward. 'I could not help thinking that was a mistake.'

THE SWERVE

The Rivers had set off on the 8:05 to London. They had Abel Darkwater's address: *Tempus Fugit, 3 Fournier Street, Spitalfields, London E1*. He had sent them tickets for the train and a fifty-pound note for expenses.

Soon after their daughter Silver was born, Roger and Ruth River had received a letter from Abel Darkwater asking them about a clock called the Timekeeper. It had come to his attention, he said, that they had recently discovered this family heirloom. Could he come and see it? Would they like to sell it?

Silver's father had been very clear; the answer was no, and no. He knew the story of the clock, though not its power, and not the prophecy, but he was determined to keep it where it had been left for safekeeping all those years ago.

'Not everything in this life is for sale,' he said to his wife Ruth. 'There are things that matter more than money. Our family was given this clock in trust. In a way, it's not really ours.'

Every year Abel Darkwater wrote again, and every year the answer was the same – no, and no.

Then one year Abel Darkwater wrote and asked if they would simply bring the clock to London so that he could show it to certain eminent collectors, and perhaps make some drawings of its workings, and take some photographs. He might even repair it for them; he understood it was no longer working.

He offered them the sum of £10,000.

'Ten thousand pounds!' Roger River said to his wife. 'We can repair the roof, fix the gutters, and have the windows painted. That would be marvellous! Poor old house is falling to pieces.'

'What if he doesn't give us the clock back?' said Ruth.

'Of course he will give it back! He is a reputable dealer. I checked up on him. And he's given us insurance – and I rang the insurance this morning. It's all above board. We need the money, Ruth.'

'I know we do. I just feel uneasy.'

'Don't worry. We'll never sell him the clock. Never.'

The train was comfortable, warm and quiet. They were sitting in First Class reading the papers and drinking coffee.

The train slowed down. The train stopped. There were no announcements. Roger got up to see what was happening. Funny, but there was no one else in the carriage now. He walked on through the buffet. Empty. He walked into the Standard Class carriages. Empty. He looked out of the window. He couldn't see anything because there was a mist.

He began to feel uneasy himself. He took out his phone. There was no signal. He walked quickly back to where he had left Ruth. She was gone. In her place was a very beautiful, rather frightening woman who smiled at him as if she knew him.

'I'm afraid there has been a change of plan,' said Regalia Mason.

THE TIMEKEEPER

'There is no need to boil her alive,' said Regalia Mason.

'She is in league with you!' said Abel Darkwater. 'I will not spare her.'

'I am in league with no one,' replied Regalia Mason. 'The Quantum is itself.'

'Only God is Himself,' shouted the Pope.

'Go back to the Vatican,' said Regalia Mason. 'We built it for you.'

She went to the alembic and passed her hand through the green flames that flickered beneath it. Instantly they died down. 'I remember a few of our old tricks,' she said, smiling her cold smile at Abel Darkwater. 'You remained as you were, I changed; that is the difference between us.'

'You abandoned the Way.'

'I abandoned magic for science, yes, and for so many years you were able to achieve by magic what science could only dream of – but now, now what do you say?'

Abel Darkwater said nothing. Cold green flames were twisting round his body.

Regalia Mason continued to speak. 'Time travel, infinite life, the secrets of the Universe, all the things that you sought, that we sought together, through the dark material of the Arcana, have become real through the ambition of science.'

Abel Darkwater answered her in tongues of flame. 'You cannot control Time without the Timekeeper.'

Regalia Mason laughed. 'Shall I tell you something, Abel Darkwater? You still believe in the world as an object. Look at you, muttering over the alembic, coaxing molten metals, liquefying fixed bodies, juggling with all the pots and pans of a Universe that is solid. But the Universe is not solid. The Universe is energy and information. Solid objects are only representations and manifestations, of information and energy. Master that and you have mastered everything.'

'I can appear and disappear as well as you can,' said Abel Darkwater, 'and I know how to transform one substance into another, but the prophecy is clear: only the Timekeeper can control Time.'

'I am controlling Time already,' said Regalia Mason, 'and without any magical device. What are the Time Tornadoes?'

'They are the beginning of the prophecy fulfilled,' said Abel Darkwater. 'They are the beginnings of the End of Time, when Time as we have known it for so many centuries will roll up like a ball, and a new god will appear. A new Lord of the Universe.' His eyes rolled like round moons.

Regalia Mason smiled her cold smile. 'In a way what you say is true. For the Quantum to assume complete control by the beginning of the twenty-fourth century, it is necessary to destabilise Time well in advance. It is an interesting trick, don't you think, to affect the past so that the future can happen?'

'Impossible without the Timekeeper!'

'Impossible for you without the Timekeeper.'

'Do you tell me that it is you, Maria Prophetessa, who is causing these rips in the Universe? Do you tell me that it is you who is the Wind that blows through the End of Time?'

She smiled. 'Your magic still has poetry, but no power. Yes, I am she who has torn the Veil. I am she who is the Wind.'

And just for a second, she changed. She was not Regalia Mason, cold and beautiful; she was Maria Prophetessa, dark and hooded, twisting and black. Gabriel looked away in fear. Abel Darkwater nodded slowly, as if he understood.

'I will prevent you!' he said. 'I have prevented you before.'

'It is too late,' answered Regalia Mason.

'You are not the child of the prophecy!' said Darkwater.

'I am not. She is here. What good has it done you to half kill her in a bottle? She has not led you to the Timekeeper.'

'I will find it if it takes me the rest of eternity,' said Abel Darkwater.

'That will not be necessary, because I am going to tell you where it is,' smiled Regalia Mason.

'WHAT?' shouted Abel Darkwater.

'Nothing that you do now will make any difference. The Time Tornadoes have begun. In a few hours – yes, this morning – Quanta will be the official research partner of every Western government. Science has won the day, not magic, though for an advanced civilisation such as Quanta will make possible, science is indistinguishable from magic.'

Before Abel Darkwater could reply, there was a terrible rumbling and grinding overhead. Great cascades of sand poured into the temple. The walls began to shake and crumble. Regalia Mason and Abel Darkwater were choked with falling sand, and Gabriel chose that moment to leap up from where he had quietly and thoroughly been wriggling out of his bonds. He ran to the alembic. With all his strength he tried to push it over, but it was too heavy for him. Then, through the sand and dust, he heard Toby's voice.

'Wazappinin? Bus is up to its armpits in sand out there. Whazzilver doin' in that jar? Come on, kids!'

The children rushed at the alembic and knocked it to the ground. It didn't shatter, but Silver had already recovered enough from the cooling of the fire to get out her double-headed axe and smash through the lead seal.

Toby and Gabriel pulled her out as Abel Darkwater came forward, his body glowing like a green fire. 'STAND STILL, ALL OF YOU!'

This time the command didn't work.

'You have interrupted the Opus!' he shouted.

'Wot?' said Toby. 'You better shut up!'

Abel Darkwater grabbed Silver by the back of the neck, as if she were a rabbit. Small as he was, he lifted her clean off the ground.

'Tell me now!' he commanded, his hands and face scaly, his eyes unblinking.

'I don't know where it is!' said Silver, wriggling round in

his grasp, and facing Abel Darkwater, as he blazed at her in his cold flames.

'Of course you do,' said Regalia Mason, 'I no longer wish you to forget.'

It was the day her parents had gone to London. Some friends of theirs were looking after Silver, but they were busy in the kitchen, and Silver, who was seven, was playing a game in the garden when a beautiful woman had appeared before her.

'Hello,' said Silver. 'Who are you?'

'I am bringing back something that belongs to you,' the beautiful woman had said. 'You will never need it, and you will never find it, but nevertheless it is yours.' She had taken a wrapped bundle and put it carefully under the . . .

And suddenly, thinking back to this moment, Silver understood why she had that strange fuzzy feeling in her head whenever she saw Regalia Mason. It was Regalia Mason who had blocked her memory, just as she had blocked Micah's memory so many years ago. Through Time, she had been the one in control, controlling everything, until the day when she would discover how to control Time itself.

'It's at Tanglewreck!' said Silver, hearing the words come out of her mouth as though someone else was speaking them. 'Gabriel, it's at Tanglewreck.'

'And so I have always believed,' said Abel Darkwater, dropping her to the floor, 'if it hadn't been for that fool Mrs Rokabye . . .'

'I may be a fool,' said a familiar voice like glass breaking, 'but I have the Hand of the Timekeeper, and I want my share of the money!'

And there she was, Sniveller by her side, holding up the glittering jewelled hand.

'You stole it from me!' shouted Silver.

'How can you steal from a thief?' asked Mrs Rokabye. 'This is no more yours than it is mine.'

'You are wrong there,' said Regalia Mason, but Mrs Rokabye was taking no notice. She looked round, dusting the sand from her mac.

'So where is it? The Timekeeper.'

'It's at Tanglewreck,' said Silver.

There was a long pause, while Mrs Rokabye digested this information.

'I hope you are not going to tell me that I have been all the way to London, and then most unpleasantly down the Walworth Hole to a ridiculous shanty town called Philippi, which is full of scrapyards and Popes, and now here to this awful place called the Sands of Time, with not a stick of rock or a donkey in sight, and for no reason at all?'

'Yes,' said Silver.

Mrs Rokabye rounded on Sniveller like one of the Furies. 'You told me this Hand would lead us to the Timekeeper!'

'It has done so,' said Regalia Mason. 'Look.'

The Hand was dragging Mrs Rokabye across the chamber towards Silver. To Mrs Rokabye's horror, Silver took the

Hand from her, and there was nothing Mrs Rokabye could do to resist. Silver dropped the shining diamond back into her duffle-coat pocket.

Regalia Mason turned to Abel Darkwater. 'There is an object called the Timekeeper. I know it well and so do you. Yet its power is linked to one person – the child of the prophecy – she of the Golden Face. You see, Silver herself is the Timekeeper.'

'Silver!' exclaimed Mrs Rokabye.

'There are Lighthousekeepers and Lock Keepers, and Housekeepers, such as yourself, Mrs Rokabye, and there are Timekeepers. I was one myself, once upon a time, but that is another story. Enough to say that on the day Silver was born, she became the Timekeeper, and the clock, emblem of her office, was discovered again that day, after its long hiding.'

'But whoever controls the Timekeeper controls Time!' shouted Abel Darkwater.

'Objects – always objects – didn't I warn you not to put too much faith in objects? Without this child, you can do nothing.'

'I can kill her!' said Abel Darkwater, stepping forward.

'Useless, all useless. Only the child can wind the clock, and unless the clock is ticking, it has no power.'

'But you said you don't need the clock,' said Silver to Regalia Mason.

'I don't need it. Shall we go?'

'Go where?' said Abel Darkwater.

Regalia Mason took her computer out of her backpack and began rapidly locating points on a three-dimensional map of the Milky Way. As she tapped in the coordinates, a familiar picture began to form on the rock walls of the temple. Silver could hear birdsong and the sound of water. Gabriel could hear voices.

Toby, the kids, Mrs Rokabye, Abel Darkwater, they were disappearing and re-forming somewhere else.

'Is it real?' asked Silver.

Regalia Mason didn't answer. Silver felt herself flowing outwards as she had done on the Star Road. She was disappearing. She was returning. She was at Tanglewreck.

TANGLEWRECK

The wide lawn. The ha-ha. The bowling green.

The hedges in the shapes of foxes and bears. The fountain. The sundial. The black and white timbered house. The oak front door. Her father's bicycle leaning against the rail.

Her father.

What?

Her mother.

How?

Coming down the path to greet her now, arms open, faces amazed, and her sister Buddleia with them too. This is not a mirage, this is not a dream. Is this how it ends?

'Not quite,' said Regalia Mason.

This was Tanglewreck. These were their lives, but slipped sideways. In the multi-universe, the multiverse, every possibility exists but none overlap.

'Think of the cat,' said Regalia Mason. 'Science calls it Decoherence. All possible states exist. The cat, I admit, is rather eccentric after years of being the most famous animal experiment in physics.'

Silver wasn't listening. She had her arms round her

parents and Buddleia. Gabriel was hanging back shyly, not knowing what to say.

'We can't understand what has happened,' said her father. 'The house isn't falling apart and we have plenty of money from a family trust. I am still an astronomer at Jodrell Bank, but we only have one child. We have Buddleia, but we don't have you!'

'You would not usually be aware of another life with different circumstances to the one you so powerfully remember,' said Regalia Mason, 'but the circumstances of the Timekeeper have made your situation rather unusual.'

'We got off the train,' said Roger, 'and we were back here but without you. I can't believe that you're here again, and four years older! Look at you!'

'I thought you were dead!' said Silver, hugging him as tight as she could. 'I've had to live with your horrible sister Mrs Rokabye and her evil rabbit.'

'I don't have a sister,' said Roger, perplexed. 'Not in any world! Who on earth is Mrs Rokabye?'

'She turned up and said she was your sister! My aunt! Look, she's over there. The one in the mac wearing a miner's helmet and eating sardines out of a tin.'

Mrs Rokabye waved sheepishly.

'We'll soon see about that!' said Roger, getting up and ready for a fight, but Ruth pulled him back.

'Roger, it doesn't matter. This is our world now, and we're all together.'

'My leg's better,' said Buddleia. 'Watch!'

And she jumped and ran and was free.

'How can that be?' asked Ruth, watching her daughter. 'In one world she fell down the stairs when she was tiny, but in this world . . .'

Regalia Mason smiled. 'Reality folds against reality, worlds are hinged against worlds.'

'Is this where we'll be for ever and ever?' asked Silver.

'If it's what you want,' said Regalia Mason. 'Did you never understand that I was your friend?'

'I'm sorry,' said Silver. 'I just thought I had to find the Timekeeper whatever happened.'

'It's so strange,' said Roger. 'On the day you were born, I was in the topmost attic – you know, the one with the sky window – and I heard something ticking, and I rummaged and rooted, and there was a bag, and inside the bag was a clock, with some papers that told me its history and its name, and that I had to keep it safe for the Child with the Golden Face. I knew that was you, my bright sunlit newborn baby.'

He kissed Silver and looked at her in wonder. 'But I don't really know what's been going on. I hope you'll tell me.'

Silver nodded happily. Abel Darkwater came forward. 'May I see the Timekeeper? Just for a moment, after so many many years of waiting?'

Regalia Mason's eyes narrowed.

Roger River looked puzzled again. 'Well no, I'm afraid not, because you see, we haven't got it.'

'Don't worry,' said Silver, 'Regalia Mason brought it back. I know where it is.'

Regalia Mason stepped forward and put a restraining hand on to Silver's shoulder. Silver felt a chill run through her, then the sun was warm again.

'Silver, I said the Timekeeper is at Tanglewreck. I didn't say which Tanglewreck. It is in the world that Roger and Ruth remember. It is at the Tanglewreck where all this began.'

'I don't get it,' said Silver.

'There are many universes, many Tanglewrecks.'

'But only one Timekeeper,' said Abel Darkwater, fastening his woollen cloak.

Regalia Mason turned to Silver, as she sat with Buddleia and her parents.

'Silver River, would you like to stay here in this world with your sister and your parents?'

'Yes,' said Silver. 'Always. Can Gabriel stay too?'

'If he chooses to stay he may stay,' said Regalia Mason.

'Then we're staying!' said Silver, full of happiness. 'All of us for ever.'

'Then it is done.'

'What is done?' asked Silver.

'Everything. You will stay here with those you love. I will return to the world you once knew. The Timekeeper has no power there now. Abel Darkwater has no power there now. You will never see him, or me, again.'

'What about Toby and the kids?'

'I will take them home. Trust me, Silver, they will come

to no harm now.'

Gabriel was looking at Silver. She got up, suddenly able to read his mind as clearly as he could read hers. She walked down the drive with him a little way, holding his hand. His face was troubled.

'Micah called her the serpent.'

'That was when she was Maria Prophetessa.'

'She is Maria Prophetessa still.'

'What do you mean, Gabriel?'

'She is tempting you like the serpent.'

'What are you talking about? I've found my mum and dad, and Buddleia!'

'That is what she desires!' said Gabriel.

'And you'll stay with me, won't you?' said Silver, her voice faltering.

Gabriel slowly shook his head. 'Not here, Silver, not if we have failed.'

'We haven't failed! Micah said that Abel Darkwater must never have the Timekeeper – well, now he won't get it. We've succeeded!'

'And given to her all the power of the world. The journey you made was more than one, it was two. It is she who must be feared, not him alone.'

Silver tried to think it through. What was it that Regalia Mason had said? That Silver was the key and that without the key the Timekeeper had no power. What power? And could that power stop Regalia Mason?

If the answer was no, why had she gone to such lengths to make an ending where Silver and the Timekeeper must not be in the same world? There was more to it than Abel Darkwater. Yes, there was more.

'Throw a stone in the long grass,' said Gabriel.

'What do you mean?'

'Micah says you throw a stone in the long grass to see if a snake be hiding there.'

Regalia Mason was sitting chatting to Roger and Ruth about the history of Tanglewreck. Silver came up and stood in front of Regalia Mason.

'I'm not going to stay here,' said Silver.

'Excuse me?' said Regalia Mason politely.

'I have to find the Timekeeper – and I haven't done that yet, have I? So I'm not going to stay. Look.'

She pulled the shining pin out of her coat pocket. It was vibrating.

'It will lead me home,' said Silver.

'But darling, this is your home!' said her mother, bewildered and frightened.

Regalia Mason nodded slowly. She looked at Silver for a minute that was a minute out of Time. It was a minute in every universe that exists. It was a minute that changed everything.

Cold and beautiful and tall, she seemed to hover over Silver, and then she vanished, yes, completely vanished, and in her place was a rearing serpent. Her tongue shot from her mouth, her small cold eyes glittered. Her body towered over the child.

'Get back!' shouted Roger, trying to shield Buddleia and Ruth.

'I'm going to find the Timekeeper,' said Silver again.

The sky darkened. Black clouds came so low over the house that the tall chimneys were hidden. The thunder boomed across the sky. Forked lightning, swift and snake-like, flashed from the clouds to the ground.

It was day no longer. Twin stars broke the sky. As each star fell, Silver heard voices calling. 'Where are you? Where are you?' One star exploded into the light, the other vanished in darkness. The lost voices could still be heard, faint and plead-ing. 'Where are you?'

The rain came. Rain like spears. All anyone could do was to lie flat on the ground as the rain bombarded their bodies. Then the quiet river at the bottom of the garden rose and reared and hit the house with such force that Silver, looking up, thought the house had been swept away.

As she looked up, she saw Maria Prophetessa in the form of a serpent, huge and old, towering in the flood of the river, her head bent towards Silver.

'I'm going to find the Timekeeper!' yelled Silver, holding on to the sundial with both hands as the water fell down in a great wave, its force sucking her through the black storm, through the stars, through Time. She held on.

Lifting her head against the water pouring off her body

like stars, she saw Maria Prophetessa rear up once more, collapse, and slither away.

There was silence. The clouds lifted. The day broke through the darkness. The river returned to its banks. She heard a bird. Voices came in and out of hearing. She stood up. She ran over to her parents and Buddleia.

Silver felt the lines of their world beginning to wobble and shift. She hugged her parents and her sister.

'Buddleia – will you stay here?'

Buddleia nodded without saying anything. She was crying.

'Mum, Dad, I'm sorry. I do love you, I don't really understand what's happening, but she was tricking me again, that's what she does, trick people, and terrible things are happening in our other world, and, and, I don't know why, but I have to find the Timekeeper, and I *am* the Timekeeper. Maybe I'll find a way back one . . .'

But already her words were thinning into the air, and she couldn't hear what her mother was saying as she held her tight, and their bodies became more and more insubstantial, and Tanglewreck itself was losing a window and a door and a hedge and a fountain, and the world she longed for was transparent as a raindrop, or her tears.

So there they were, on the unmown grass, her and Gabriel, and Toby and the kids, not knowing anything that was happening, or where they were, and Abel Darkwater had disappeared and Regalia Mason had disappeared, and Silver knew exactly what she had to do.

She went to the sundial, and pushed it with all her strength. It began to scrape and move backwards, and there, underneath, was a stairway, and on the third step was a box, and in the box was the Timekeeper.

The Timekeeper. At last. Centuries. Stars.

She lifted it out, jewelled and dusty.

She opened it, and touched the wheels, moving one against the other, like other worlds.

There were the pictures, lapis and gold; the chariot, the lovers, the wheel of fortune, the world . . . and the child at the End of Time. It was a picture of her.

The clock wasn't ticking, two of the pictures were missing, and there was only one hand on the dial. Carefully, Silver felt in her pockets, and first of all she put the pictures in place, one by one, and then she took out the diamond pin. She clicked the hand into place on the enamelled dial, and there was a hesitation, and then the clock started to tick.

TICK!

In London, Abel Darkwater heard it and lay down in his twilight study, the blinds drawn. He had failed to sacrifice the child. If she had set the clock in motion once again, and he had taken it from her, and offered her to the dark gods, the mysteries of Time would have been his. Now there was nothing.

TICK!

At the airport, Regalia Mason was boarding her private jet. There had been no more of the Time Tornadoes and Time was as steady again as most people expected it to be. Quanta's assistance was no longer required by the perplexed scientists of the West, and the sinister man from MI5 was thinking of looking a bit deeper into Quanta himself.

She could not use the future to distort the present; now that the Timekeeper was ticking again, it would regulate the last few hundred years of ordinary Time, and the birth of the new god would remain a mystery. Perhaps the Quantum would become all-powerful, but perhaps it would not.

Nothing is solid, nothing is fixed. The future forks with new beginnings and different ends.

She thought about it; if the child had not begun the journey, the Timekeeper would never have been found. If the child had done what Regalia Mason had predicted she would do, and stayed with her parents and her sister in a happy free world, not like this one at all, then the prophecy would have been fulfilled very differently.

Abel Darkwater had never understood the importance of the child and the decisions she would make.

But then, Regalia Mason, who always read the small print, had overlooked the simplest thing of all; that one true heart can change everything.

TICK! She heard it beating.

At Tanglewreck, Gabriel and Silver had been amazed to see

Micah and Balthazar and the Throwbacks emerging from the steps under the sundial.

'We have come with food,' said Eden. 'Vindaloo, korma, saffron rice.'

'Yippee!' shouted Toby, and the kids fell upon the food, shouting and celebrating, and hugging each other and the Throwbacks and Silver.

'Party!' yelled Toby. 'This is the best! The total best!'

'But how did you get here, and under the sundial?' asked Silver, bewildered.

'All things connect,' said Micah simply. He held the clock in his hands, and stroked it lovingly, telling Silver again how he had worked on it all through the long sea-voyage.

'I never knew its power,' he said, 'but I knew what power it had.'

While they were talking, they hardly noticed a bedraggled pair of thieves climbing wearily up from the hole, followed by a man in pantaloons with a red beard.

'My clock!' said the man, looking delightedly at the Timekeeper. 'Roger Rover at your service.'

'I think you're in the wrong century,' said Silver.

'I think I'm in the wrong life,' said Thugger. 'Can you lend us a few quid to get back to London? Fisty 'ere needs to see a man about a dog.'

Fisty emptied the dead Elvis on to the grass.

'I reckon I can fix him for you,' said Micah.

And the day went on. Micah offered to take Toby and the

kids back down to London, if they would go through the tunnels. The kids were so excited about seeing their parents again, and Silver had to try hard not to cry. She kept hoping that Roger and Ruth and Buddleia would be sitting out on the lawn when she looked, but she knew that they wouldn't be there.

'Thazzit then, Silver,' said Toby, as Micah began to round up the kids. 'This is my mobile number, yeah?'

'Yeah, Toby, thanks. Thanks for everything.' She hugged him.

'You call me and you come down to Brixton, yeah?'

She nodded, too full of feeling to say what was in her heart.

The kids set off down the tunnels in single file, led by Balthazar, with Eden bringing up the rear to keep them safe.

It was almost night.

'Excuse me,' said a familiar voice. There was Mrs Rokabye.

'You are not my aunt,' said Silver, in a voice that told Mrs Rokabye the game was up.

'No, well, strictly speaking that is true, but when I read in the paper of the mysterious disappearance of your poor parents, and your obvious difficulties, I wanted to make myself useful. I have always loved children, you know.'

Silver didn't know.

'And I didn't have anywhere to live.'

'Oh no . . .'

'And Bigamist . . . here he is, yes, he is quite reformed, the

412

best of rabbits, all repentence and good deeds from now on – that's right, Bigamist, isn't that right?'

Bigamist had a carrot in between his teeth. He dropped it humbly at Silver's feet. It was true he had stolen it from her vegetable garden in the first place, but, well, perhaps . . .

Mrs Rokabye was wringing her hands. 'It was all that wicked man Darkwater, you know. He hypnotised me, he threatened me, and . . . you will need someone to cook and clean for you until you get older, and . . .'

Sniveller came loping forward.

'And if you say no, I shall have to marry this man.'

Sniveller looked hopeful.

And in a world of all possible outcomes, somewhere Mrs Rokabye is married to Sniveller, and somewhere she has never met Silver or been to Tanglewreck, and the train is still moving towards London, and Roger and Ruth will come home to this house in this world, and . . .

TICK!

Micah was speaking very seriously to Gabriel. He came over to Silver and bowed to her.

'What you have done, none but you was able to do. Thank you, Child of Time.'

'I couldn't have done it without you,' said Silver. 'You rescued me, you looked after me, you gave me the map – oh, here it is.' She fished in her pockets and gave it back to Micah. 'You held on to Gabriel in the Black Hole, and you kept reminding me about her, Regalia Mason. I know she's bad but I wanted to believe her. She made me trust her.'

'She be skilled in all the arts,' said Micah. 'Only you has she not deceived.'

He turned to Gabriel. 'You know all the ways and where we shall always be. Shall you return with us, or shall you remain here?'

Gabriel looked at Micah and looked at Silver, then he walked away awhile, and the two of them were deep in talk. Silver watched them, her heart heavy. She would be alone for a long time now. Years. Until she grew up.

My name is Silver. I have lived at Tanglewreck all of my life, which is to say, eleven years.

My name is Silver. I have lived at Tanglewreck all of my life, which is to say until this time happened, but what happens now, I do not know.

Night came. Silver was sitting alone in the dark on the grass damp with dew. She was thinking about her mum and dad and her sister, and wanting them to be happy in the world she couldn't find any more.

She looked up at the stars. Ora was there and Dinger the cat, and lives so far away from hers that they would never touch again. And lives so near hers that they could almost touch. So many lives, and this night and these stars.

The Timekeeper was in the house, ticking through Tanglewreck like a heartbeat. Her own heart was beating too fast. Sometimes you have to do something difficult because it is important. But it still hurts, and you still cry.

She heard a noise behind her. It was Gabriel. He sat down and put his arm round her.

'I will stay here with you,' he said.

'But you have to live underground.'

'Not now. I can live here with you. Shall I stay with you?'

'I'd like that, Gabriel. I don't know what happens next.'

And they sat together all through the night until the morning came, and she thought she saw three suns rising, and she thought that whatever happened next, she had done the task that had been given to her to do, and that is as much as anybody can do, in this strange life of ours.